SIX

#2 THE DOCTORS CLUB SERIES

TAMSEN SCHULTZ

ALSO BY TAMSEN SCHULTZ

THE DOCTORS CLUB SERIES

THE WINDSOR SERIES

WINDSOR SHORT STORIES

THE TILDAS ISLAND SERIES

To friends, who come in all shapes and sizes

ACKNOWLEDGMENTS

While this book is a work of fiction, the abuses workers and communities suffer at the hands of palm oil plantation owners and operators are a very real thing. In fact, as I prepared this book for publishing, an expose hit the news calling attention to the pattern of coercion and violence against local communities in Papua New Guinea related to the palm oil plantations. And Indonesia is considering extending the current moratorium on new plantations, citing environmental and labor rights issues. While many companies *do* hold their suppliers accountable, sadly, that's not a universal truth.

While I want to thank all those people critical to my writing journey, I also want to acknowledge those people—some we may know, some we may only read, or hear, about—who have courage. The courage to speak, the courage to act, the courage to stand up for those who aren't able to stand up for themselves. "Thank you" is an almost pitiful thing to say considering the risks many of you take. But from the bottom of my heart, thank you.

CHAPTER ONE

"HELLO, ROSEY, HOW ARE YOU TODAY?" Six asked her paralegal as she stopped by the older woman's desk on the way to her own office. Located on the fourth floor of the building occupied by the regional US District Attorney staff, the suite of rooms bustled with activity as the workweek kicked off for most employees.

"Sorry to see you in today, Vi," Rosey responded. Six's legal name was Violetta Salvitto, and while her friends called her "Six"—a nod to the first two letters of her name—everyone in her professional world called her "Vi." Only they pronounced it "Vie," and not "Vee," which it should be, since the Italian pronunciation of her name was "Vee-oh-letta." When she'd first moved to the US, she tried to correct people, but she'd long ago given up that fight. Some battles couldn't be won, and some weren't worth fighting.

Taking the folder Rosey handed her, Six smiled. "What's a little murder between friends?" she said with a shrug. "This is all that he wanted me to see?" she added, surprised.

The file, which was the reason she was in the office on her day off, was thin. Thinner than she would have anticipated for

1

the federal murder and drug trafficking charges it covered. Her colleague, Mitch Greene, had called her in as a second set of eyes on the case. The young man involved had made a series of bad decisions that started with transporting eight kilos of heroin from Miami and ended up with him shooting and killing his "partner" as well as an innocent bystander not ten minutes from the federal courthouse in Boston. As an attorney for the DA's regional office, it wasn't Six's usual type of case. But as macabre as it sounded, murder was an interesting change from the financial crimes she usually prosecuted.

"Mitch said he doesn't want to taint your opinion. Those are the essentials." Rosey nodded to the file. "He asked that you take a look and form your own opinions. He'll be back from court in about an hour."

Six tucked the file under her arm. "Thanks, Rosey. Can you let him know I'm here when he returns?"

"Of course."

"And—"

"Hold your calls," Rosey finished.

"You are my very favorite person in Boston," Six said, grinning at her paralegal, who shook her head and smiled.

"The only people you know who are actually *from* Boston are in this office," Rosey shot back.

Tossing Rosey a wink, she started toward her office, acknowledging to herself that as usual, Rosey was right. She had work colleagues in Boston, but her friends—her true friends—all lived in Cos Cob, a small seaside town an hour north of Boston. Her good friend Cyn had been the first to buy a house there, then Six had followed. Shortly after, the other two members of their fearsome foursome—Nora and Devil—moved as well. Other than work, her life was in Cos Cob.

Six had only taken a handful of steps when her attention snagged on Gavin Cooper, a paralegal who'd joined the department nearly five months ago in January. Sitting at his desk, he moved his fingers over the keyboard, but lifted his eyes to meet hers. Gavin was an enigma that she hadn't quite figured out yet —but only for lack of trying. In fact, she'd been trying—and mostly succeeding—at ignoring him since he'd joined the office. Six knew a mistake when she saw one, and Gavin Cooper was most definitely a mistake that she had no intention of making.

At six foot three with light brown hair, deep brown eyes, and an easy smile—not to mention his more than eye-catching build and demeanor—he'd captured the attention of his fair share of single people in the office. In the first month or so, he'd flirted with and teased men and women alike. But to the best of her knowledge—and the office grapevine—he hadn't ever followed through on any of those flirtations. About the only thing she could confirm about his personal life without asking—which she wasn't going to do—was that he was single. Whether he was into men or women or both or neither, she didn't know, and she didn't think anyone in the office did, either.

Professionally, Gavin was assigned to Mitch. She'd heard from her colleague more than once about what an exceptional paralegal he was—whip-smart and with an attention to detail that eased cases through the courts. He was also military-sharp on his timing. Not once had Gavin even come close to pushing up against a deadline, let alone missing one. That was to be expected, though. Prior to joining their office, he'd been a paralegal for the British Army and a Special Forces officer before that. Why he hadn't finished out his career in the military, she didn't know and, again, had no plans to ask.

Of course, even though he was the mistake she wasn't going to make that didn't mean she couldn't sneak an appreciative look every now and then. Thankfully, because they didn't work together, she wasn't presented with the temptation to ogle too often.

Pushing thoughts of Gavin Cooper, Special Forces paralegal, to the side, she closed her office door. After setting Mitch's file down on her desk, she hung her jacket and purse before taking a seat. Thirteen years earlier—when her placement in the office had been sanctioned by the US State Department—Mitch had been the only one told about her double life as an agent for *Agenzia Informazioni e Sicurezza Esterna*, or AISE, the Italian foreign intelligence agency. As part of the quid pro quo of allowing a foreign asset to work in the office, she often reviewed cases that he suspected might have ties to activities either AISE or another foreign intelligence agency might want to know about.

It was an odd balance to keep—her work as an attorney for the US DA's Office and her obligations to her home country. But she, Cyn, Nora, and Devil all did it—although Cyn, Nora, and Devil were agents for the United Kingdom, Jordan, and China, respectively. They'd been raised—literally—to do the work they did as embedded agents. Each of them had also managed to create a successful life outside of her agent activities. It was odd, for sure, but she wouldn't have it any other way.

Out of habit, Six flicked her computer on before turning to the file. An hour and a half later, she lined the papers into a neat stack and sent Mitch a quick text. Rosey had said he was expected back from court thirty minutes ago, but court didn't operate like a subway and often ran on its own time.

"Stop by when you're back," she typed.

"Walking in. On my way," he answered.

Setting her phone down, she turned her attention to the big window in her office that looked north and toward the city. From where she sat, she couldn't see the ocean, but she took in the peekaboo views of the iconic Boston skyline and—at least on this day—a bright blue sky.

Six smiled, she loved this time of year—the three-week stretch that fell sometime between April and June that New Englanders called "spring." Regardless of how fleeting it was, though, it was her favorite time of year. The weather wasn't yet humid, the trees and flowers had budded out, and the barren browns of late winter were no more. Life was full of color, and without the humidity, she could be outside to enjoy it.

A knock on her door interrupted her reverie and because no one else would interrupt her when her door was closed, she called for Mitch to enter.

"What do you think?" Mitch asked without preamble as he took a seat across from her. He was nearing his seventieth birthday, and as a tall, gaunt man, he slightly resembled a skeleton. A well-dressed skeleton, in his high-end navy suit, but a skeleton nonetheless.

"Are you ever going to retire?" she asked. Seriously, the man should have retired five years ago. Or even before that given that his wife, a scientist, had sold her company for an astonishing amount of money fourteen years earlier. There was no reason the two of them shouldn't be boating around the world and sipping cocktails in exotic locations.

"No, I hate golf, and Marcia likes having the house to herself. I figure I'm still useful here. I may as well keep the peace at home and stay out of her way."

Mitch was only sort of joking. Marcia loved her husband, but she definitely liked having her space.

"So, what do you think?" he repeated.

"You mean about your druggie murderer who was probably an errand boy for the Agosti family?"

Mitch grinned and leaned back. "I wondered. Talk to me."

Familiar with Mitch's shorthand way of speaking, Six proceeded to give him her opinion on the file. The evidence—circumstantial though it was—pointed to his being tied to the Agosti crime family; a small Italian syndicate with big aspirations that'd broken into the international drug trade in a major way three years prior.

"So, do you think he knows anything?" Mitch asked, taking the file she handed back.

Six started to shake her head, then stopped. "Unlikely, but not impossible. The family isn't big—not yet. Because of that, it's possible that someone as low-level as your guy knows something or someone. It's a long shot, but there's still a shot."

"You'll help?" Mitch said more than asked.

Six didn't hesitate. "I'll reach out to a few folks and see what I can find. Give me a few days?"

He nodded as he stood. "He was arraigned yesterday, so we have some time. Thank you," he added as an afterthought.

She nodded and rose as well, wanting coffee from the kitchen. She didn't really want to work, but rush hour was already starting. If she didn't want to get stuck in traffic, she'd be better off spending a couple more hours in the office before getting on the road to Cos Cob.

"What's on your docket?" Mitch asked as they exited her office.

"One case. Embezzlement from an employee retirement program," she answered. Her caseload was much lighter than the rest of the office because she worked part-time. When not in trial, she only worked two and a half days a week. When she was called away by AISE, it was even less than that, and she was out for as long as the job required. The arrangements were not always easy to manage. But apparently the powers that be in both countries—the US and Italy—had decided to make it work, and she'd never encountered any issues with her erratic schedule.

"Fun," Mitch said as he peeled off and headed to his office. Mitch had approximately zero interest in any case that did not involve blood and guts, and he hadn't bothered to modulate his sarcasm.

"Yes, well, you know what they say about one man's fun being another man's..." She let her voice trail off, not sure what the rest of that saying was or if it was even the right one. She'd lived in the United States since starting college twenty years ago, but she still hadn't gotten the hang of all the American idioms even though she loved them.

"Hah," Mitch said, not bothering to turn back as he marched into his office. "Go get yourself some coffee, Vi. You brought that fancy machine in for a purpose. Put it to good use." Six's gaze lingered on his now-closed door, then drifted to where Gavin sat. Not surprisingly, he was watching her.

"Everything all right?" he asked.

She nodded but instead of saying anything, she pivoted on her heel and walked to the kitchen. Sandy and Laura, two paralegals, were chatting when she entered. Both women were relatively new and in their late twenties. Six had heard Laura wasn't long for this job, but Sandy was quite good, despite her apparent desire to be considered pretty more than smart.

"Did you see him? I was surprised, in a damn good way, to see him. He doesn't usually work today," Laura asked.

"Hard *not* to see him," Sandy replied.

It was also not hard to guess who they were talking about. Six wondered if Gavin's ears were burning. Then again, if they were, then they were probably always burning given how often he was a topic of conversation. Ignoring the two women, she walked to the fancy coffee machine she'd bought and installed in the office kitchen. It was extravagant, but if there was one thing she couldn't do without, that was good coffee. Or maybe that was wine...

"Damn, I'd like to lick him all over," Sandy said with a giggle that drew Six's attention, and not in a good way.

"I'd love to get him home on a Friday night and fuck him seven—or fifteen—ways to Sunday," Laura said.

And that was crossing a line Six couldn't—and didn't want to—ignore.

"Ladies, I'm quite sure you are familiar with the terms 'hostile work environment' and 'sexual harassment.' Have some respect for this office and for yourselves. If he hasn't shown an interest in you so far, you need to take a hint. And if you're going to continue to talk about your colleagues in that way, we're going to have issues."

The women stopped and gaped at her. Abruptly, they both spun around—in a move that looked almost orchestrated—and left the kitchen.

Six watched them go, then shook her head and turned to the task of making herself some coffee. A few minutes later, as the water was still heating, Gavin walked in.

"Frick and Frack flew out of here like bats out of hell. What'd you say to them?" he asked, leaning his hip against the counter and crossing his arms.

"You don't want to know. Coffee?"

He considered her response and question, then nodded. "Thanks."

Six packed another coffee filter and locked it in place. Once the light came on indicating the water was the right temperature, she hit the button, and the elixir of gods started pouring from the two spouts.

"Milk?" she asked. Gavin hadn't said a word—or moved— since he'd thanked her. His stillness was a little disconcerting.

He shook his head and continued to watch her. Once the cups were full, she whisked one away and handed it to him, hoping he'd leave. Why he made her so uncomfortable she didn't know. Yes, he was an attractive man, and yes, she was attracted to him, but she was also a grown-ass woman. She had zero interest in pursuing something with a man who flirted with everyone as easily as he breathed. The stereotype of the jealous Italian was not based on fiction, and that was a level of crazy Six was not going to stoop to.

"What were they saying?" Gavin asked. "Before they fled."

Six glanced over at him as she poured a dash of steamed milk into her mug. She rinsed the small metal carafe, then, setting it to dry, unlocked both filters. "Like I said, it's not important," she said, then emptied the coffee grounds into the small bucket the cleaning staff left for that purpose.

"You didn't say it wasn't important, you said I wouldn't want to know. What if I do want to know, Violetta?"

Six raised her gaze to his as she rinsed the filters. Only her parents used her full name—and apparently Gavin. The asshole even pronounced it right, with an impeccable Italian accent.

She sighed and picked up her mug. If he wanted to know, he had a right to know. "Sandy wanted to lick you from head to toe, and Laura wanted to fuck you fifteen different ways over the weekend. If you want to file a sexual harassment claim, I'll support you in that."

The side of Gavin's mouth tipped up. "And what did you say that had them scurrying away like mice?"

Her own lips twitched. "I reminded them that sexual harassment and a hostile work environment weren't complaints that only women could make."

The hint of a grin turned into a smile. "You defended my honor."

Six rolled her eyes and shook her head. "I'm certain you don't need me to do that. I did, however, defend the integrity of this office."

Gavin's smile turned into a frown, but the teasing kind. "I like the idea of you defending my honor."

Six snorted. "Did you not just hear what I said about a hostile work environment? Stop flirting with everything that walks and get back to work, Cooper. I'm sure Mitch has some document you can format or edit or something."

He grinned again and pushed away from the counter. Holding his mug up, he spoke. "Thanks for the coffee, Salvitto. And for the record, if you paid attention, you would have noticed that I don't flirt with everything that walks. Until today, it was only those who don't matter."

Six shot him a skeptical look, but he didn't stay around to

clarify his statement. Her shoulders relaxed with every step he took away from her. She was glad to see him leave. Not only would she not be able to argue with him—something she felt compelled to do given his blatant lie—but honestly, the view wasn't too bad, either.

CHAPTER TWO

THOUGH HE KEPT his head down, Gavin watched Violetta exit the kitchen and head to her office. Not once did she look his way. Which was fine with him. Really. No, really.

In collaboration with the US government and the government of Italy, MI6 had dispatched him to be her backup should she require it. He did not need to be thinking all the lascivious thoughts that he somehow couldn't keep buried whenever she was present. And often when she wasn't. His orders might have been somewhat vague, but he was quite certain that they did not include fantasizing about the fifteen ways he'd like to fuck her over the weekend—*thanks for the inspiration, Laura*—let alone acting on those fantasies.

Besides, he was also certain that Violetta had no idea who he was or the real reason he was now part of the DA's office. If he got close to her, he'd have to tell her. And it didn't take a genius to know what her reaction would be to learning that her government thought she needed backup. So, no thanks; he liked his balls right where they were, thank you very much.

Her office door closed, and he switched his attention to the brief he was editing. Originally, he'd become a paralegal so that he could help his teammates with their wills and other life affairs. Everyone on his former team had seen more than one family struggle through the legal system when no will or directive had been in place. And over the years, he liked to think he *had* helped. But supporting his teammates hadn't prepared him for the work MI6 had him doing at the field office for the federal district attorney. Writing briefs, filing motions, and all the other things that went along with supporting a federal prosecutor in a legal regime he wasn't familiar with had led to more than a few long nights as he tried to catch up and learn. Five months in, though, he was definitely enjoying it. It wasn't quite what he'd had in mind for this stage of his career, but he liked working for Mitch—one of the most ethical men Gavin had ever met—and he got to watch Violetta every day.

Yes, *every* day.

His part-time schedule was the same as hers, and since his orders were to be her backup, he'd taken those seriously and rented an apartment in a town just south of Cos Cob. He would have preferred to be closer. But he'd weighed his options and decided to live where he wouldn't be recognized. And where, as a newcomer, he wouldn't be the topic of a conversation Violetta might overhear. But on each of their shared days off, he usually took a jaunt up the coast to her picturesque little town and checked in on her. Now that the weather was getting better, he'd even taken a boat out a few times and cruised by her house —an iconic New England-style home with three stories, paned windows, storm shutters, and a wraparound porch. Her yard flowed from the house down to the sea, and on sunny days, he could usually find her in her garden or on her porch.

Or at her friends' homes. The older agent who'd briefed him had given him dossiers on her three closest friends—Cyn Steele, a fellow MI6 spook; Lily Devillier, known as Devil; and Nora Amiri. The four had been thick as thieves since the age of twelve, when they'd all met at a boarding school they attended in Switzerland. A school so exclusive that only one girl from each of the eighty sponsoring countries was invited each year to attend. If anyone dropped out or was asked to leave at any time during her six years of study, the vacated spot remained unfilled.

When Gavin had first been told about the school, he thought his superiors were having him on. It sounded a little too much like Hogwarts for it to be real. But no, St. Josue was a real school —a real school that not only educated girls and young women, but trained them to be spies. Yes, spy school was a real thing.

During the months he'd watched Violetta, he'd been tempted more than once to ask her what it was like to attend St. Josue and have her country more or less determine her life's path when she was just twelve. But back to his earlier point, if he asked, then he'd have to explain how he knew about the school in the first place, and he was too fond of his balls to risk it.

Returning his attention to the brief, the minutes, and then the hours, ticked by. The next time he looked up, the office was empty. He remembered mumbling some goodbyes, but to whom, he couldn't say. Although Violetta wasn't one of them. As his target—in a good way—he was more attuned to her than to anyone else in the office. At least that's what he told himself to explain his awareness of her.

Still, he glanced at her office door. It was closed, and he could see a thin light coming from underneath. He considered asking her if she wanted to go grab a drink, then nixed that plan and considered offering her another coffee. He was about to rise from his seat when he heard a noise coming from her office.

It wasn't unusual to hear Violetta going off on a tirade in Italian when a case wasn't going her way, or a witness wasn't cooperating. But this wasn't that same sound. No, this was more like a mix of surprise and pain.

In an instant, he was up and moving toward her. He knocked once on the door, then, taking his life in his hands, opened it.

Violetta sat behind her desk. Her honey-brown hair fell in waves over her shoulders and her cognac-colored eyes were fixed on her computer.

"Violetta?" He moved quietly in to the room and shut the door behind him. After a beat, she dragged her attention from her computer and looked at him. And damn, she was tearing up. Never did he think he'd see her cry at the office. He assumed that she, like everyone else, cried sometimes. He just hadn't ever expected to see it happen here.

"What's happened?" he asked, wondering if maybe he'd missed some major news event as he'd had his head buried in work.

She blinked, then caught her lower lip between her teeth. This vulnerable, almost uncertain, side of her was nearly too much for him to resist. He shoved his hands in his pockets and gave his feet a firm directive to stay put.

"What's happened, love?" he asked again, the endearment slipping out. It was a common enough one in the UK that hopefully she wouldn't read too much into it.

She blinked again and looked away, clearing her throat as she did. "I apologize, I didn't mean to disturb you."

That statement pissed him off more than it should, but he persevered. "You didn't disturb me. You're upset. What happened?"

Her gaze drifted to the window, then rising, her body followed until she stood staring out into the darkness while he kept his focus on her. She wore heels and a skirt suit, as she did nearly every day she came to work. She was both a runner and a swimmer, and her legs were long and strong. Her curves made his fingers twitch, as did the fact that in her four-inch heels, she was less than two inches shorter than him. Which made her eminently grabbable.

"Violetta?"

She turned her head and looked at him over her shoulder. He wouldn't force her to talk, but she looked as though she needed to.

The silence stretched between them and just when he thought she might not speak at all, she answered. "I was perusing the news as I was getting ready to leave. Did you hear about that hit-and-run this afternoon? The one that killed the pedestrian?"

He nodded. It was actually a wonder more pedestrians and bikers weren't killed every day in Boston. Sometimes the only reason he could think of as to why he hadn't been taken out yet by a Boston driver was all the evasive driving training—and practice—he'd had.

"They just released the name of the victim and he's..." She cleared her throat again and turned around. Bracing herself against the window, she finished, "He is, or should I say *was*, a good friend of mine."

CHAPTER THREE

Six MANAGED to drag herself into the office the next morning. Since she'd been in on Monday, typically one of her days off, no one would have faulted her for staying home. But she knew herself well enough to know that she was better off doing something productive than sitting at home and remembering her friend, Jeremy Wheaton.

Of course, it didn't help that she had the mother of all hangovers. On her way home the night before, she'd phoned Cyn to let her know about Jeremy. Her friends, along with Joe, Cyn's partner, had been waiting for her when she pulled up her drive. They'd brought food and dessert and wine. Lots of wine. Too much wine for a Monday night, but the right amount for a grieving Italian.

It had helped that her friends—except Joe—had all known Jeremy as well. Six, naturally, had been the closest to him since they'd been at Harvard Law School together. But given that Cyn had done her PhD at Harvard and Devil her MD at the same university, while Nora had completed her DVM at Tufts in Boston, they'd all known him. And they'd all been able to share Jeremy stories and reminisce about the amazing man he'd been.

16

Now, as she rode the elevator to her floor, she held on to those feelings—the smiles and laughter—of the night before. Even as she recognized that Jeremy's being gone still didn't feel quite *real*.

She managed to trudge through the day and get much of her administrative work for the month done—one thing they didn't teach in law school was that there was more to being a lawyer than the glorified days in court. In fact, as a federal prosecutor, those adrenaline-pumping days of arguing a case only happened a few times a year—maybe a few weeks a year if it was a busy one.

Still, the rote work gave her something to do that she didn't have to focus on too much, and it kept everyone else out of her office. In fact, no one had stopped by, and glancing at the clock, Six was surprised to see it was nearly five. Which meant that Rosey, who was off work at four thirty, had left without saying goodbye. Not that the woman was prone to interrupting her, but she usually checked in a few times throughout the day to see if Six needed anything.

Frowning, she wondered if maybe Gavin had said something to Rosey about Jeremy, which would explain Six's uninterrupted day. The thought was quickly followed by a flash of irritation. Gavin had no right to share Six's loss with her paralegal.

Filled with a sudden need to move, she rose from her desk and walked to the window that looked toward Boston. Cars, bikes, and people bustled on the streets below. Planes were lined up to land at Logan Airport, and a traffic helicopter was visible in the distance.

Jeremy was gone, but life went on.

As that thought seeped into her soul, she recognized that her irritation with Gavin wasn't quite fair. First, she didn't know for certain if he *had* said something to Rosey. But more importantly, if she were honest with herself, her annoyance most likely stemmed from the fact that he'd caught her at such a vulnerable moment. And being vulnerable with anyone other than her friends irritated her to no end. Rosey's odd behavior served as a reminder of what Gavin had witnessed the night before—something Six had no desire to recollect.

Not that Gavin had been anything other than a gentleman. After she'd told him the news, he'd listened as she'd gone on to talk about how she met Jeremy and what a remarkable man he was. Gavin had even brought her a glass of cold water and handed her a handkerchief when a tear—or two—had escaped. Then, when the pressure cooker of her emotions had released enough for her to feel as though she could breathe again, he'd walked her to her car and made sure she was settled and on her way home before leaving himself. She suspected that if she'd lingered in the parking garage a little longer, he would have offered to drive her. Thankfully, she'd pulled herself together before he had the chance.

Shoving her memories from the night before back into the recesses of her mind, she returned to her desk and closed out her work-related programs. Her mouse hovered over the power button, though, and her eyes darted to the police database application on her desktop. What she knew about Jeremy's death was limited to what she'd read in the news. Did she want to know the details?

Reading a case file on someone she didn't know was one thing, but accessing one on her close friend? She knew what it would contain—witness statements, CCTV video of the intersection from when he'd been struck, pictures. Was that how she wanted to remember her friend? Not to mention the fact that it wasn't entirely ethical for her to open a file that had nothing to do with her caseload.

She sighed, then clicked on the power icon. And hesitated again.

Fuck. She couldn't do it; she couldn't let it alone.

Not wanting to risk any censure, she placed a call to a

contact of hers in the Boston Police Department and received approval to access the file. Three minutes later, she was staring at photos of the scene and feeling grateful that the first ones she opened were from later in the investigation. Jeremy's body was covered with a tent, giving Six the ability to pretend it wasn't the scene of her friend's death.

After scrolling through the photos, she opened the report and read the witness statements. Eyewitnesses were notoriously unreliable. Remarkably, though, of the six people who'd been interviewed, all had roughly the same thing to say: the car had come from nowhere, seemed to speed up, then took off after impact.

It was possible that the car had sped up to make a yellow light and the driver hadn't seen Jeremy in the crosswalk. But the conviction in each of the statements caught Six's attention.

Knowing that what she was about to do, what she was about to see, would be difficult, she braced herself, then opened the file taken from the traffic cam. The video, like most traffic cam video, was grainy, and at first, it was hard to get her bearings. She could see several people standing on all four corners of the intersection, but she couldn't make out which was Jeremy.

Then a light changed, and a familiar form stepped off the curb. Six's stomach clenched, then pitched. It was like watching the worst kind of horror film, knowing what was coming next but not being able to turn away.

Less than ten seconds later—ten grueling, painful seconds— Jeremy lay dead in the street. And the light-colored compact SUV, which had indeed sped up as it rounded the corner and appeared to aim for Jeremy, was long gone from the field of the traffic cam.

Six rewound the video, then played it again in slow motion. From the reports, she already knew that the car had no license plate, so what she thought she might see, she didn't know. Regardless, she felt the need to at least try to search for some clue as to what had happened. And she couldn't ignore the question hovering in the not-so-distant corner of her mind—was it really an accident?

She watched it another four times, and when she finally closed the case file, she'd come to the conclusion that there was more to Jeremy's death than just an accident. In fact, she was nearly certain it was murder. But why would someone kill Jeremy? He was a civil litigator who'd had some contentious cases during his career, but nothing that would drive someone to kill him.

Or so she thought. As the early evening light began to soften outside her window, Six wondered what he'd been working on recently. Without hesitation, she pulled up the state court docket and searched for any filings associated with Jeremy and the law firm he ran with his sister, Heather.

There were six active cases tied to the firm and of those, four appeared to be Jeremy's. Of those four, only one was a big-money case—a faulty equipment suit that had resulted in the death of a construction worker. But even if the family were awarded the full amount they sought, it would be little more than a drop in the bucket to the corporation. Certainly not enough to kill over.

At a loss, Six closed out of the application and leaned back in her chair to consider the limited facts. It didn't take her long to go through them, because there simply weren't that many. From the video, it looked as if Jeremy had been targeted. But even having watched it the number of times she had, she couldn't rule out the possibility that someone had been trying to make a yellow light and miscalculated how quickly it would turn red.

But what if it wasn't a mistake? What if someone had intentionally killed him?

Unable to come up with any answers, Six grabbed her phone and placed a call—a call she'd intended to make anyway, but now she had more reason.

"Hello?" the woman answered.

"Heather, it's Violetta. I'd ask how you are, but I can't imagine."

Heather Wheaton, Jeremy's younger sister, sniffed before answering. "Vi, thank you for calling. It's a shock, that's for sure. Two nights ago, we were talking about taking a trip to Germany to see the Christmas markets this winter." Her voice broke as she finished her sentence. Then she cleared her throat. "I can't believe he's gone."

Six's heart ached for the woman. Jeremy and Heather's parents had died when Heather was in college, and it was just the two of them. "Me neither," Six said softly. "He was one of the good guys."

Heather sniffed again, then silence fell over the line as Six considered how to word her next request. Deciding that honesty was best, she was about to ask Heather whether she thought it was truly an accident when Heather spoke.

"I saw the police report," she said. "They didn't want to show it to me, but I made a pest of myself. It's not right, Vi. I know the police think it was a random hit-and-run, but I *saw* the car speed up. I *saw* it aim for Jeremy."

Six had had a hard time watching the video of her friend dying; she couldn't imagine the strength Heather had to watch her brother's death.

"I know," Six said softly. "I saw it, too, and agree, it doesn't look like an accident." In addition to the fact that the car had picked up speed and seemed to aim for Jeremy, there was the fact that it hadn't slowed down after it hit him. If it had truly been an accident, she would have expected the driver to at least hesitate a fraction before taking off.

"Is there any reason why someone would target him?" Six asked.

Heather hesitated. "Not that I can think of, but he was

working on a few things I wasn't involved in, so maybe there's something there?"

"Want me to look into it?" Six offered. She planned to anyway, but if Heather handed over the reins freely, it would make things easier.

"Would you?" The relief in her voice let Six know she'd made the right decision in calling and offering. "I have so much to do with arranging his funeral, managing his estate…"

"Of course," Six said. "It's the least I can do. Would you mind if I stopped by his house to look through his things?"

"I'm here now. Can you come by?"

In no traffic, Jeremy lived twenty minutes away in the heart of the city. At this time of the evening, it would be closer to forty. Still, Heather said she was already there, so Six agreed. Five minutes later, she was heading down to the parking garage.

When she stepped out of the elevator, a familiar dark blue SUV pulled around the corner. For a millisecond, Six wished she could hide from the too-attractive driver. Since there was nowhere for her to go, though, she did the next best thing and stared at her phone as she continued to her car. She had no desire to speak to, or acknowledge, Gavin, not after last night and not as she was preparing to look into the death of her friend. Mercifully, he continued on, and a few minutes later, she pulled out into the Boston rush-hour traffic in her Tesla Model X.

The parking gods smiled on her, and when she arrived in Jeremy's neighborhood, she found a spot less than a block from his apartment. The next thing she knew, she was wrapping Heather in a big hug.

"I am so very sorry," Six mumbled.

"Thank you, Vi," Heather replied as she pulled away. "It still doesn't feel real, you know? I *know* he's gone. I saw the video. But it still feels like he's going to walk through his door and ask what I'm doing riffling through his things."

"More likely he'd be on your case about messing things up," Six said with a sad smile, but at least Heather chuckled.

"You're right about that," Heather replied, her eyes tearing up even as she, too, smiled. Jeremy had been meticulous about his stuff and his space, easily one of the tidiest, cleanest people Six had ever known. "Come in. Can I get you some tea or coffee?"

"If it's easy," Six responded. "And then maybe you can walk me through anything you've found?"

Six followed Heather into Jeremy's kitchen, where a big pot of drip coffee sat in a machine. Pouring them each a cup, Heather then gestured to the small bistro table that sat in the breakfast nook.

"I haven't found anything," Heather said after she'd taken a seat. "The police were here yesterday and had a quick look around, but it was clear they thought it was nothing but an accident, so they didn't take anything."

"What about his laptop and phone?"

Heather's gaze dropped. "They were both with him when he...yesterday. They're destroyed."

Six reached over and put her hand on Heather's. It was a paltry thing, but all the comfort she could give the younger woman. At least for now. If Jeremy had, in fact, been murdered, Six would stop at nothing to bring the perpetrator to justice.

"And his paper files?"

Heather bobbed her head. "We don't have too many of those these days, but what we have is at the office. That said, most of them are for older, closed cases. With the exception of the basics, like retention letters, contact information, and things like that, the files for all our cases are electronic."

"Are they backed up?" Six asked.

Heather's gaze lifted to meet Six's, and the woman blinked, then slowly nodded. "Of course. I don't know why I didn't think of that. We have a cloud storage provider. All the systems are backed up every hour."

"You've had a lot on your mind, and it's been less than forty-eight hours. Why don't you let me look through his files? I'll sign what I need to so that you don't run into any confidentiality issues with your clients," Six said.

A beat passed, then Heather nodded. "You know," she said with a half-smile, "I'm so out of it that I would have just handed over the passwords. Thank you, Vi. Thank you for looking into this. I don't have any reason to think someone would intentionally kill my brother, but after watching the video, I can't get the thought out of my mind."

Six squeezed Heather's hand, then let go. "I'll do everything I can to find out what happened," she said. "Now, why don't you draw up that confidentiality agreement and I can get to work digging through his files."

CHAPTER FOUR

BY THE TIME Six was back on the road and headed toward Cos Cob, night had fallen and along with it had come a storm. Crossing the Tobin Bridge, her rain-sensing windshield wipers ratcheted up a notch as she maneuvered around a semi-truck that was kicking up enough spray to power wash her car. Knowing the drive home would be longer than usual, she smiled when her phone rang as she crossed over Admirals Hill. At least she'd have some company.

"Are you driving in the storm?" Devil asked. Of the four of them, she and Devil were the only ones who worked in Boston. Cyn worked at a university about forty-five minutes northwest of Cos Cob, and Nora traveled for her work as a veterinarian.

"Yes, you?"

"No, I'm home. The ventilation system at the lab had some trouble today so they didn't want anyone in the building." Devil was a medical doctor who worked primarily in research. What precisely she researched, Six hadn't a clue, but she did know that it sometimes led to Devil and Nora working jointly on a project.

"How are you?" Devil asked, her voice uncharacteristically

sympathetic. Not that Devil was cold, but she was, well...*reserved* would be the closest word Six would use to describe her friend. Together they were like fire and ice. But somehow, their differences made their friendship stronger. Devil needed Six to remind her that human emotions were a real thing, and Six needed Devil to remind her that maybe not everything needed to be emoted about at all times.

"Was hungover this morning, thank you very much. But other than that, I'll be fine." Because she'd always be *fine*, that's how they were all raised. A country couldn't afford to have an agent be *not fine*.

Devil made a little "hhmm" noise. Her friend saw through—but understood—the lie. "Is there anything we can do? Have you talked to Heather?"

"Actually..." Six proceeded to fill Devil in on her discussion and visit with Heather. By the time she finished, she was merging onto Highway 128, and the storm had amped up to include thunder and lightning.

"Want me to reach out to the medical examiner?" Devil asked. "I can see if there's anything in the injuries that might tell us something."

That gave Six pause. "Would the injuries look different if it were an accident versus intentional?"

"Not usually, but sometimes there's an anomaly that isn't consistent with a true accident."

Six didn't have to think about her answer. "Yes, please do. Even if there's nothing, at least we can close down that avenue of inquiry."

They chatted for a few more minutes about the logistics of the case, then ended the call. She was less than ten miles from home and despite the raging storm, Six's body started to relax. It always did when she returned to Cos Cob, whether she'd been gone for a day or a month.

Flicking on some music to drown out the sound of the

storm, she glanced in her rearview mirror and started at the sight of a car right on her tail. Frowning, she alternated her attention between the mirror and the road. There were fewer than a half a dozen cars in sight. There was no reason for someone to be driving so close—not on a good day and definitely not during a storm—and no reason they couldn't pass her.

Turning on her rear camera—an aftermarket perk she'd had installed—she tried to get a glimpse of the driver. Or at the very least, of the license plate. Unfortunately, both were a bust. The vehicle had no license plate and it was too dark to see anything inside the white SUV except for the outline of a person behind the wheel. The hairs on the back of her neck stood on end as the similarities between the car that had killed Jeremy and the one behind her clicked into place. Then the lights from an oncoming car illuminated the one following her, and her heart stuttered. In that brief moment, she'd caught a glimpse of the SUV's front. To the left of center, a dramatic dent ran all the way from the hood to the bottom of the bumper.

Rage flowed through her body at the very real possibility that the car behind her was the one that had killed Jeremy. Whoever they were, they must have followed her from his apartment. Little did they know, they'd just thrown a match into a hornet's nest.

She accelerated away easily and switched lanes so that her camera caught as much of the white SUV as possible. She didn't think she'd be lucky enough to get a clear picture of the driver, but if the light from another oncoming car hit it right, she might. Although with the rain-slicked roads, she had to focus her attention on driving, rather than whatever the camera might be recording.

To her surprise, the SUV caught up to her, its lights glaring through her back window. Glancing down at the screen displaying the rear camera, it wasn't hard to guess the driver's intent as the vehicle inched closer to her back bumper. A spinout on the wet road and at the speed she was traveling would be a death sentence, but Six remained calm. This was far from her first high-speed chase.

She allowed the SUV to creep up within six inches from her bumper, then, increasing her speed a touch, she switched lanes and slowed down. Her tail shot ahead of her and she quickly switched the camera angle to be forward-facing as she trailed the vehicle.

It didn't take long for the driver to regroup and try another plan. In a move that was amateurish, even for an amateur, the SUV slowed down. Six scoffed and rolled her eyes. As if she'd pass right by and let him get behind her again. Slowing her own pace, she stayed a steady twenty feet behind the car as she waited to see what the driver would try next.

And that was when everything went to shit.

Light from an oncoming car lit up the cab of the SUV and in that moment of illumination, a figure rose from the back seat. Other than their profile, she could see no details about this second person. But the one thing that was easy to make out was the outline of the gun he, or she, carried.

Again, she wasn't all that worried. Her car, along with all her friends', was specially made and included bulletproof glass. She, Cyn, Devil, and Nora had all laughed at Franklin—their handler —when he'd issued the order that their vehicles be built with the same security features as the President of the United States. None of them worked *as agents* while in the US, and the order had seemed overkill to the extreme. But now, it appeared that not only was she going to have to eat crow, she'd have to thank Franklin for his foresight.

With an annoyed sigh, she pulled closer. While she may not be worried about herself, she had no interest in instigating a shooting on a major highway. Peak traffic hours had passed a few hours earlier, but there were still innocent lives around them.

The first shot hit her window as she changed lanes to come up behind the SUV. The glass held, but she wasn't going to lie to herself—the sound startled her enough that she swerved back into her lane.

Then, to her horror, the headlights of another vehicle reflected in her rearview mirror. She considered switching lanes to prevent it from coming up behind the white SUV. But the car was traveling fast. So fast that if she cut it off, she was worried it wouldn't be able to stop, or swerve, in time. Quickly deciding on a different tactic, she slowed down, leaving enough room for the newcomer to move into her lane and pass the SUV on the right.

Only that's not what it did.

Surprised, confused, and somewhat concerned, she watched as the dark-colored vehicle flew past her, right up onto the bumper of the white SUV. The brake lights of the darker car tapped, as if signaling to her, and on instinct, she slowed down even more. A second later, the white SUV went spinning across the highway. Passing less than ten feet in front of her, it then hit the side railing of the highway and flipped over. And over. She watched in her rearview mirror as it rolled three times before slamming into a large maple.

She slowed down enough to confirm the car had come to rest against the tree, but she didn't stop. She wasn't equipped to traipse through the woods or take on unknown assailants if the driver or passenger were still alive. Not in her suit and heels. Besides, there was likely nothing she could do. The car was an older model, before airbags. A spin and roll at high speed was second only to a head-on collision when it came to fatalities. She doubted either had survived.

She also wanted to know more about the dark SUV that had inserted itself into her situation. She hadn't needed saving—

she'd had everything under control—but her ego wasn't so big that she couldn't admit that whoever it was, they'd definitely helped.

Pushing on the accelerator, she closed the gap between her car and the Good Samaritan. It slowed down as she approached, and she had a moment's hesitation. Yes, it had intervened and ultimately helped, but that didn't necessarily mean that the driver was friendly.

Easing back again, she finally had a chance to look at the license plate. The sequence of numbers and letters looked familiar, but she couldn't place it. Luckily, it would take less than thirty seconds to trace it once she got home. Assuming the plate wasn't stolen.

So intent on trying to place the numbers from memory, Six was startled when the SUV threw its brakes on. Unprepared for that turn of events—even though she'd just done it herself—she flew by the car. Despite the rookie move on her part, at least she had the presence of mind to look over as she passed.

Oddly, the light in the cab was on. And in the two seconds that she could see inside, she caught sight of something she'd never expected.

Behind the wheel of the SUV—one she now knew was blue, though in the dark and with the storm, it looked more like black —sat Gavin Cooper.

He winked and gave her a cheeky salute. Then he slipped his car in behind her and took the next exit off the highway, leaving her alone on the road.

And wondering what the hell had just happened.

CHAPTER FIVE

"*CLUB MEETING, ten minutes, Cyn's place*," Six texted her group of friends through Bluetooth as she turned off Highway 128 toward Cos Cob. The reference to the "club" was her doing—well, hers and Cyn's—from years ago. There wasn't a category of genre fiction that Cyn didn't read, and every time Six had picked one up, especially one of the romances, it seemed to be about some sort of male club. Motorcycle clubs, billionaire clubs, and secret clubs abounded in mass market fiction. When Cyn finished her PhD, the last of the four of them to earn a degree with the word *doctor* in it, Six had decided that there was no reason the men should have all the fun, and she'd dubbed them the "Doctors Club." They could have been a billionaires club or even a secret club. But since none of them liked to call attention to their money—except for Cyn's outrageous house—and they legit couldn't speak about their secret with anyone other than a few, Doctors Club seemed the best fit. After so many years, it had been shortened to just "the club."

"*On my way*," Nora wrote back. "*I'll pick you up, Devil.*"

"*See you soon*," Devil wrote.

"*I'll be sure we're dressed*," Cyn chimed in, making Six smile.

Back in January, Cyn had met Joe Harris, the new chief of police of Cos Cob, and the two had more or less been together since that first meeting. He was a good man and a good partner—Cyn had a tendency toward recklessness, and Joe managed to help ground her without stifling her.

On the dot, Six pulled up to the main gate of Cyn's behemoth of a house, which sat a mile up the coast from her own. Once the massive gate opened, she zipped up the quarter-mile driveway and pulled to a stop near the front door. Not surprisingly, Nora's car was already there.

"What happened?" Cyn asked the moment Six walked in. For being so tiny—barely five foot two and a hundred pounds soaking wet—Cyn had a commanding presence. With her big gray eyes, perfectly styled hair, and natural elegance, it wasn't hard to remember that although her parents might be hippies at heart, they were still a marquess and a marchioness. And Cyn was Lady Hyacinth Steele—though she'd legally changed her name to Cyn twenty years earlier.

"I'll explain. Coffee?" Six asked, moving past her friend toward the kitchen.

"Of course, but you're okay?"

Over her shoulder, Six threw Cyn a smile. Prior to Joe, it would have taken Cyn at least ten minutes to remember that was something she should ask.

"Fine. Confused, and you'll understand why in a minute," Six answered as she stepped into the kitchen. Devil was perched on a stool at the island with her hands wrapped around a glass of wine. Her bright turquoise eyes swept over Six, no doubt cataloging her health. Six flashed her a ghost of a smile, letting her know she was fine. Relief danced across Devil's face, though she remained seated.

"Here," Nora said, handing her a latte. Nora was about an inch and a half taller than Cyn and had a lot more curves. With her deep olive skin, green eyes, and curly black hair, Six had always thought she resembled a Mesopotamian queen. "Thank you," Six said, taking the drink and dropping a kiss on her friend's cheek.

"Where's Joe?" Six asked, looking around the kitchen.

"He decided to work out while we catch up. He said to call if we need him," Cyn answered. And by "call" Cyn literally meant phone him. He may be in the same house—in the third-floor gym—but in Cyn's forty-thousand-square-foot mansion, sometimes phoning someone was the only way to find them, or speak to them, without having to walk ten minutes.

Six nodded, then took a sip of her coffee. She hesitated, not because she didn't want to speak, she just wasn't sure where to start. Her friends all sat down at the round kitchen table, but Six started to pace. Which was easy to do in a kitchen that was bigger than many people's homes.

"I filled them in on your visit with Heather," Devil said. Which meant that Six didn't have to go over that and could start right where things got interesting. Taking a deep breath, she relayed the events of the last thirty minutes. When she got to the part about the white car spinning and flipping, Cyn pulled out her phone, probably to ask Joe to pull the police report.

But whether the two passengers in the vehicle had survived the crash or not wasn't the most pressing question.

"Gavin Cooper?" Nora repeated when Six finally revealed who she'd seen in the other car.

Six nodded.

"That superhot paralegal that everyone is trying to bang?" Cyn clarified.

Six slid her friend a look.

"What?" Cyn demanded. "It's true, isn't it?"

"Not everyone," Six muttered. "But yes, the very same."

"Do you think he's stalking you?" Nora asked. Six hadn't considered that, but it only took her two seconds to dismiss the possibility.

"No," Six said with a shake of her head. "If he were a stalker, I think he would have wanted to stick around and keep playing savior."

"I think you're right about that," Devil said. "You said he's ex-Special Forces. Does he live around here? Maybe he was on his way home, saw your predicament, and stepped in to help."

Cyn snorted. "Sorry, Devil. Most normal people step in to help by calling the cops. They don't casually cause a spinout that probably killed two people before giving a jaunty little wave and going on their merry way."

"It definitely killed two people," Joe said, jogging down the back stairs and walking into the kitchen. "There were a few weapons in the car, but no IDs on the bodies yet," he added.

"I think they were the same people who killed Jeremy, so you might want to let your people know about the connection," Six said as Joe crossed the room and poured himself a glass of water. Joe Harris, with his dark hair, sharp cheekbones, piercing blue eyes, and dimples, was a good-looking man. He stayed fit as well, but Six couldn't imagine Cyn—or any of the them—with men who didn't. Fitness was important in their line of work, and they each spent a lot of time staying at the top of their physical game.

After Joe finished downing the water, he nodded and pulled out his phone. "I'll let them know." Then switching to coffee, he started the machine, obviously deciding to stick around.

"I honestly don't know what to think," Six said. And she didn't. Gavin was obviously trained in combat driving techniques; his Special Forces years would have seen to that. But the whole scenario didn't make any sense.

"Are you sure he's ex-military?" Cyn asked.

Six nodded. "He was definitely in the military."

"I don't think that's what Cyn was asking, was it?" Nora said. Joe joined them at the table and took a seat beside Cyn. Six looked at her friend.

Cyn shook her head. "It wasn't. What I meant was, do you think he's really *ex*? Is it possible he's still serving?"

All four of them turned their attention to Joe. When he'd been hired on as the chief of police, none of them, not even Joe, had known that he'd been handpicked by Franklin—their handler and Cyn's uncle—to provide aid to the women when and if they needed it. Six was pretty sure that Franklin had hoped to keep his machinations a secret for at least a few months. But things had escalated quickly after Cyn found a dead body on her property. Interestingly, now that Cyn mentioned it, Six realized that Gavin had started at her office a few weeks after Joe arrived in Cos Cob.

"I don't know why you all are looking at me. I have no insight into Franklin's decision-making. Hell, I didn't even know *my* role in your lives until after I accepted the job and moved up here," Joe said.

Cyn reached out and took his hand. "No one is privy to what goes on in Franklin's mind, and frankly, I think that's a good thing. We were looking at you, babe, in speculation, wondering if maybe Gavin could be another you. Not *you* you, of course," she said, pointing to him. "But a *You*," she added, waving her hand in his general direction.

With more than twenty-five years of friendship between them, Six knew exactly what Cyn was saying. Had Franklin sent Gavin to…well, not watch over her, but be her backup? If so, she might have to fly down to Florida and have a little come-to-Jesus with the man. Having Joe around made sense. They didn't ever run ops in the US, but they often ran investigations, and many times, what they were looking into had ties to the US. Having a law enforcement ally helped with that.

But a former British Special Forces soldier?

What could he provide them other than brawn?

"I think it's possible," Devil said. Six looked around the table to find her friends all nodding.

"I don't know why Franklin would have picked him," Nora said. "But I think it's worth asking."

Devil let out a small laugh. "You don't know why Franklin would pick him? Really? Have you seen the man? He's too delicious to look at for very long. He could foil any nefarious plan by just standing there in all his glory."

Six frowned. "Aren't we beyond judging people solely on their looks?"

Three sets of eyes swiveled to her. Joe looked down at his coffee, but Six would swear she saw his lips twitch.

"We are most definitely not above judging someone by their looks," Cyn said. "And Gavin Cooper looks every bit the Special Forces soldier he is. While I agree, he's a good-looking man—not as attractive as you, babe," she clarified as an aside to Joe, who rolled his eyes and took a sip of coffee. If there was one thing Cyn and Joe were, it was confident in the other's commitment to them. "I think we all know two things. First, part of what makes Gavin attractive is the fact that he's confident and capable, so yes, we're judging based on looks, but not the superficial kind."

"Speak for yourself," Devil said, arching one eyebrow, then taking a sip of her wine.

Cyn gave her the side-eye but continued. "And second, *if* Franklin sent him, we know he's qualified to do something that he thinks we need."

"Fill a gap in our capabilities?" Nora suggested.

"We have no gaps," Six said.

"No, we have no gaps that you want to consider because if you do, you might find a reason that it's a good idea for Gavin to stick around," Nora said. "I'm curious why you're so against it."

Six wasn't born yesterday and was well acquainted with her friend's style of conversation. Nora was trying to lead her down a path Six wasn't interested in going down.

"If there is a legitimate reason for him to be assigned to work with us, then I would have expected Franklin to call attention to the gap in our capabilities prior to sending him," Six said.

Cyn snorted, and Six was sure a little coffee came out of her nose. Yep, it did. Joe reached over and snagged a napkin, then handed it to Cyn.

"Sorry," Cyn said, wiping her nose. "It was almost like you were serious about expecting Franklin to tell us anything. I can't believe you kept a straight face while you said that."

Six glared at her friend, though in her heart, she knew Cyn was right. Franklin may be Cyn's uncle, but that didn't mean he felt any compunction to share his plots and plans with them. Joe was proof of that.

"There's only one way to find out if Franklin sent him or not. And if he did, why," Devil said.

"Oh, believe me, I plan to call him when I get home," Six said, narrowing her eyes in anticipation of that conversation.

Again, Cyn snorted. "Did you not just hear what I said? Franklin isn't going to tell you shite. You need to ask Gavin."

Six's stomach did a little swoop at the thought of confronting Gavin. Again, Cyn was right—she'd get more out of the soldier than Franklin. But her gut was telling her that once she spoke with Gavin, things would change. She didn't know how they'd change, only that they would. And she wasn't ready for that. She liked her small circle of friends and even believed Joe had been a good addition. But Joe was Cyn's to deal with. Did that make Gavin *hers* to deal with? Was Franklin playing matchmaker again, as they were all certain he'd done with Joe and Cyn?

If that's what he was trying to do, he'd learn soon enough that he didn't always get what he wanted. She might be pissed about him sending Gavin without speaking to her about it first, but from a professional perspective, she could almost understand that decision. If, on the other hand, he was trying to interfere with her personal life, they were going to have some issues.

She sighed. When she'd arrived at Cyn's thirty minutes ago, she'd been confused about Gavin's actions. Now the answer seemed obvious, even if she didn't like it.

"I'm going to fucking kill Franklin," she muttered in Italian. Everyone around the table chuckled. They didn't need to be fluent in the language to get her meaning.

"It worked out for me," Cyn said, baring her teeth in a cheeky smile as she leaned into Joe.

"That," Six said, waving her finger between Cyn and Joe, "is not in the cards for me. Aside from not being interested in a relationship of any kind, you forget, Gavin and I still work together. I refuse to become an office romance cliché."

"Don't let a label define you, babe," Devil said with a grin as she rose and started gathering their empty cups.

"I agree," Cyn said. "When it's love it's love."

"Stop teasing her, you two," Nora said.

"Thank you, Nora," Six said, joining Devil at the sink and placing a cup she'd rinsed in the dishwasher.

"The more she denies it, the more worked up she'll get," Nora continued. "Then she'll go full on Violetta-Italian on us. We'll be here all night trying to keep her from flying down to Florida and killing Franklin, and I have an early morning tomorrow."

Six glared at all her smiling friends. "Have I ever told you all how much I hate you?"

CHAPTER SIX

SIX PACED her living room as the storm still raged outside. Spring storms didn't usually last more than an hour or so, but this one had staying power. She paused in front of a big picture window. During the day, she had a clear view down her lawn, to her dock, and out onto the Atlantic. But now, everything was pitched in darkness except the occasional lightning striking the turbulent gray waters.

A bolt hit the ocean, and the sky lit up like a strobe. Six closed her eyes and focused on the feel of the thunder rolling over the land. Like most storms, her temper was brief and intense. But as her house shuddered around her and the clap of thunder rolled on and on, she wondered if Mother Nature had created this night just for her—it was a keen reflection of her mood.

Her mind swirled with reasons Franklin might have sent Gavin. Nora had suggested that maybe he was supposed to fill gaps in their capabilities, but for the life of her, she couldn't figure out what those were. She and her friends had been active agents for their respective countries since the age of eighteen— twenty years. Why now? What had changed? And why would they need any assistance here when none of them operated *as agents* in the US?

She'd called Franklin, of course. Even knowing that Cyn was right and she'd never get anything out of him, Six had felt the need to try. So far, in the hour she'd been home, she'd left two voice mails. She didn't think Franklin had much of a life other than playing the spymaster, so she was quite certain he was avoiding her.

That left Gavin, though.

She hadn't yet been able to bring herself to pick up her phone and dial his number. She was self-aware enough to recognize the age-old evasion technique—if she didn't ask the question, she wouldn't know the answer. And if she didn't know the answer, then she wouldn't have to confront the truth. An option that held more appeal than it should.

If, on the other hand, she confirmed what she and the club suspected about his presence in her life, then she'd have to talk to him. And talking to him about what had happened that night would be just the beginning. From there, he'd no doubt expect to be brought into her circle of spy friends, and being honest with herself, she didn't want him there. She liked her life the way it was and didn't need him upsetting the balance she and her friends had created for themselves over the years.

Still, as she tried to push thoughts of Gavin from her mind and stoke her irritation at Franklin, she could all but hear Devil's voice inside her head telling her she needed to pull on her big-girl panties and call Gavin. *If* Franklin sent him, then Gavin wasn't going anywhere. Not just that, but if Franklin did send him—which was the only explanation that made sense—there had to be a reason. And despite how much she'd enjoy disemboweling him at the moment, she was woman enough to acknowledge that Franklin never did *anything* without a good reason.

That reason might not be clear to her right now, but taking

her annoyance with him out of the equation, she had to admit, his track record was flawless. Granted, she wasn't privy to everything he was involved in. But when it came to his work with her and the rest of the club, not once had he led them astray or made a bad decision. And that was saying a lot for a man who'd been in the spy game for nearly a half a century.

With a resigned huff, Six grabbed her phone and sank into one of her comfy upholstered chairs. In the mornings, it was her favorite place to sit and watch the sun come up. But with her mood the way it currently was, staring out into the storm wasn't a bad view either.

Bringing her phone to life, she realized Gavin's contact was on her work device, not her personal one. Contorting her body into an unnatural and satisfyingly uncomfortable position, she reached into her bag that she'd tossed on the floor and grabbed her other phone. Pulling up the office directory, she found Gavin's cell.

"Violetta," he said when he answered, his voice rolling through her with his annoyingly perfect Italian accent. "I wondered when you'd call."

"Franklin sent you, didn't he?" There was no point in beating around the bush. When she decided to pull her big-girl panties on or rip the Band-Aid off, she went in all the way. She smiled to herself as those thoughts formed; there were so many good American idioms and clichés—they were one of her favorite things about living in the US.

"Officially the orders came from my commander. But is Franklin an older gentlemen who looks a bit like Prince Philip did in his younger years, but better-looking and with more hair?"

"The very same," Six muttered in English before adding a few choice laments in Italian. There was no going back now. They both knew who—and what—the other was. "Franklin didn't deign to tell me anything. Did they give you a reason?"

"Have dinner with me and I'll tell you all about it."

Six snorted. "Just because we're supposed to work together —although to what end I haven't a clue—does not mean we are suddenly going to be spending time together."

"It's dinner, Violetta, not a lifelong commitment."

"That's cute how you tried to make it sound like I was being unreasonable," she shot back. "Your offer was a power play, short and simple, Cooper. 'I'll tell you what you want if you do what I say.' I don't play that way, Gavin. You may not know me well, but you should know that by now."

Silence fell over the line. Six had a fleeting thought that given how good they both were at holding on to the power of silence, they might still be on the line come dawn without another word spoken. She pulled the phone away from her ear and glanced at the display. Actually, she'd run out of power long before dawn since she'd forgotten to charge her phone.

Finally, Gavin sighed. "You're right, that wasn't called for. But I do think what we need to discuss is best discussed in person. Can we meet? Please," he added.

Six grinned. "See, that wasn't too hard to ask now, was it? And yes, I agree we should meet in person. How about dinner at Kearney's here in Cos Cob tomorrow?"

A beat passed, then Gavin chuckled. A real one...she hadn't realized until now that his easy humor in the office was an act. But hearing him now, the difference was clear as night and day. This chuckle was fuller, deeper, a little richer.

"This is going to be interesting, isn't it?" he mused.

"I suspect it is, yes."

"Tomorrow night at seven thirty, then?"

"Tomorrow night at seven thirty," she confirmed. "Good night, Gavin."

He didn't respond right away, and she wondered what he was thinking. Then his voice rumbled out low and thick with speculation, and his tone had her body tightening with anticipation.

"Good night, Violetta. Sweet dreams," he said, and then the line went out.

At the age of thirty-eight, Six was well familiar with her own sexuality, and she fought the urge to fan herself. She could readily admit Gavin was an attractive man and that there was an attraction between them. But it hadn't been until she'd heard those five words—in that tone of voice—that she acknowledged how *attracted to* him she could be. If she let herself.

She glanced up at the ceiling knowing her bedroom was overhead and let out a long breath.

Yes, sweet dreams, indeed.

———

Six slept late the next morning. It was one of her days off, and after ending the call with Gavin, she'd hit the gym in her attic hard and hadn't made it to bed until after midnight. Dragging herself from under the covers, she padded into the bathroom and stopped in front of the sink. Looking in the mirror, she cast a critical eye on her hair before pulling it into a ponytail and deciding to deal with it later. She was turning away when a flicker in her reflection caught her attention. Pausing, she eyed herself. She knew she was a reasonably attractive woman. And she wasn't blind to the attention men paid her. But forcing herself to stare into her own eyes, it was the darkness she saw there, the demons, that held her attention, not her physical looks.

Placing her hands on the counter and leaning closer to the mirror, Six forced herself not to look away. She wasn't scarred or damaged, not in the way some might think, given the life she'd led. There wasn't a single defining moment that had brought about the shadows she now saw. But rather, it was all the little tears in her soul that were staring back at her. The missions that had taken her to dangerous and depraved places, the colleagues in AISE that she'd lost, the lives that she'd witnessed be destroyed. For a field agent, her career had been relatively charmed, in no small part thanks to Franklin's oversight and intelligence. But twenty years as a spy, and six years of training before that, wasn't something a person escaped from unscathed.

She pushed away from the mirror before her thoughts turned too maudlin. She was what she was and she—mostly—liked the life she'd built. There was no point in dwelling on the darkness.

After brushing her teeth and rinsing her face, she threw on a pair of yoga pants, pulled on her favorite Harvard Law sweatshirt, and headed downstairs for some coffee and a *cornetti*—the small Italian pastry her personal chef, Sylvia, made for her.

Settling into her office with her drink and food, she answered a couple of texts from the club letting them know that Gavin had confirmed their suspicion and that she was meeting with him that night. When she was done, she opened her personal email to find a message from Heather that included access to the cloud service she and Jeremy used. After jotting off a quick note to let Heather know she planned to start looking that day, she logged into the service and began poking around.

Several hours later, she'd gone through all but ten files and found nothing that would give rise to murder. In line with his previous cases, Jeremy had some suits against a few big corporations, but nothing that was significant enough to damage the reputation—or bank account—of those corporations.

Needing a break, she locked her computer and headed toward the kitchen. Dumping her dishes in the sink, she continued on to the mudroom and pulled on a pair of tennis shoes. The storm from the night before had moved on, leaving behind a warm, slightly humid, clear spring day. Perfect for a short walk.

Stepping out onto her porch, she inhaled the heavy, earthy air, so very different from Rome, where she'd grown up until she'd been shipped off to St. Josue. At this point in her life, she'd lived in the US longer than she'd lived anywhere else. But even so, those memories of her early years still had a firm hold on some of her mental real estate.

It wasn't that she missed Italy—she wouldn't move back even if offered the opportunity—but somehow, she still longed for it. Or perhaps she longed for the carefree days of her early childhood, and she confused that with her love of the place.

As if sensing her darkening mood, her phone rang, and Nora's name appeared on the screen. Six jogged down the steps of her porch, intent on following the path to the back of her house then onto the dock as they talked.

"Nora," she answered.

"How are you?" Nora responded. Not that Six liked to label her friends, but Nora was the caregiver of the group. She was as badass as the rest of them, yet still managed to stay humane and sympathetic.

"We're always fine, aren't we?" Six countered. She'd just put her shoes on, but she opted to kick them off when she stepped off the path and onto her lawn. The grass was still wet from the rain the night before, and the damp blades tickled her toes.

"Of course we're *fine*, but how are you?"

Six almost smiled at the question. Leave it to Nora to get to the heart of the matter—because in her world, a person could be many things at once, including both *fine* and *not fine*.

Six took a few steps, enjoying the feel of the earth under her feet while contemplating her answer. "I think I am fine," she responded. "I'm not entirely sure what to think about the Gavin development, but it will sort itself out. I started looking into

Jeremy's files today, though, and I haven't found anything. Not yet anyway."

"You will," Nora said, making Six smile. Always so much faith.

"I hope so," Six said. "I don't like the idea of his murder going unaccounted for. I know none of us do. But it will be an uphill battle given the police still think it was an accident."

"Someone almost ran you off the road after visiting his apartment. I think it's safe to say Jeremy's death wasn't an accident. Not unless you've been making some interesting enemies you haven't told us about."

Six snorted as she stepped onto her dock, the worn wood warm under her feet. "If I were making any enemies, you can be damn sure they wouldn't have caught me off guard last night."

Nora let out a low laugh. "Of course not. That said, I don't believe this, but I feel compelled to ask, is there *any* chance it could be something, or someone, from your other life? Someone who's found out who you are and what you do outside of your day job?"

Six had considered this the night before as she worked out. It was a possibility—it always was with the work she and her friends did—but her gut was telling her the events of the night before were about Jeremy. Coming on the heels of her visit to his apartment, she couldn't see the incident being sparked by anything else. Still, Nora's question had her rethinking the possibility.

"I don't think so, but I'll run it by Franklin. Maybe if I leave a message for him asking that specific question, he might call me back." True to form, Six still hadn't heard from him, despite the two additional messages she'd left. She suspected that Gavin had checked in with his people and that his people were talking to her people. Which meant that Franklin would know about their dinner, and coward that he was—though he'd chalk it up to strategy—he wouldn't call her back until after she and Gavin talked.

"Hhmm," Nora said, by way of agreement. "If he thinks you think you might be in danger, that *is* his Achilles' heel—he feels that way about all of us. He may be a prickly little lord who enjoys playing chess with people's lives, but he does have a soft spot for us."

"Either that or our countries have threatened him with death if anything happens to us," Six countered, only half joking. She had no clue how a member of the British aristocracy and handler for MI6 had ended up being the handler for all four of them. They all assumed it had something to do with Franklin's relationship with Cyn and his ability to convince anyone to do what he wanted. But she also liked to think that a part of the decision was because he liked them. And Nora was right—on the rare occasions when any of them had felt uncertain or in danger in a way that wasn't *normal*, he'd always gone to the mat for them.

"So what are your plans now?" Nora asked.

Six stopped at the edge of her dock. The water was calm but murky after last night's churning. In a few weeks, she'd have her boat brought out from its dry dock up the coast. But day trips out on the water were a vague desire at the moment.

"I have a few more files to look through before my dinner tonight. If I don't find anything going through those, I'll do a deep background on Jeremy. We all knew him, I don't think he was involved in anything nefarious, but maybe he inadvertently got caught up in something. If there's anything there, I'll find it." She hated the minutiae of tracking people's movements, but she'd do it. Even if she hadn't promised Heather, she would have done it for her own peace of mind.

"You'll let us know if you find anything?" Nora asked.

"Of course. You'll be the first to know." It went without saying, and yet it was something they always said to each other.

As odd as it might seem, it was their way of ensuring they never took each other—and their unique friendship—for granted.

After ending the call, Six slipped her phone back into her pocket and tipped her face up to the sun. The gentle heat warmed her skin, and a subtle breeze lifted the end of her ponytail. As she listened to the water and the birds and the rustling of the tree leaves, she couldn't help but feel things were changing. It wasn't as though she hadn't ever investigated anyone or anything before. She'd done plenty of that in her role at the DA's office. But Jeremy's death was different. It was like the work she did for AISE—filled with more questions than answers. It wasn't an approach she'd ever brought to the US and certainly not, metaphorically speaking, into her home.

Cyn had done something similar in January when a "friend" of hers had left a dead body on her doorstep. Thank god she had decided to investigate, though—thank god they all had— because hundreds of lives had been saved. But still, it was an uncomfortable place to be. Six didn't like to mix her two lives. Her life in Massachusetts, despite some of her cases, was her refuge. She wanted to keep it that way.

A seagull screeched, and Six opened her eyes. A lone boat bobbed on the water. It was a beautiful day to be out; she wondered if maybe they were fishing. She wasn't a fisherman, but she'd heard that sometimes, after storms, the catches were good. She watched the small boat trawl slowly up the coast, then she turned back toward her house.

She paused and looked at her home, her sanctuary. She could keep the status quo or she could investigate Jeremy's murder. There was no question Jeremy won that contest.

And if that meant things would change, then so be it.

CHAPTER SEVEN

SIX PLACED A PLATE OF CHEESE, crackers, and fruit on her desk, then sat down at her computer again. She had ten more of Jeremy's files to go through and then, if she still had nothing, there were some decisions she'd need to make. Not yet ready to concede to the possibility that the files would tell her nothing, she dived in.

Two hours later, she leaned back in her chair and stared at her screen—not so much looking at the content but considering her options. The last ten files had all been minor cases and mostly a reflection of the pro bono work he did with a few immigrant communities.

Six had said that she'd do a deep dive into Jeremy if she didn't find anything in the files. But her instinct wouldn't let go of the idea that what had happened to her friend was tied to his work. There was no explanation for how strongly she felt this *knowing*. Before he'd died, it had been about a month, maybe six weeks, since she'd seen Jeremy. Anything could have happened in that time. Maybe he'd witnessed something he shouldn't have. Or maybe one of the abusers of the women Jeremy had helped had found him. There were all sorts of things that weren't associated with his work that could have made him a target of a killer. And yet she found it hard to believe it could be anything but.

As she considered her options, her gaze drifted over her monitor, the screen showing an exact replica of Jeremy's laptop. She was about to jump back into the files again and see if she'd missed something when the recycle bin on the screen caught her attention. The one place she hadn't looked.

She clicked the icon, and the file manager popped up. There were dozens of items, so rather than reading the names, she filtered them by date, showing the most recently modified document on top.

Six's skin tingled, and she felt a welcome rush of adrenaline. The file at the very top, titled simply "SJC," had last been modified the morning Jeremy was killed. She'd found it. She knew she had. She didn't know what it was, but her instincts were rarely wrong in these situations.

Taking a deep breath, Six opened the file to find several more items inside.

The first was a photographed image of a business card, Austin Fogarty, VP of Sales for Shanti Joy Cosmetics, LLC. Six had no idea who Austin Fogarty was, but she was definitely familiar with Shanti Joy. It was one of the largest cosmetic companies in the world that ethically and sustainably sourced, developed, and delivered all its products.

Needing more context, she clicked on the next few files. One was an itinerary for a flight from Indonesia to Boston. The other looked like a journal entry containing random thoughts about Jeremy's own trip to that country the prior January. None of the notes made much sense—not yet, anyway—so she closed that document out and opened another. A scanned image of a deed to a piece of property about an hour and half west of Cos Cob filled her screen. The deed was in Jeremy's name. He'd never mentioned buying or owning the land to Six, and she made a note to ask Heather if she knew anything about it.

The last item was another file with the name "Indonesia Pictures." If the situation had been different, Six would have smiled. In all the years she'd known him, Jeremy had taken maybe a handful of good pictures, though he loved doing it and always had a camera ready. But given that the files had intentionally been hidden away, *smiling* wasn't on the list of things Six felt like doing.

As the mouse hovered over the icon, a sense of dread slithered down her spine. She had a feeling she wasn't about to see a series of images celebrating the beauty of Indonesia. On a deep breath, she clicked the file open, then enlarged the view of the images so she could see thumbnails of all sixteen on her screen. Most were too dark and blurry to see much, but on a few, she could make out a circle of men, some holding drinks, some not. Clicking on one that looked clearer than the rest, a single image filled her screen.

Six's stomach dropped. It was indeed a circle of men, and some were indeed holding drinks. But what caught her attention were the two naked women kneeling on the floor, blindfolded and with their hands tied over their heads.

Not letting herself contemplate the fate of those two women yet, Six instead focused on the details. Zooming in on various parts of the picture, she gathered what data she could from the moment in time that the image had captured.

The women appeared to be Indonesian, although Six's assumption was based only on the color of their hair, the tone of their skin, and their general build. When she found nothing more that might tell her who they were, she shifted her focus to the four men in the picture. Scanning their faces, she didn't recognize any of them, but wondered if they had something to do with Shanti Joy. The company wasn't shy about marketing its ethical practices, and Six knew it sourced a lot of oils from

Indonesia. Nothing in the picture looked remotely ethical, though.

Breaking the image up, she saved four individual files, each a picture of one of the men. She'd run them through her facial recognition program as soon as she finished going through the rest of the photos.

Deciding she needed the full impact of what Jeremy had deemed important enough to save, she closed the image she'd opened and started at the top of the list. There were only sixteen pictures in all, but Six had a feeling those sixteen images were going to pack a punch. And with each one that she opened, that feeling proved more and more true.

Ten minutes later, Six closed out the last and rose from her seat so abruptly that her chair tipped back. Catching it before it fell, she set it to rights, then stalked into her living room, where she paced in front of her picture window.

What the hell had Jeremy been a part of? No, not a part of, Jeremy would *never* do what the men in the pictures had been doing. Those were the types of things Jeremy dedicated his free time to *preventing*.

After the death of their parents, Heather had rebelled a bit and gotten involved with a man who hadn't been good. It had taken Jeremy a year, and Heather nearly getting killed by her abuser, before the two had been able to extricate her.

Once Heather was back on her feet, they'd both dedicated significant amounts of time to helping other victims of domestic violence. What was depicted in the images on Jeremy's computer wasn't domestic violence in the true sense of the word. But it was very clearly violence against women. Something Jeremy never would have countenanced.

She continued to pace. If she started the facial recognition program now, it wouldn't be out of the realm of possibility that she'd take her anger and disgust out on her poor computer. Stalking from one side of the room to the other, a litany of

Italian flowed from her mouth as she cursed the men involved with limp dicks and pustules. Oh, she still intended to bring the men to justice, but having limp dicks and pustules would make them very popular in prison.

Her phone dinged with a text, but she wasn't ready to talk to humanity quite yet, so she continued pacing and ignored it. She should have known better, though. Within ten minutes, she received three more texts.

Forcing herself to stop pacing, she let her friends' concern ground her, and she picked up her phone. Two messages from Cyn and one each from Devil and Nora awaited her—all wanting to know if she was getting ready for her dinner. Opening a group text, she invited them over. Devil texted back that she was twenty minutes from home and would come straight to her house, while Cyn said she'd be right over. Nora was finishing with her current client and promised to be there as soon as possible.

After telling Cyn to make herself at home when she arrived, Six jogged upstairs to take a shower. She wouldn't have much time with them before she'd need to leave to meet Gavin, so she wanted to at least get her hair into a manageable state.

She'd just turned off her hair dryer when she heard Cyn's voice greet both Devil and Nora. Yes, Six had the five-minute-shower down to an art form, which left her just enough time to dry her hair enough that it wouldn't frizz in the humidity.

"I'd make some snarky comment about getting dressed up for your dinner, but I think we have bigger things to tackle, don't we?" Cyn asked as soon as Six joined them in her living room. She hadn't put on her makeup yet, but she did have on her favorite pair of jeans and loose-knit silk top.

"Follow me," Six said, leading them to her office. After opening the file with the images, she pulled up the first, then gestured for one of her friends to take over. Taking a seat, Cyn started clicking slowly through the sequence. The images got progressively more graphic from the first to the last, presumably as the night went on and the men drank more, got more aggressive, and felt more invincible.

When Cyn closed out the last of the images, she leaned back in her chair. "What was Jeremy doing with those pictures?"

"You mean was he there and took them?" Six clarified the question she thought Cyn really meant to ask. Hesitantly, Cyn nodded. "I have no idea," Six said.

"He wouldn't stand there and let that happen," Nora said. A little knot of stress in Six's stomach untangled at Nora's certainty. Six didn't think so either, but it was nice to know she wasn't alone.

"I agree, but that still doesn't answer the question of how he got them," Cyn said.

"Or why he has them and what he planned to do with them," Devil added.

"Who are the men?" Nora asked.

Six shook her head. "I don't know. I'll run their faces through the recognition program when I leave to meet Gavin. Hopefully, we'll get hits quickly and we'll know by the time I'm home." She hesitated, then added, "I think they may be associated with Shanti Joy."

Cyn frowned. "The cosmetics company?"

"Aren't they all about ethical and sustainable business practices?" Nora asked. "Hardly in line with what we saw in the pictures."

Six showed them the image of Austin Fogarty's business card. "This was in Jeremy's file as well."

Silence fell over the group, no doubt each playing through the scenarios. It wouldn't be the first time a corporation had lied—or even the hundredth. But it somehow seemed more egregious coming from the kind of company Shanti Joy claimed to be.

"We don't know for certain," Six said, acknowledging they all had legitimate reasons to doubt. "But—"

"Yes, we do," Devil said, turning her phone around for them to see the screen. She'd done the obvious and googled Austin Fogarty. The image of the smiling, well-dressed man staring back at them was a familiar face. Yes, Shanti Joy, or at least one of its execs, was most definitely involved in the rape and exploitation of those women.

"His behavior is a little off-brand, wouldn't you say?" Cyn said. It had taken Six about a year after meeting Cyn to fully grasp the British affinity for understated sarcasm.

Devil let out a little chuckle. "Just a bit, but it's not just his behavior." Again, she turned her phone around to show them the website that depicted Shanti Joy's executive committee and board of directors. Two more familiar faces smiled back at them. Based on the pictures and bios, they were Kaden Fogarty, the COO and brother of Austin Fogarty, and Julian Newcross, member of the board and husband of the founder, Julia Newcross.

Six let out a long breath. "Well, I guess that explains Jeremy's interest. Between the bad behavior of the corporation—or its execs—and the exploitation and abuse of the women, he wouldn't have been able to *not* get involved."

"To what end though?" Cyn asked.

"And who is the fourth man?" Nora interjected.

Six glanced at her watch. She had the same questions, but she was also due to meet Gavin in thirty minutes. She shook her head. "I have a few ideas about how, and why, Jeremy might have gotten involved, but I'll need to do a little research. As to the fourth man, I'll run him through the recognition program and let's see what we get. His picture isn't as clear as the others, and it's mostly a portion of his profile, but let's see if anything pops."

"Do you need to finish getting ready for dinner?" Nora

asked. She must have caught Six looking at her watch. The question sounded innocent, but when she saw the grinning faces of her friends, she knew it was anything but.

"Yes, but before I do," Six said, deciding not to react to her friends' subtle provocation, "does Joe have any updates on the two people in the car from last night?" she asked Cyn.

Cyn shook her head. "Not yet. He said he'd text us all when he had something."

"Still no ID?" Six asked. It was unusual that twenty-four hours after an accident they wouldn't have at least a fingerprint ID yet.

Cyn made a face. "One of them didn't have fingerprints. Or rather he did, but he'd scarred his fingers enough that he's unidentifiable. Although with such unusual prints, the police were able to tie him to a couple of arsons in Miami from a few years ago. They just don't know who he is."

"What about the other?" Devil asked.

"As of this morning, they were running them both through the system, but I know nothing more than that," Cyn answered.

"You'll keep me posted?" Six asked as Cyn rose from the seat.

"Of course," she said. "And you'll do the same?" It came as no surprise that her friends would want to know everything about her dinner with Gavin tonight. They were her friends, so their interest was expected, but Six knew that despite all their teasing about her and Gavin, his presence in her life meant a change to theirs as well. He was one more person in a small but growing number of people who knew who they were and what they did. The role he was sent to play didn't just affect her, and she owed it to them to keep them informed. Not that she wouldn't have anyway.

"I'll call you all when I get home," Six confirmed.

The four of them exited her office and headed toward the door. "I know this sounds unlikely, but you might want to try to enjoy yourself tonight," Cyn said. "As you said, the situation is what it is. If Franklin thinks he's someone we need in our lives, maybe we should give him a chance."

Six appreciated how Cyn had made Gavin's entrance into their lives about the group, rather than just her, and her observation was logical and sound. But Six was still going to withhold judgment until she had a better sense of what Gavin Cooper's orders were regarding his duty to her and her friends.

"At the very least, you'll have something pretty to look at while you eat," Devil added with a grin.

Six rolled her eyes and shook her head. "Out, all of you. I need to throw on some makeup and finish with my hair. I'm not sure if he'll prove to be an ally or not, but either way, I'm going dressed for battle."

"And by battle, I assume you mean killer clothes, hot lingerie, and perfect hair and makeup?" Nora said with a smile.

Six grinned as she opened the door. There were all sorts of armor and weaponry a person could carry, and confidence was one of the most powerful. She didn't need the right clothes or hair to be confident, but they for damn sure didn't hurt.

CHAPTER EIGHT

GAVIN WAITED at the entrance to the restaurant and watched the townsfolk go about their evening business. Cos Cob was a picturesque seaside village that, on the weekends, filled with people from the city wanting to breathe the fresher air. But on the weekdays, and especially during this time of year, it was primarily a place for the locals, of which there were only about two thousand.

It was a far cry from the industrial city in northern England where he'd grown up. Small boutiques lined the few commercial blocks of Main Street, and interspersed were useful shops, such as a pharmacy, a co-op, and a bookstore, as well as several well-rated restaurants. Including the one he was currently standing in front of—an upscale pub with a very Irish name, but a very Parisian patio for outdoor dining.

He glanced over at the outdoor tables; three couples and a family were enjoying themselves. If the conversation he and Violetta needed to have wasn't so sensitive, it would be a nice place to enjoy their meal. But of course, their meeting tonight wasn't about the meal.

He looked up when he heard the distinct sound of her car. It was an eerily quiet SUV and what little noise it did make, it seemed to do so hesitantly, as if apologizing for the racket. He smiled as she whipped into a spot across the street, and he wasn't going to lie to himself, his heart rate kicked up in anticipation.

He'd seen her in suits, and once she'd stopped by the office in her gym clothes after running some 10K charity race. He'd even seen her in all sorts of other outfits when she hadn't known he was watching out for her. But he looked forward to seeing what she'd wear when she came to meet him. Would she dress up or down? Casual or businesslike?

Him? Well, he'd decided to start as he meant to go on. Outside of work, he had no intention of ever wearing a suit, so he'd donned a pair of jeans, an off-white button-down, and a pair of black shoes. Eventually, he planned to ditch the button-down for a T-shirt, but he still had some winning over to do before he became *too* familiar. Not that she had a choice in working with him, but still, he'd much rather she agree to it willingly than because she'd been ordered to.

His breath caught in his throat when she slid from her car. Wearing a pair of jeans that fit her like a glove, heeled sandals, and a silk top that matched the color of her cognac-colored eyes, she was stunning. He'd been attracted to any number of women in his forty years, but he'd never had the kind of physical—almost uncontrollable—response to a woman as he had to Violetta Salvitto. From day one, there'd been chemistry between them. But his reaction to her had only grown stronger and more intense over time. Now, how she looked and carried herself was only a portion—and not even close to the biggest portion—of his attraction.

She caught his eye as she stood on the other side of the street waiting for a few cars to pass. She didn't offer a smile or a wave, but at least she looked relaxed. Well, more accurately, she didn't look as though she was coming to do him murder.

She glanced left and when the cars cleared, her long strides brought her to his side of the street. When she stopped in front of him, he considered leaning forward and brushing a kiss against her cheek in the European style. But pushing any familiarity on her would get him nowhere and he needed, wanted, to earn her trust. So instead, he opted for a simple nod and a smile.

"Thank you for coming tonight," he said.

He didn't miss the way her eyes swept over him before meeting his again. "Shall we?" she asked. She had her hair tied back in a loose bun, and as she gestured with her head to the door of the pub, a long strand escaped.

He nodded, then shoved one hand in his pocket and opened the door with his other. Not two seconds after the door closed behind them, an older man came forward, his hands outstretched and a big smile on his face.

"Vi, I heard you were coming. It's been too long," he said.

Gavin's eyes narrowed as the two brushed cheeks.

"It's been two weeks, Ambrose. If you had your way, the club and I would be in here every night," she said with a light laugh.

"And I would be honored if you were," the man replied.

"And bankrupt," Violetta added with another laugh. "Ambrose, this is Gavin Cooper," she said, stepping aside and gesturing to him. Gavin took the older man's hand and didn't miss how Ambrose sized him up.

Then, casting Violetta a curious look, he spoke. "I booked your usual table, but I could move you to the patio or somewhere...else."

Violetta offered the man a grateful smile. "The usual table would be perfect."

Ambrose's eyebrows shot up and although he held his tongue, his gaze darted back to Gavin in question. It didn't take a genius to figure out that Ambrose knew *something* of Violetta's other life and now understood that Gavin was also somehow a part of that.

As they made their way to a table in the back corner, Violetta waved to a young man sitting at the bar then to a couple cuddled side by side in a booth on the other side of the pub. He didn't know why, but her openness, her friendliness, surprised him. Not that she was *unfriendly* at work, but she certainly never went out of her way to make friends in the office. Then again, if he led the life she led for the number of years she had, it was probably much simpler to keep her private life just that, private.

"The usual?" Ambrose asked Violetta once she'd taken her seat. Violetta nodded. "And you, sir?" he asked, turning to Gavin.

"What's your usual?" he asked Violetta.

"An IPA from a Vermont brewer that's just across the border. It's hoppy, so if you don't like hops, I'd pass."

Honestly, being British, he wasn't a huge fan of the American-style hoppy beers. But there was a subtle challenge in her words. She'd assimilated to the US, could he?

"I'll have the same, then," he said to Ambrose, who nodded, then disappeared.

"You come here a lot?" he asked, handing a menu over to her though he suspected she wouldn't need it.

She inclined her head. "Ambrose is a good friend, and while there are a lot of very good restaurants in town, no one does comfort food quite like he does."

He arched a brow. "Are you feeling the need for some comfort food?"

Her gaze drifted toward the bar behind him. She'd taken the seat with her back to the wall, leaving her with a full view of the restaurant. He didn't enjoy not being able to see what was happening behind him. But while he didn't think she'd intentionally set out to test him, he could use the situation to show her that he trusted her enough to watch his back. At least he hoped that she would.

"Violetta?" he asked, drawing her attention to him. For the

first time since she'd stepped out of her car, he noticed the worry in her eyes. He didn't think he was the cause, and he wondered if she'd learned something about the two people in the vehicle from the night before.

She shook her head. "I apologize, I'm distracted. As for comfort food, yes, I do need it. I just lost a friend, and the little escapade last night erased any doubt I had that he was murdered. The police disagree, though. It isn't going to be a pretty next few weeks as I convince them otherwise."

He inclined his head. "Fair enough. Do you want to talk about it?"

"About Jeremy? No," Violetta said. They paused their conversation when Ambrose brought their drinks.

"Do you need a few minutes, or would you like to order now?" Ambrose asked.

Violetta flashed a brilliant smile, one that had Gavin blinking. He'd seen her smile and laugh with colleagues, but he hadn't realized how restrained those interactions were until this moment. Because the smile she'd given was big, genuine, and filled with a warmth and a humor he hadn't expected.

With an internal sigh, he acknowledged he was done for. As in, off the market for good—not that he was ever really on the market, but to the extent he had been, he wasn't anymore. He wanted Violetta. He wanted that smile. He wanted to know what else about her changed when she truly let her guard and walls down. And he wanted to be the man who earned that privilege.

He wondered if his superiors had contemplated this scenario and came to the quick conclusion they hadn't. The man she'd called Franklin might have. On the day Gavin had been issued his new orders, he'd been the only person in the room who knew Violetta Salvitto. To everyone else, she'd been just another op. And no doubt, his superiors were just waiting for the day when MI6 would recall him, and they could check the box on this joint MI6 and British Army cooperative effort.

But was that what he wanted?

"Gavin?" Violetta asked.

He blinked, and his gaze bounced between his dinner companion and the restaurateur. They both looked at him expectantly.

"Sorry, woolgathering. Was there a question?" he asked.

Violetta frowned, but picked up her menu. "Do you know what you want to eat?"

"What are you having?" he asked.

"Shepherd's pie," she answered. "It's the Wednesday special from Labor Day to Memorial Day. He changes it to a chicken and vegetable curry for the summer."

"Shepherd's pie it is, then. Thank you," he added when Ambrose nodded. Gavin waited for the man to be out of earshot, then he raised his glass. Violetta eyed him but did the same.

"Cheers," he said.

"Salute," she replied, and they clicked glasses before each taking a sip. The flavor of the hops came through strong, but to his surprise, the beer was smooth, almost creamy. All in all, not bad.

Not one to beat around the bush, Violetta set her glass down, pinned him with a look, and asked, "What are your orders?"

He didn't hesitate to divulge. If he wanted her trust, he'd have to offer her his. "They were vague, but the gist of it was that I needed to stick close to you and offer any assistance should you need it."

Violetta frowned. "Do you know who I work for?"

He took another sip of his beer and smiled. "I think the real question is why was an MI6 spook allowed to order the assignment of a British Special Forces officer to essentially take up residence in the United States in order to protect an Italian intelligence asset who has never had an assignment in the United States and so who, in theory, shouldn't need backup."

The smile she gave him wasn't as brilliant as the one she'd given Ambrose, but it had started with her eyes and was genuine. "Yes," she said. "I did wonder that."

He smiled back and raised his glass. "You and me both," he said.

She searched his face, looking for any untruth. Nearly a minute passed before she picked up her own drink again and leaned back in her chair. "Why did you take the assignment? There is zero reason why I'd need any backup. I'll grant you that on a few ops I've been on, it would have been nice. But here? In Cos Cob and Boston? It doesn't make any sense."

He lifted a shoulder. "I agree, it doesn't." He didn't take issue with her statement about not needing any help. Sure, he'd stepped in last night, but that was only because he figured if his car got a little banged up it would be easier to fix than hers. She'd had the situation under control, and if he hadn't been around, she still would have been fine.

"So again, why would you take the assignment?" she pressed.

"Because I didn't have a choice," he answered baldly.

She leaned forward again, and the tips of her fingers slid over her glass as she studied him. After a beat, she spoke. "No choice?"

He shook his head. "I may be a senior officer and I may be decorated out the arse, but I'm still a soldier. I go where they tell me to and do what they order me to." It wasn't quite that straightforward or mindless, but it was close.

Her brows dipped, but it was a few seconds before she spoke again. "Do you *want* to have the choice?"

It was his turn to frown. "You mean do I want out of this assignment?"

She nodded.

He hadn't considered that would be an option. Now that

Violetta had asked, though, and asked in such a way that led him to believe she could make it happen, did he *want* that to happen? As he mulled the question over, he realized the answer was a complicated one.

If she'd asked him five months ago, he would have said yes, he wanted out. But now? Now that he knew her in the ways he did, and knew the ways he *wanted* to know her better, it wasn't so clear-cut. He wanted to be here. He wanted to work side by side with her. But he also wanted out because as long as he was *in*, the British Army owned him. His contract gave them the right to pull him at any moment.

"The assignment? No, I like it here. I like the work I'm doing, and I like the idea of working with you even if neither of us understands why or how this all came into play."

"But?"

"No buts," he said. "I don't like the idea that the army could pull me at any time, which tells me that I like this assignment. Probably more than I should."

She stared at him for a long time, then finally, she lifted her drink and gave a shake of her head. "I honestly have no idea what Franklin must have been thinking. This could, quite possibly, be the world's most boring assignment for you. Aside from what happened last night, my life here is quiet. I work, I hang out with my friends, I pretend to garden, and I play auntie to my friend Nora's various strays."

It actually sounded quite idyllic to him. But he hadn't been sent to Massachusetts to become a part of her life in a way that would allow him to partake of those simple joys with her. Even if he wanted to.

"I think it's safe to say that neither of us knows why I'm here. But I am here, so if you need an extra set of hands, you know you have one."

Something flashed in her eyes, but it was gone before he could place it. She'd just learned about him the night before, and, so far, all her questions had sounded genuine. She didn't seem to understand his assignment any more than he did, but a suspicion sneaked up on him that she did, or might, know *something*.

The moment to ask was interrupted when Ambrose brought their dinners. And after Gavin took his first bite, he all but lost interest in what Violetta may or may not know. He'd never imagined finding a good shepherd's pie outside of the UK, but the one that was now his for the taking couldn't be more perfect. The flavors were rich, but not heavy. The balance between the meat and the veggies at the bottom and the potatoes at the top was the way he liked it—about a fifty-fifty ratio. And the potatoes themselves were seasoned with the perfect amount of salt and pepper.

After his third bite, he realized that Violetta had stilled, and he looked across the table to find her staring at him.

"It's good, yes?" she asked, her fork held halfway to her mouth.

"You know it is," he countered, then took another bite.

She inclined her head and slipped her own bite between her lips. When she was done, she swallowed a sip of her beer, then spoke again. "It is good. I think it's very good. But just because I think it's good doesn't mean you have to like it. Devil swears by a certain type of foie gras. She says it's the best in the world. She might be right, she probably is, but I can't stand the stuff, so the quality is irrelevant."

He filed that little tidbit away in his head for future reference. He'd learned a lot about Violetta from the files they'd given him, but he didn't know she didn't like foie gras. Which worked out well, since he'd didn't like it either.

"There are lots of reasons not to like foie gras. But so long as you're not a vegetarian, there is absolutely no reason someone would not like this," he said, pointing to the shepherd's pie with his fork.

SIX

She smiled, a small upward tip of the left side of her mouth. And just like that, his body was once again focused on her and everything he wanted to do to, and with, her.

He cleared his throat, then sipped his drink. "So, what about last night?" he asked, bringing the topic back to something that might dampen his reaction to her.

She looked at him without a hint of guile. "What about last night?"

"The car that tried to run you off the road. You remember that? They took a shot at you." She remembered; she just didn't want to talk to him about it. She might be coming to accept that he was one of the good guys, but like the food, that didn't mean she had to like him or the job he was sent to do.

"I can't do my job if you don't talk with me," he pointed out.

She snorted. "I don't actually care if you can or can't do your job. That seems like a *you* problem."

Gavin couldn't help it, he barked out a laugh. Her answer was *so* Violetta. And he didn't doubt her veracity in the least. In some ways, he didn't blame her. If AISE sent someone to be his backup as he went about his daily life, he wouldn't care about their job either. His loyalty was to England and its subjects, and hers was to Italy and its subjects. Their interests might overlap at times, but they had no duty to each other.

She might not have a *duty* to care about him, but he had every intention of making sure she *grew* to care.

"Fair enough," he said. "Will you answer questions if I ask them?"

"Depends on the questions."

He hadn't expected anything less. "Was the incident last night related to your friend's death?"

"His murder," she corrected, giving him his answer. He hadn't hesitated to flip the small SUV when he'd seen what the two people inside were trying to do to Violetta. Now that he

67

knew they were responsible for, or at least involved in, Jeremy Wheaton's death, he had even less sympathy.

"They followed you from his apartment," he said. It wasn't a question. He was taking a risk letting Violetta know he'd followed her, too—first to Jeremy's, then home—but again, if he wanted her trust, he had to offer his.

"Apparently they weren't the only ones following me," she replied, her right eyebrow ever so slightly elevated. It was the subtlest reaction he'd seen from her, and it made him a little nervous.

"I haven't followed you before," he said, meeting her stare with a direct one of his own. "I have checked in on you, but until last night, I'd never actually followed you."

"Still, the fact that you did, and I didn't notice—or the fact that *they* did and I didn't notice until they were nearly on my bumper—is...well, it's disconcerting."

"I can see how you might feel that way. I would too. But the truth is, you have no reason to think that anything like what happened last night would happen here. For all intents and purposes, you're a civilian in this country. So am I. There should be no reason anyone here would want to harm you." It was a little bit of a stretch—intelligence agents gathered enemies faster than flies on shit sometimes. But he'd seen her dossier, or the parts of it that hadn't been redacted, and the kind of ops she ran would be impossible to tie back to her unless there was a leak at AISE.

She took the last sip of her drink and set her glass down. "I've noticed a boat occasionally trawling by my house, about a hundred yards out. Any chance that's you?"

He grinned. "I always wanted a boat. I negotiated it into my assignment, saying it would be an easy way to keep an eye on you given the security at your house."

She paused, then, to his delight, threw her head back and laughed. A big, honest laugh. When she settled down, she reached for her napkin and dabbed her eyes before taking a sip of the water that had been left at the table with their beers. "I wish I could have seen those negotiations," she said. "I've met a few ranking officers from the British Army. They don't tend to have a great sense of humor and probably had no idea you were poking at them, did they?"

Gavin smiled. "They did not. It was all *very* serious. Except your friend, the spook. He took my side and argued for a bigger boat, saying the waters around here could get rough and I needed something more substantial than a dinghy. Personally, I think he was having as much fun poking at the army as I was."

She let out a small laugh at that. "Yes, Franklin takes great joy in manipulating people."

A waiter came over to clear their plates, asking if they wanted dessert or another drink. Gavin looked to Violetta. He wasn't ready for the evening to be over, and he still wanted to talk to her about Jeremy. But if she didn't want to talk, he couldn't force her.

To his surprise, she ordered an amaro, as did he. Not only did they appear to share the same taste in drinks, but by ordering, she'd willingly prolonged their time together. It was a small thing, but he felt as if he'd come out the winner of a prizefight.

"What was Jeremy like?" he asked. If he was going to be her backup, he needed to know everything there was to know— about the crime and about Jeremy, but also about what Violetta was thinking. She wasn't willing to share anything about the crime or her thought process, but maybe he could get her talking about her friend. He had a feeling that she'd inadvertently stepped into a hornet's nest, and the more he knew, the more he could watch her back.

A soft smile touched her lips at his question, and she glanced away. It was dark out, but the lights from the patio and the street gave them a view of the world that carried on.

"We were in law school together," Violetta said. "We met the first day in Civil Procedure. It was a god-awful class, and we commiserated together. From there we started studying together, and we've been friends ever since. He is—was—one of the good ones, you know?" she said, looking up. He hadn't met Jeremy, but he knew the kind of person Violetta was referring to. The kind of person who is just *good*.

He nodded. "What kind of work did he do?"

Violetta paused while their waiter brought their drinks. When the young man was gone, she picked up the small tumbler filled with two fingers of the rich honey-colored liquor and rolled it between her palms.

"Mostly civil litigation," she answered. "He liked to take on corporations who were taking advantage of the little guys."

Another little tidbit Gavin filed away. It wasn't unheard of for a corporation to go after someone who was causing them trouble. Granted, killing a man was extreme, but that would depend on the type of threat Jeremy might have posed.

"But he did a ton of pro bono and volunteer work, too. Mostly to support women coming out of unhealthy relationships, but immigrants as well. He also served as a child advocate." She paused, took a sip of her amaro, and tipped her head back. Her eyes closed for a moment, but Gavin didn't know if it was in memory of her friend or in enjoyment of the liquid traveling down her throat. Or, he supposed, it could be both.

"Like I said," she said when she again met his gaze. "He was one of the good ones."

"You told me he was murdered. Is there proof or is that conjecture?" He was pressing a bit, but she'd been the one to mention murder, so she shouldn't be surprised that he'd ask about it.

Her eyes studied him as she took another sip. After a beat, she answered. "Nothing concrete. I saw the video of the car that hit Jeremy. It was the same make and model as the one from last night. I also have video from my car's rear camera that shows damage to that car that could be in line with a hit-and-run."

"And there's the fact that they followed you from his apartment," Gavin added before sipping his own drink. She was right —it was all conjecture at this point, but pretty damn good conjecture.

She inclined her head. "I have someone in the police keeping an eye on things. But even if they can tie the car from last night to Jeremy's death, they still don't have evidence proving it was murder versus an accident."

"Which is where you come in, isn't it?"

"I'm worried about Heather, Jeremy's sister," she replied, ignoring his probing question. She'd more or less admitted to looking into Jeremy's life and death, but clearly wasn't yet decided on how much to share with him.

"In what way?" he asked, going with the flow.

"I was only at his apartment for thirty minutes before they decided to follow me home. Heather's been in and out of the place since they first notified her of her brother's death. Why did they follow me? Or more to the point, why did they try to run *me* off the road?"

Gavin didn't have an answer for that, although it was a damn good question. Presumably, if Heather gave Violetta access to any files, it would make Heather, who would also have access, a target as well. But that wasn't what had happened.

"It might be worth having someone watch over her," Gavin suggested. "But as for why *you*, maybe it has to do with the fact that you're a federal prosecutor? Maybe they don't know you're a friend of Jeremy's and saw you as a threat because of your job?"

Violetta seemed to mull this suggestion over. It wasn't a great one, but unless there was a reason that she was *specifically* targeted, it wasn't illogical to treat the incident as just being in the wrong place at the wrong time. It was possible that her friendship with Jeremy and her life with AISE might unnecessarily be muddying the waters.

If he hadn't been watching her so closely, he would have missed how Violetta drew back, almost infinitesimally. As if she'd discovered something.

"Violetta?"

Her eyes jumped up to meet his.

"What are you thinking?" he asked.

She held his gaze and for a moment, he thought she might take him into her confidence. But then she shook her head. "Just something I need to look into."

"I can help," he said, throwing in a cheeky smile that was more a flash of his teeth than anything else.

She had the grace to give him a rueful laugh. "I'm sure you can, but I'm also sure you'll understand if I don't take you up on that offer. I have three best friends that I've known since I was twelve. They are all exceptionally bright, exceptionally wily, and exceptionally loyal. And then we also have Joe, Cyn's partner. I think I have all the backup I need, thank you very much."

He smiled in response. Violetta's words might have been intended to put him off, but what she'd done was throw the gauntlet down. He had every intention of being included on the tiny list of people she trusted—those she considered the most loyal. And he was going to have a hell of good time proving it to her.

CHAPTER NINE

SIX STRETCHED IN BED, wiggling her toes against the cool cotton of her sheets even as she burrowed under her fluffy duvet. Once again, she'd been up late. First filling her friends in on her dinner, then doing some research into an idea she'd had about what Jeremy might have been investigating before he died. After she'd wrapped that up for the night, she again hit the gym. Technically, she was supposed to be in the office today. But given that she'd been in on Monday and Tuesday, she'd emailed Rosey and Mitch to let them know she'd be working from home.

She was staring at her ceiling, contemplating how unfortunate it was that her coffee machine wasn't right beside her bed —something she might have to rectify—when her phone dinged letting her know someone was on her property.

Grabbing her device, she pulled up the app connected to the security cameras to see Gavin's SUV making its way up her drive. She frowned as she watched him park, then slide from his seat. In jeans and a T-shirt, he looked better than any man had a right to. It didn't hurt that he appeared to be carrying coffee and what looked to be a bag of pastries.

He jogged up the steps of her porch and rang the bell. She considered ignoring him—having him in her house wasn't something she was looking forward to—but then she spotted the label on the cup. Her favorite coffee.

Still, she debated. Was she really going to sell her soul for a cup of coffee? The thought made her smile. Apparently, she wasn't above a little bribery among colleagues, or whatever they were, because she was definitely considering letting him in. The doorbell rang again and with a growl, she threw the covers off and stalked downstairs. She might be getting coffee out of this deal, but that didn't mean she was happy about him showing up.

She flung the door open and glared at Gavin.

"Good morning," he chirped. Then wisely, he held out the cup holder so she could see the latte with her name on it.

She held his gaze as she reached for the cup. Once she had it securely in hand, she turned and stomped to the French doors leading out to her back porch. Throwing them open, she stepped out into the cool morning sunshine.

"You need to reset the security, Violetta," Gavin called. She ignored him and took a sip of her latte. Octo Coffee, one of her favorite places in Cos Cob, made the best coffee on the eastern seaboard. They also made excellent pastries.

Spinning to face Gavin and demand the pastries, she was startled to find him right behind her. He'd set the bag and second cup of coffee down, and his free hands came out to steady her. His fingertips slid under the hem of her short sleep shirt and rested against the top of her boxers. The rough skin of his palms gripped her waist.

"You need to reset your alarm, Violetta," he said.

She reached up and gently pinched his top and bottom lips together. "You're interrupting," she said, holding her drink up. He arched a brow but said nothing more. She took another sip of her coffee while his hands remained at her waist, and her fingers remained on his lips. She was well aware their positions were crossing a line she hadn't intended to cross, but he smelled good, and his lips felt nice under her fingers. Beyond that, she hadn't had enough coffee to contemplate anything more.

"Security system, Salvitto," Gavin said through his pinched lips. He sounded ridiculous, but he did not appear to mind having her fingers on his mouth.

"Give me thirty more seconds," she said, lifting her cup and taking another sip. Although when his thumbs started caressing the skin at her waist, she didn't think she'd need the rest of her coffee to wake up. He was doing a damn fine job of sending sparks of adrenaline, and attraction, through her.

Slowly, she let her fingers drop from his lips, and her palm came to rest on his chest. Her hand was on the opposite side as his heart so she couldn't feel it beating, but she could feel Gavin's tight breaths.

She glanced up to find him staring down at her. His gaze dropped to her lips, and his fingers flexed on her waist. Abruptly, she stepped away. She did not need to fall under his spell and much to her chagrin, she realized that it wouldn't be all that hard to do just that.

Thankfully, he took her distance in stride and reached for the pastries. "I'll give you all of these if you go reset your alarm," he said, holding the bag out.

She rolled her eyes and swiped the bag from his hand before he knew what hit him. It was cute he was concerned, but he'd need to learn not to barter with pastries. It was a sure way for him to get taken down. "When I answered the door, I used a code that automatically resets the alarm thirty seconds after the door closes," she said, digging through the bag. "It helps with things like deliveries, or whenever I'm carrying stuff into the house and have my hands too full to stop and deal with the alarm."

Having removed his own coffee from the cup holder, Gavin

took a sip as he turned and considered her house. "You have a different system on your back door?"

"I have a setting that allows me to determine which of the five doors into my house I want the alarm on for. It's currently set for all but this one," she responded, gesturing to the open door between her porch and living room that they'd walked through. "What are you doing here?" she asked, once she'd selected a *bombolone* from the bag. The doughnut-like pastry had been a favorite afternoon treat when she was a little girl, but it served as a breakfast delight just as well.

"You're here, so I'm here," he said, withdrawing a *cornetti* sprinkled with raw sugar from the bag before taking a seat on the porch swing. The *cornetti* had been her second choice, but since Sylvia made her some the day before, she was happy to leave it to him.

"Why aren't you at work?" she clarified, taking a seat on the small couch perpendicular to the swing. When she curled a leg under her, she realized how little she had on. Her short T-shirt barely reached the top of her rolled-up boxers, and her boxers most definitely showed a lot of leg. She stared at her bare thighs, debating whether to change. Then she decided, fuck it, it was too much work to go to for someone who invited himself over when he knew damn well he wasn't particularly welcome.

"I work when you work," he said. She lowered her *bombolone* and stared at him. "Well, to be accurate, I mostly work when you work. I do pop in on occasion when you're not there so it's not obvious to the rest of the staff that my schedule is tied to yours." When he finished, he took a sip of his drink and stared out toward the ocean as if his response answered anything.

Her eyes narrowed. "Does Mitch know why you're really here?"

Gavin took a bite of his *cornetti* and shook his head. Once he'd swallowed, he answered. "He's a smart guy. He's probably figured something out, but as far as the British Army is concerned, he's just following orders, too."

Well, that put a pause on some of Six's resistance. Not because she suddenly trusted Gavin. But if, unlike hers, his cover story was being kept secret from Mitch, then he had some powerful people behind him who wanted him here.

"*Fanculo,*" she muttered before ripping a bite off her *bombolone.*

Gavin chuckled and started to gently rock the swing. "You're starting to realize this isn't going to go away, aren't you?"

She slid him a narrow look as she took a sip of her coffee.

"Are you cursing me in your head? And by *curse* I don't mean swear, I mean curse me with like saggy balls or something?"

She couldn't help it—her lips twitched. "I wasn't thinking anything as drastic as that, but I'll keep that one in mind."

He chuckled, then took the last bite of his *cornetti* before turning to face her. "What have you found out about Jeremy Wheaton's death?"

She still hadn't talked to Franklin. And she still hadn't a clue as to why he would assign Gavin to help her while she was non-operative. But she *could* see the earnestness in Gavin's expression. He truly wanted to help. Then again, he'd been in the area five months with zero action—he was probably bored and looking to fill his time.

"Thank you for the coffee and pastries, Gavin," she said, before finishing off her *bombolone.* In the past five minutes, she'd accepted she'd have to work with him—their higher-ups would see to that—but that didn't mean she had to jump right in feet first. She wanted to talk to Franklin, if only to unleash her annoyance on him, before making any decisions.

He sighed. "You'll have to call on me at some point, you know."

She shot him a saccharine smile. "Perhaps. But now is not that time."

He held her gaze, then gave a little shake of his head. "If I walk out the front door will the alarm go off?"

She gave a single nod. "You can trot along that path though," she said, pointing to the decomposed granite path that ran between the back and front of her house.

He rose, and the look he gave her hovered somewhere between resigned and amused. "Here," he said, pulling out a small white card and handing it to her. "It's my number. My real number. Use it when you're ready."

"And if I'm not?"

"There will come a day when you will be. Trust me, Violetta, I know that for a fact."

She wasn't quite sure what to make of that comment, but he didn't give her a chance to react. He leaned over her, brushed a kiss across her cheek, then jogged down the steps and disappeared around the corner of her house. A few seconds later, his SUV started and his tires crunched on her gravel drive as he departed.

She reached for the bag of pastries he'd left on the swing and pulled out a honey *cornetti*. As she nibbled her way through it and sipped her coffee, she acknowledged that her response had been a childish one. It might reflect what she *hoped* would happen—she didn't want to need to use his number—but it didn't reflect reality. If the powers that be had decided they needed to work together, then they'd have to figure out a way to work together. As was often the case in her life and with the line of work she'd chosen, what she wanted and what she hoped were irrelevant.

After Gavin left and she'd had her fill of Octo pastries, she retreated to her room and dressed for the day. Based on what she'd discovered the night before, she had more than a few things to follow up on. But before she had the chance to turn her computer on, her phone rang. By all that was holy, Franklin was finally calling her back.

"*Questo gibboso, ributtante rospo.*"

Ignoring her Shakespearean insult about being a bunched-up toad, he replied, "It's lovely to speak with you, too, Six." Even though she'd known him more than twenty-five years and he'd only ever called Six and Devil by those names, the sound of her nickname coming from his mouth always sounded awkward enough to give her pause. Like her grandmother talking about TikTok or Snapchat.

"What the fuck, Franklin?" she demanded.

He chuckled. The asshole. "You sound like Hyacinth when she realized New Joe was sent to replace Joe." Cyn's Joe had replaced his uncle, who also happened to be a Joe. It was confusing at first, and on occasion, they still referred to Cyn's Joe as "New Joe."

"He's a good man, Six. I picked him myself," he added.

Yet another statement that gave her pause. "Picked him for what?" Six asked, almost wishing she hadn't. If Franklin confirmed her suspicion that he was playing matchmaker, she was going to castrate him. Or maybe go into hiding.

There weren't many things that scared her, but the thought of Franklin playing puppeteer to her love life was one of them. But only because he was a man who didn't fail. He was a legend in the field and a legend for a reason. If he'd decided she needed a life partner, then she was screwed.

"For you, dear. Of course."

That ambiguous statement helped not at all. Deciding she didn't want to pursue this line of questioning, she changed her tactic. "What exactly is he supposed to do? I get why you sent New Joe. Having someone in law enforcement is helpful. But having someone like Gavin? Someone who has as much right to operate in this country as I do—which is none—makes no sense." Oops, she'd opened the door she hadn't wanted to. Not that she thought Franklin would suddenly say, "You're right! I picked him for you because I thought you'd make beautiful babies." But she needed to stay far away from any line of discussion that could lead to her personal life.

"Never mind," she muttered. "Just tell me, you *did* send him, right?" She believed Gavin about that, but she wanted to hear it from Franklin himself.

"Six, you will need to learn to trust him. I know he told you about meeting me."

"Yes, well, I just learned who he was less than thirty-six hours ago, so thank you very much but I'll continue to withhold judgment."

He sighed. "The four of you. You give me so much trouble."

She snorted. "If by trouble, you mean we question your interference in our personal lives, then yes, we do." Franklin was Cyn's uncle, but he'd more or less adopted the rest of them as his nieces once Cyn claimed them as her new best friends. Six was aware that he traveled a thin line being both their handler and a surrogate uncle. But he'd chosen that path more than twenty years ago, and he hadn't walked away yet. If he was going to treat her like family, then she was going to return the favor.

He sighed again. "He's a good man, Six. Give him a chance."

"I don't have a choice, do I?"

"Not really, no."

"What, exactly, is he supposed to do?"

"Whatever you need him to," Franklin answered. Well, that didn't sound so bad. "Or whatever he thinks he needs to, to keep you safe." All right, that sounded less good.

"This is the part I don't understand, Franklin. I *don't operate* in the United States. Why is he here?"

"I heard about your little run-in the other night. Or should I say near-run-in."

The point he was trying to make was clear, but still wasn't strong. "Once in the twenty years I've lived in the US, I've had a *run-in*. That hardly lends itself to needing a babysitter."

"And Jeremy Wheaton's murder?"

It was her turn to sigh. "There was no way you could have predicted that when you sent Gavin here in January."

"Not that, specifically." He paused, and in that moment of silence, Six knew she was finally going to get to the heart of the matter. Or at least part of it. "You—all of you—have been in the game long enough to accumulate enemies. Yes, the work you do isn't likely to lead back to you, but the longer you are in the game, the higher the odds become that something will come back on you. Believe me, Six, I know. I'm just taking precautions. With all of you."

It was entirely possible Franklin was bullshitting her, but her gut told her he wasn't. As a seasoned agent of nearly a half a century, his perspective wasn't one she could, or should, discount. His comment also spoke of experience, and she wondered what had happened to him. He might be all up in her business, but that was not a two-way street.

She let out a long breath. "I don't like that you keep springing these *backup* assets on us without talking to us first. I'll be honest, Franklin, it feels like a test. It feels like you're testing if we've lost our ability to judge a person's character or intent. And, as you pointed out, we've been in the game long enough that that kind of a test starts to feel like you're doubting our abilities in general."

"What would you have said if I'd told you what I was doing?"

They both knew full well what she, or Cyn, would have said if he'd told them ahead of time, so she didn't bother answering. "But your point is well taken. I'm still pissed as hell at you. But I'm also woman enough to recognize that you have decades more experience than I and you may know more about what the future might bring to our doorsteps."

"Gracious as always, Six." *That* British sarcasm wasn't hard to miss.

"You're lucky I didn't curse you with saggy balls," she shot back, then winced. Franklin was in his early seventies, maybe cursing him with saggy balls wasn't as dramatic as it would be for someone like Gavin. But what did she know? She'd never seen a naked seventy-year-old.

"That would be the least of my worries, dear."

"Gross. Stop. Please."

He chuckled, then sobered. "He's a good man, Six. He has a past. We all do. But he's exceptional at what he does and has a lion's heart."

Franklin was only confirming what she'd already sensed, though hadn't acknowledged. His warning had given her something to think about, and she owed it to him to do that. But she needed time, so she changed the subject. "You want to know what I think happened with Jeremy?"

"You already know why he was murdered?"

"Not for certain, but I have a lead," she replied.

"Are you going to be able to follow it?" His question wasn't second-guessing her ability, but a commentary on the limits of what she could do within the United States.

"So far, yes. If that changes, well, that's why you sent us New Joe, isn't it?"

"Indeed, it is," he answered. "I don't need to know the specifics, but you'll let me know if you need anything? And you'll be careful?"

"Yes and yes," she said without hesitation.

"Then that's all I need to know," he said.

Silence fell over the line, then Six spoke. She might still be stewing over his tactics, but there was never a doubt that Franklin cared. And each time she went on assignment, if she happened to meet other agents, it was reinforced. He demanded excellence from her as an operative. But he also recognized and encouraged her to be *human*.

"I'm not ready to thank you yet for sending Gavin, but I can say it for everything else," she said. "I don't know if any of us would have survived in this game as long as we have without you, our fairy godfather." It was a sincere compliment, even though he hated that moniker Devil had given him years ago.

"Call me should you need anything," he repeated.

"Pinkie promise," she said, yet another Americanism she loved. It somehow managed to sound both playful and serious at the same time.

He made another indecipherable sound, then ended the call. Six set her phone down and stared at it for a moment—just a brief one. Then she leaned forward, flicked on her computer, and got down to business.

CHAPTER TEN

SIX STARED at the image on her monitor. The night before, she'd uncovered a file that documented four trips to Indonesia that Jeremy had made since the first one in January. She had an inkling of what he'd been doing, although so far, she hadn't found any real evidence to support her theory. Hacking into his phone or credit card records was on her agenda, but right now, she was staring at a satellite image of the property Jeremy held the deed to. The property Heather had confirmed earlier that she knew nothing about.

The forty-two acres were heavily wooded, and it was hard to see much more than a green canopy of leaves. As she continued to look at it, the more strongly Six felt that this remote parcel of land was the piece that didn't quite fit in with Jeremy's other files. And because of that, it was interesting.

Joe had texted earlier and they'd all agreed to meet that night to discuss some updates on the white SUV and the two men inside. Glancing at the clock, Six decided she had time to drive over and check the property out. It was only ninety minutes away, and she wasn't due for dinner at Cyn's with the club until half past five.

Without another thought, she shut her computer down, changed into a pair of jeans and Stan Smiths, and headed out the door. Once she had the map and directions up on her display, she headed out to discover, hopefully, just what Jeremy was doing with such a big piece of land two hours from his home.

The two-lane country roads wound west through beautiful forests and fields. Still, their loveliness didn't distract Six from noticing a certain SUV occasionally showing up in her rearview mirror. That Gavin was following her didn't bother her as much as it would have a few days ago. She still thought it was a colossal waste of his time and talent, but who was she to decide how the British Army deployed their resources?

Ignoring the sporadic glimpses of his car, she focused on the road and let her mind wander. There was no doubt that Jeremy had been trying to help the women in the pictures. If Six were a betting woman, which she was, she'd bet that he'd met one or two of them on his first trip to Indonesia in January. Somehow, he must have gained their trust enough for them to tell him what was going on. His subsequent trips were likely more fact-finding missions. His goal? Well, Six hadn't found any paperwork yet, but she'd bet he'd been planning to file an alien tort claim against Shanti Joy in order to bring to light its behavior and hypocrisy.

The infrequently used, and old, law—the Alien Tort Claims Act—was originally drafted to allow non-US citizens to file a civil claim in US federal courts for violations of international law committed by US citizens. But since the 1980s, it had been used to facilitate claims by non-US citizens brought against US corporations for human rights violations, including rape, torture, child labor, kidnapping, and murder.

If Shanti Joy knew about the abuses happening to the women in Indonesia—which, given they were perpetrated by several senior-level executives and a board member, was highly likely—then going after the company was exactly something Jeremy would do.

Six mulled this over as she continued her drive. She prosecuted criminal cases and knew very little about the act other than what she had dredged up from law school memories and the brief research she'd done that morning. Maybe that was something she could have Gavin look into. She smiled at that... she was pretty sure his idea of helping her wasn't acting as her paralegal.

Six glanced at her dashboard screen as she turned onto an even more rural road. According to the map, Jeremy's parcel fronted the road she was on, and the property line started about a mile from the turn. The lot was long and deep, and the frontage was limited, which should, she hoped, make it easy to find the driveway. Not that she intended to use the driveway. No, she'd scoped out the area, and there was a nature preserve a mile up the road that bordered the property. She planned to park there and walk in.

Coming up on where she thought the property line started, Six slowed her car. Sure enough, about a hundred yards past the line, she spotted an overgrown driveway and, tucked back from the road, a gate. She didn't stop, but her speed allowed her to see that some of the overgrown grass was trampled in a way as to indicate a car had been through recently.

Continuing on, she pulled into the parking lot of the preserve and found a spot two over from a Subaru. She gathered her gear, including a small gun she tucked into an ankle holster and a knife she slipped into her back pocket. Being well acquainted with the bug and insect population in the New England forests, she also pulled on a lightweight jacket that would at least protect her arms from being eaten alive.

She was just exiting her car when she paused. Last January, Cyn had gone running off on her own and come back with a knife wound. It wasn't so much that she'd gone on her own that had been the problem, but the fact that none of them, not even Franklin, had known what she'd planned to do. If anything more serious had happened, it would have taken them precious hours to figure out where to even start looking for her.

Pulling out her phone, she sent a group text to her friends letting them know where she was and what she was doing. They'd be at her side as fast as their cars could get them there if they weren't all working that afternoon. Still, that didn't stop first Cyn, then Devil and Nora, from admonishing her for going on her own.

There was some truth to their comments. It might not be the smartest thing to go traipsing onto private land on her own. But she'd been in worse, far worse, situations. And if something went down, it wasn't as though she wasn't prepared. But again, she didn't often have the luxury of working with a team, and if she'd talked to her friends before she'd left, this could have been one of those times.

"*Text Gavin,*" Cyn's second message appeared on Six's screen. He wasn't exactly the *team* she'd been thinking of. But even though his car hadn't driven past the preserve parking lot, she knew he would be nearby.

A chorus of agreements came from Nora and Devil. And now she'd sound petulant if she didn't. She sighed, then typed in the number he'd given her that she hadn't yet saved in her phone.

"Hello, Violetta," his voice rumbled over the line. With only the tiniest bit of gloating in his voice.

"I'm headed to a piece of property Jeremy bought in February. I know you're here. My friends seem to think it would be good to have some backup."

"Your friends, of which I count myself one, agree."

She let out a huff. "Where are you?"

"Look up and into the trail at your three o'clock."

She glanced to her right and found the trail. When her eyes

adjusted to looking into the dim, filtered light of the forest, she saw him standing near a large maple.

Ending the call, she sent a quick text to her friends letting them know she had backup. She also promised to call them as soon as she was on her way home. Then sliding the phone into her jacket pocket, she exited her car and walked to the trail.

Dressed as he was that morning, in jeans and a T-shirt, he stood with his arms crossed and his phone dangling from his fingers. He wore a smile that had her bracing for some arrogant comment about it not taking her very long to need him. To her surprise, though, he gestured to the trail with his head, then turned and started walking.

Once they were deep in the forest, he spoke. "I received Jeremy's file last night," he said over his shoulder. "The financial transaction for this land was in it, which is how I knew. Did you receive the same?"

She shook her head, then realized he'd turned back around. "No, his sister gave me access to their cloud storage account. I found a copy of the deed hidden in his files."

"We should compare files when we get back," he said. She wasn't looking forward to spending that time with him, but he was right, and she'd do it for Jeremy.

"I agree. Where did you park?"

He glanced back again before answering. "There's an abandoned house on the other side of the road about five hundred meters farther up from the driveway to Wheaton's property. I tucked my car back behind the house."

"Did your file tell you anything about the property? I just pulled up a Google satellite image," she said. Then a thought occurred to her that should have come to her earlier and she let out a quiet curse in Italian.

"You know I speak Italian, right?" he asked, throwing a grin in her direction.

She rolled her eyes. "Between your reactions and your flawless pronunciation of my name, I assumed."

"So what was that swear for?"

"I just realized that once again, Franklin might know what he's talking about."

"Meaning?" As he asked, he stepped off the trail, holding a branch for her.

She put her hand on it to hold it in place as she passed, then let it swing back. "I have access to all sorts of intel, but up until now, I've been using only the means that a normal—or civilian —would use. I *had* planned to hack into his phone and credit card info. But because this investigation is for personal reasons, and not professional ones, I've been putting it off." Cyn hadn't been so cautious when the dead body showed up on her front door, but Cyn was well acquainted with recklessness.

"And?"

"And now I realize a benefit to having you around."

He stopped and turned toward her, his eyes dancing in amusement. For a moment, she wondered if he was ever *not* amused. Franklin had said he had a past, but it sure as shit didn't look like one that bothered him.

"There are a lot of benefits to having me around, but I'm pretty sure the one I'm hoping you're thinking of isn't the one you're thinking of."

She arched a brow at him and tried to give him her best "are you kidding me?" look, but ended up letting out a huff of a laugh and shaking her head. His grin turned into a wide smile.

"Stop that," she said.

Instantly, his smile turned down. "Stop what?" he asked, confused.

"Smiling at everything. It's annoying. Aren't you ever mad or sad or any other emotion other than happy?"

He cocked his head to the side and studied her. "Is *that* why you don't like having me around? Because I'm too *happy?*"

She narrowed her eyes. "No. I don't like having you around because it makes me feel like I'm being babysat—which I'll admit, that's more a me issue than reality. But also, you flirt and grin your way through life, and it makes you seem shallow and untrustworthy."

Again, another tip of his head. "And you don't want me to be shallow or untrustworthy? You want me to be something else?"

She looked up to the canopy in an attempt to find some patience. She shouldn't have said anything in the first place, but now that they were here, and going to be working together, perhaps she needed to get it all out.

"Look, before I knew who you were, you being shallow and untrustworthy didn't even show up on my radar. You were just a pretty man who liked to flirt with everyone in the office. But now that we have to work together, yes, I care. You *can't* be happy all the time. No one is. If that's the only side of you I see, then I'll start to wonder what else you're hiding."

He shoved his hands into his pockets and regarded her. "You think I'm pretty?"

Her stare turned flat, then she pushed around him and continued in the direction they'd been heading before they stopped. He followed behind.

"It's a beautiful day, and I'm on an op with a talented and beautiful woman who intrigues me more than I should admit. Of course I'm happy."

She sliced him a look over her shoulder. He had a weird way of finding joy.

"But you never answered my original question," he continued. "What benefit did you suddenly realize about working with me?"

"As you said, you're on an op," she said.

"And?" he asked, grabbing her elbow and turning her sixty degrees to her right as he pointed in the new direction. So maybe he was handy for something else, too.

"Now you can access all those things I'd been hesitating to access because I'm *not* on an op. I assume, other than state secrets, we have the same kinds of files and access to information. Since your op is to help me, you can help me by looking up all the info I haven't yet." She would have used her resources as she saw fit. This way, though, she could keep Gavin busy *and* not have to explain to AISE—or the NSA—why she was accessing the phone records of a US citizen.

"See, another silver lining on this beautiful day," he said, and she was pretty sure he'd said it specifically to annoy her.

She was about to snap a retort when he tugged her jacket, pulling her to a stop. Stepping close behind her, the heat of his body pressed against her back and shoulders.

"There's a small cabin on the property," he said, keeping his voice low. "No utilities and no signs of life, but that was just from visuals." He pointed up, indicating his information had come from satellite imagery. "We didn't have a chance to run the heat sensor over it."

"How small?"

"About seventy-five square meters."

She'd been in the US long enough that she had to do the calculation in her head. About eight hundred square feet. "I assume it's close, since you stopped me?"

He nodded, and she could feel his body shift. "Two hundred meters straight ahead."

She stared into the foliage but could see nothing. Behind her, Gavin was silent. And still. The stillest she'd ever seen him. She twisted around to look at him. It was remarkable, really. All the amused, happy energy that had been zinging off his person since she'd set foot in the woods was suddenly gone. His focus remained on the cabin, but she didn't turn around. Instead, she let herself relax and feel him, feel his intent, feel his energy, and feel his resolve. Maybe that was a little woo-woo of her, but sensing energy, not in a supernatural way, but more in a primal sense, had always been a skill she'd possessed. And it was one that had served her extraordinarily well over the years.

It didn't take her long to pick up on what he was feeling—strength, patience, focus, concern, and determination. Intellectually, she knew he had these qualities, or at least some of them, to get to where he was in life. But it was unsettling to suddenly be experiencing them with him.

"You okay?" he asked, his eyes flickering to her.

She nodded, not sure what else to say.

"I wish we had better intel on the house," he said.

"You're worried," she stated.

He bobbed his head to the side once. "We're about to approach a building that was bought by a man who was just murdered, and we don't know why he bought it or why he was killed. I don't know if I would go so far as to say I'm *worried*, but I'm definitely on alert."

"Are you ever not?"

This time his head came around so he could look at her. Their faces were inches apart and from this distance, she could see flecks of green and gold in his brown eyes. "These days? No." She expected him to say more, but instead he returned his attention to the woods. "What's the plan, love?"

Her gaze drifted over his profile one more time before she, too, refocused on the cabin—or at least the general direction of the cabin. Since she'd just learned about the building, she quickly went through their options in her mind, then answered. "We need to recon. Let's get as close as we can and see if there's any activity. I have something that might help, but we have to be within ten feet of the building. Do you think that's possible?"

He lifted a shoulder. "Only one way to find out."

She stepped to the side and gestured for him to move ahead of her. He seemed to know where the cabin was, so there was no reason she needed to be in the lead. With a nod, he moved around her and together, they made their way toward the building.

They were almost on top of it by the time Six caught her first glimpse. Stopping in front of her, Gavin held up a hand, then, after a beat of hearing nothing but the forest noises, he gestured for her to move to his side.

"We need to circle the cabin and get a lay of the land," he said. "Normally I wouldn't suggest splitting up, but what do you think? I go clockwise, you go counterclockwise, and we meet on the other side?"

She surveyed the land, then nodded. The cabin sat in a small —very small—clearing. She wasn't keen on the idea of splitting up either, but at no point would they be more than fifty meters from each other.

He caught and held her gaze. The moment was brief but intense, and she sensed that he wanted to say something. Then he shook his head, turned, and silently started making his way through the forest around the back of the house. Not wasting any time, she did the same although in the opposite direction. When they met up again on the other side, Gavin came walking toward her shaking his head.

"I saw nothing, no movement, nothing that looks like this land is being used. You?" he asked.

"I had to cross the driveway, and it looks like it's been used, but not frequently. Other than that, nothing."

They both turned to face the house. They were a little closer to it on this side, maybe ten meters. The forest would give them cover for another five, but then they'd hit the clearing. The good news was that this side of the cabin only had two windows set high in the wall. So high that it was unlikely anyone on the inside—if there was anyone on the inside—would be able to see them if they stayed low.

"How's your running crouch?" she asked.

He chuckled softly. "You're not questioning my stamina, are you, love?"

His response wasn't worthy of one of her own, so instead, she led the way. Keeping low to the ground, she made it to the side of the house in less than fifteen seconds with Gavin right behind her. They both turned and sank to their haunches with their backs to the wall.

Silently, she withdrew her phone and earbuds. After handing one to Gavin and inserting the other in her own ear, she opened an app on her phone that would amplify sound from inside the house. Hitting the button, she and Gavin listened.

Thirty seconds of silence passed, but Six knew better than to make any rash decisions. Signaling to Gavin to stay put, he nodded and they continued to listen.

Another thirty seconds passed then finally, the unmistakable sound of feet shuffling across a wood floor filtered through their earbuds. Her eyes shot to Gavin's. At least one person was in the house.

Then a voice. And another. Then another.

All three were women, and all spoke very softly. Six turned up the volume and hoped that they would continue their quiet conversation. After a beat they did, although the language they spoke was a difficult one to follow. Six strained to hear, and after a few more comments, she recognized it. It wasn't one she spoke, but she'd heard enough Malay interspersed into the conversation that she was certain the language was from Indonesia. Though which one, she didn't know.

But that knowledge, and the questions it raised, all suddenly seemed secondary. Because in a flash, she knew exactly who the women were and what Jeremy had been up to.

CHAPTER ELEVEN

VIOLETTA SHIFTED BESIDE GAVIN. He met her gaze, waiting for her to indicate what she wanted to do next. He didn't recognize the language, but judging by the way Violetta cocked her head in concentration, she did.

She pushed herself to her feet, and he followed her back into the woods.

"You know who they are?" he asked, keeping his voice low even though they were a good twenty meters away.

"Not specifically, but yes. You've seen Jeremy's file, you know he traveled to Indonesia quite bit recently?"

He nodded. He did know that, but he didn't know why. His file didn't contain that information.

"Did you have access to the photos?"

His stomach sank. "What photos?"

Violetta's eyes narrowed and her jaw tightened. Her gaze darted to the house, then back to him. "Several executives from Shanti Joy Cosmetics, or maybe still are, raping and abusing women who work at the palm oil plantation the company sources their oil from."

He stared at her for a beat, then spun around, unwilling to face her as he gathered himself together. He had no wish to fall down the rabbit hole he'd long ago thought had closed, especially not in front of Violetta. Even as he fought it, though, images of another battered body, weak from abuse and mistreatment, flashed in his head. Then just as quickly, that image was replaced with one of a sad smile, and a wave, followed by the screech of a train. And then nothing but Gavin's hollow cry for help.

Ruthlessly, Gavin shoved those memories down deep. There might have been no way to help then, but there was now. When he was sure no trace of his memories would be written on his face, he turned back around.

"Those women, specifically?" he asked, pointing to the house.

Violetta inclined her head. "That's my guess, yes."

"And Jeremy's role?"

"Have you heard of the Alien Tort Claims Act?" When he nodded, she continued, although as soon as she'd said the name he knew where she was going. "I think he was going to help those women bring a claim against the company, and he brought them here to keep them safe and have them close by."

"And if he happened to make his intentions known to Shanti Joy, that's probably why they came after you when you left his place. It's a federal civil case, but who better to advise him than a federal prosecutor?" he said, putting two and two together. She hesitated, then nodded.

"We need to get those women somewhere safe," she said.

He agreed. If Jeremy had poked the corporate bear, then it was possible the women were in danger. It was unlikely Jeremy would have said anything about the women being in the US, but it wasn't a stretch to think the company, or the people involved, might look.

"You recognized the language?"

Violetta shook her head. "Some, not all. Part of it was Malay."

"Do you speak it?"

She gave a half shrug. "Well enough to get by."

That piece of information wasn't in her files either, but he'd fill those gaps over time.

Violetta crossed her arms and stared at the cabin. "Those women have likely been abused, flown to another country, and are now living in a cabin with no access to anyone other than Jeremy, and I doubt they know he's dead. I think I should be the one to approach them," she said.

He sliced a look in her direction. If she thought she was going in alone, she had another think coming. Although her points were well taken. "You go first. I'll join you after you convince them you're one of the good guys. Or gals," he corrected himself. "Any idea how to do that?"

She nodded and started typing into her phone. Then, after a beat, she flipped it around for him to see. On the screen was a picture of her and Jeremy Wheaton at what he assumed was their law school graduation. They both wore mortarboards, graduation gowns with some sort of drape, and tassels around their shoulders. Jeremy was dipping her back as if they were ballroom dancing. Someday he'd ask her how close she and Jeremy were, but not today.

"I have dozens of pictures of us," Violetta said. "And I can speak enough Malay to hopefully convince them."

"You have protection if you need it?" He didn't need to ask the question, and if she'd been the one to ask, he would have been insulted, but she just nodded. He didn't know what she was carrying, but at least she had something. "I'll wait at the corner of the cabin," he said, pointing to an area near where they'd crouched.

She glanced in that direction one more time, then nodded, took a deep breath, and walked toward it. He followed behind until he needed to peel off to stay out of sight, then he leaned against the cabin and placed his ear to the siding to better hear.

Violetta knocked and called out softly in what he assumed was Malay. Silence greeted her first attempt and after no movement from inside, she tried again. Whatever she said the second time took her longer to say and he assumed she was doing her best to persuade the women to answer the door.

It didn't work.

Violetta took a deep breath and tried again. This time, she spoke and continued speaking. Finally, Gavin heard the quiet murmuring of voices, then the equally soft shuffling of feet. He let out a long, slow exhale when the door creaked open.

Violetta continued to speak. He couldn't see her, but he assumed she was showing whoever answered the door the pictures of Jeremy while trying to convince her that she was a friend. A woman spoke and Violetta answered. A long pause followed, then Violetta called out for him.

"You can come out, Gavin."

Slowly, so as not to startle the occupants, Gavin emerged from his spot. He stopped several feet away from the three stairs that led to the front door and let the women—there were three of them that he could see—have a look at him.

Violetta said something to the one closest to her, but all eyes stayed fixed on him. He kept his hands loose at his sides and tried to remain as still and nonthreatening as possible. He didn't miss the fear in their gazes, and it tore at him. They'd been abused and misused by a man just like him—tall, white, and in their eyes, powerful. He wanted to swear he was nothing like the men who'd done what they'd done to them. But not only did he not speak their language, he doubted they'd believe him.

Violetta spoke again. Whatever she said must have

convinced the women to let them enter. All three moved back and opened the door enough for them to slip through. Staying close to Violetta, he followed them inside to a small living room area, then took a seat on the sofa one of the women directed him to.

"They don't know about Jeremy," Violetta said, taking a seat beside him. "They know I'm his friend, and they know I know why they are here, but they don't know he's dead."

On her last word, the woman sitting in the chair beside Violetta sucked in a sharp breath. Apparently, at least one of them knew some English. Both he and Violetta turned to her.

"I am Abyasa," she said, haltingly. "I speak little English. Jeremy is dead?"

Violetta reached over and covered the woman's hand with her own, then nodded. "I'm sorry, but yes," she answered, her voice cracking at the news.

A tremble went through the woman's body, but then she straightened in her seat. "You will help us now?"

Without missing a beat, Violetta nodded. "Yes, I will help. And my friends. We all knew Jeremy."

Abyasa studied Violetta for a long moment, then gave a small nod before turning to her companions. Judging by the way they drew back, then clung to each other as their gazes darted back and forth between Violetta and Abyasa, Gavin assumed Abyasa had translated what she'd learned.

One woman cried silent tears, and Gavin desperately wanted to go to her. His comfort wouldn't be wanted or appropriate, but even knowing that, it was a struggle not to offer. With her attention still focused on Abyasa, Violetta's hand came down and rested on his thigh. He didn't know if she sensed his internal battle or if she'd done it for another reason altogether; regardless, the feel of her gentle and sure palm on his leg steadied him.

"Can you tell me your names?" Violetta asked, her gaze switching to the two women seated opposite them before shifting back to Abyasa, who translated.

"Candra," said the one on the left.

"Shinta," said the other. All three were petite and had big dark eyes and black hair. But those were about the only features they shared. Abyasa's face was round, as were her eyes and mouth; even her nose was what his nan would have called a button nose. And her thick, almost wavy hair was pulled into a loose ponytail at the nape of her neck. Candra's face was long and angular, and her straight hair hung to her shoulders. Shinta had short black hair and a heart-shaped face with almond-shaped eyes. All were dressed in Western-style loose-fitting pants and sweaters.

Violetta started to speak but was cut off when something in the kitchen area dinged. The women all looked at one another with wide eyes and confused expressions on their faces. Even without knowing the reason, Gavin knew that whatever had caused that sound wasn't going to be good news.

"Abyasa?" Violetta asked.

A second passed before the woman answered. "That ding is to let us know when Jeremy is coming. It is something, I do not know, something he put on the gate. He did not want to surprise us, so he put it there. When he comes, it dings." She paused, and Gavin could already feel Violetta getting ready to spring into action. "If Jeremy is dead, who is coming?"

No one good was Gavin's thought, though he didn't voice it. Didn't need to.

Violetta shot him a quick look before rising and issuing an order to the women. "Gather your passports, we need to leave," she said.

Jeremy had prepared the women well and they all pulled their passports from their pockets even as Violetta started herding them out the back door. Gavin moved to the front window. "I don't see anyone yet," he called out to Violetta as he reached for the gun tucked into his ankle holster. She said something in Malay and Abyasa, Candra, and Shinta all slipped their passports back into their pockets for safekeeping.

"We're going to head out the back and into the woods," she responded. He could hear the sound of the women slipping on their shoes followed by the creak of the back door. "Gavin," Violetta called, an entreaty in her tone.

"Go," he said. "As soon as you're in the woods, I'll follow." He wanted to give them cover during their retreat, if needed, and staying in the house, with the view he had, was the best way. Once they were safely in the shadows of the forest, he'd follow.

"Gavin," Violetta admonished.

"Get the women to safety, Violetta."

He didn't want to take any chances that Violetta or the women would be seen, but his words didn't galvanize her into action. He was aware of her hesitation even as he kept his attention on the driveway. It wasn't a long stretch of road, but how fast the car arrived depended on how fast it was being driven. Finally, the shuffle of feet on the small back porch greeted his ears and a few seconds later, he saw all four of them slip into the forest. He still couldn't see the car, but he could now hear it. Without wasting another second, he tore through the house and bolted out the back door to the woods. Once he was well camouflaged, he dropped to his haunches and watched. A few seconds later, Violetta joined him. They were well hidden, and he wasn't worried about being seen, but that didn't stop the adrenaline from pounding through his system with a beat that would make any DJ envious.

The forest had gone silent at the initial intrusion of so many people into its space. But as the seconds ticked by, bugs began to buzz and birds began to call.

"The women are thirty meters back," Violetta said, keeping her voice low. "Did you see anything?"

"Heard it, but didn't..." He fell silent when a vintage Mustang nosed its way through the overgrown drive and into the clearing. It was a sweet ride, but what Gavin appreciated about it most was its low-slung carriage. It had slowed the driver down enough so that they'd all been able to clear the house.

The car rumbled to a stop and a few seconds later, the engine switched off. Violetta placed a hand on his back and the two remained crouched, watching. Casually, as if they'd come off a long road trip, two men emerged from the car. On the driver's side, the side closest to them, stood a tall, thin man—perhaps in his early thirties—dressed in a suit, of all things. He had dark hair that was slicked back and a cigarette hanging from between his teeth. He looked to Gavin like a bad cross between the Godfather and John Travolta's character from *Saturday Night Fever*. The other man was younger, maybe mid-twenties, and had cropped blond hair and a build that could rival a Mack truck.

Thankful for the dampening effect the woods would have on any sounds they made, he reached into his pocket and pulled his key fob out. "Take my car and get the women out of here," he said. "It's closer than yours. Follow alongside the driveway and when you get to the road, you'll see an abandoned house five hundred meters north."

He didn't take his eyes from the two men as Violetta slipped her hand into his and took the device. A second later, he felt her hand in the back pocket of his jeans, sliding over his ass. Something he would have quite enjoyed under different circumstances.

"The fob to my car. You know where it is."

He gave a sharp nod as she started to rise. "Stay safe, Gavin," she said. "Call me when you're in my car. I'll have a plan." He chanced a glance at her and let his gaze linger as she silently made her way into the depths of the woods, the trees enveloping her form not far from where he remained. When she was no longer visible, he returned his attention to the two men and the cabin.

Just in time to see each of them throw a Molotov cocktail through the front window.

CHAPTER TWELVE

THE TWO HOMEMADE devices the men had hurled through the window exploded into flames. The old timber of the cabin wouldn't last long, and after watching the curtain disintegrate in less than twenty seconds, Gavin decided that was a good thing. The fire would destroy all traces of the women. Those two morons were doing him a favor.

The sounds of the fire masked any noise he might have made, and he rose from his crouch and watched as the assholes each tossed another device. The front door was already burned away and judging by the sounds that followed the second volley, Gavin would bet that at least one of the bottles had hit the concrete countertop in the kitchen.

As if orchestrated, the two men pulled guns from waistbands and waited, presumably for the inhabitants to come running out. Gavin didn't fight the smile on his face when no women came rushing out and into their primitive trap.

The men looked at each other and one said something, though what it was, Gavin couldn't hear over the sound of the flames. Flames that were now lapping at all sides of the small cabin as black smoke billowed up. The area was remote enough that it was possible no one would notice and call the fire department. But even if someone did, it was probably a volunteer department and it would take them at least twenty minutes to arrive, if not longer.

Confident the men wouldn't leave until the women came out or the cabin was fully destroyed, he left his position and circled back behind the Mustang. His targets were standing at the front of the car and Gavin quickly unscrewed an air valve on one of the back tires, then moved to the other side and did the same with the second tire. Shoving the caps into his pocket, he considered his next move.

He had no intention of letting the men get away, but ideally, they'd get taken into custody rather than, well, something more drastic. He wasn't opposed to something more drastic, but his desire to know who had hired them outweighed his personal beliefs on the value of their lives.

Studying the men, it wasn't hard to determine who the leader of their merry duo was. Mr. Saturday Night Fever would be the one who would have the information Gavin wanted. Which meant incapacitating the young Mr. Mack Truck. Damn, but some days were better than others.

With a grin, he crept forward along the passenger side of the car, keeping his gun at the ready. The heat from the fire wrapped around him, and sweat dripped down his back. Ignoring the discomfort, he tossed out a silent thank you to Mother Nature for the wet spring that would keep the flames from spreading too far into the woods.

When he was three feet from his target, he popped up to a standing position. The Mack truck didn't even have time to complete his turn before Gavin had the man on the ground. A well-placed knock to the head with the butt of his gun was a beautiful thing. The heavy body hit the grass, and Gavin kicked the young man's gun well under the car.

The fall of Mr. Mack Truck happened so fast that by the

time Mr. Saturday Night had his gun trained on Gavin, Gavin had his up as well.

"Fancy meeting you here," Gavin said. "Although I don't think we've been properly introduced."

In a move that was no less obvious than a blinking sign, the man communicated his intention with a slight bracing of his shoulder. Gavin had to give him props for not hesitating, but Mr. Saturday Night was a moron if he thought he could outshoot a Special Forces soldier.

Less than a heartbeat later, Mr. Saturday Night lay on the ground. Blood poured from his shoulder and his useless fingers barely retained their hold on his weapon. Keeping his eye on the gun, Gavin approached slowly, then just as slowly, reached down and picked it up. Tucking it into his jeans, he moved far enough away to keep an eye on both men. The knock he gave Mr. Mack Truck should keep him out for a while, but Gavin didn't feel the need to risk having his back to him.

"You fucking prick," Mr. Saturday Night said, gripping his bleeding shoulder with his good hand as he tried to push himself up into a sitting position.

"Tsk tsk tsk. You hardly seem in a position to be name-calling, mate. Who hired you?" Gavin demanded.

The man gave him a look that told Gavin to go fuck himself. Gavin raised his gun and fired a shot two feet from Mr. Saturday Night's hip. The man jumped, then let out a string of epithets that Gavin almost wished Violetta were there to hear. She would have appreciated his inventiveness.

"I'm not sure I know anyone by that name," Gavin said when the man finally quieted. "Would you care to repeat yourself?"

"Fuck off," the man spat.

"Well, mate, if that's the way you're going to be, no one can say I didn't give you a chance, can they?" Gavin stepped forward and Mr. Saturday Night shrank back, keeping his attention trained on the gun in Gavin's hand. This man, whoever he was, may be playing a tough guy, but at least he was smart enough to be worried now.

"One more chance, Tony," Gavin said, raising his gun. The man looked confused, but that could have been from the reference to the *Saturday Night Fever* character rather than any questions he had about Gavin's intent.

The sound of sirens drifted toward them, and the man flickered Gavin a cocky smile. "I ain't tellin' you shit," he said. Although why he thought the arrival of the fire department would sway Gavin from his path, Gavin hadn't a clue.

"Again, wrong answer," he said, then swiftly, he brought the gun down in a single blow and Mr. Saturday Night collapsed fully back to the ground.

Knowing the men had come for the women—to either capture or kill—Gavin figured they might have something in the car they'd intended to use to restrain them. Sure enough, after covering his fingers with his shirt, he popped the trunk and found a fresh packet of zip ties. Grabbing a rag from the floor, he used it to open the packet without leaving any prints. When he had several ties in hand, he tossed the package back in the trunk, stuffed the rag into his back pocket, and circled around to the two men.

Kneeling beside Mr. Mack Truck, Gavin withdrew his phone, opened an app, and placed the young man's right hand, then his left, on the screen. The handy program, provided to him by Britain's finest, would digitally record fingerprints.

After using a couple of zip ties to bind the man's wrists and ankles, Gavin moved on to Mr. Saturday Night and went through the same process. The sirens were getting closer, and he hoped that the police were close behind the firefighters. A volunteer force wasn't prepared to deal with what were essentially two hitmen.

Once they were secured, Gavin debated whether to leave their guns. If they'd committed other crimes, it could help law enforcement link them to those crimes. Leaving them could also serve as a warning to the first responders not to assume the two men were victims. On the other hand, if he left them, and one of the men woke and managed to break free, or if one of the first responders cut them loose, there'd be live weapons in the area.

With a sigh, he crouched down and used a stick to pull Mr. Mack Truck's gun out from under the car. Checking the safety, he slipped it into his ankle holster. It was an awkward fit, but he'd rather carry his own weapon as he made his way to Violetta's car.

With one last look at the scene, he contented himself that all was as good as it could be before turning toward the woods. Then, as the tires of the heavy fire truck crunched on the driveway, he slipped into the foliage and jogged his way north.

CHAPTER THIRTEEN

"ALL'S GOOD," Gavin said, his voice sounding a little tinny on speakerphone. Her phone wasn't hooked up to his Bluetooth system, and Abyasa held it in her hand so that Six could keep both hands on the wheel while they talked. Driving while juggling a phone was something she could do practically in her sleep, but she wasn't going to risk getting pulled over for something so stupid.

"I'm taking the women to Cyn's house. I assume you know where it is?" she asked. She'd called her friends the second she'd turned onto the main road and was certain they weren't being followed. She trusted that the three of them were taking care of everything and would make Abyasa, Candra, and Shinta more than welcome.

"I do, I'll head there. Any chance you can give Joe a heads-up on the two men?"

"Already done," she answered. As soon as she'd finished talking with the club she'd called Joe. Although by the time he picked up, Cyn had already texted him and he was looking up the number for the local sheriff.

"You good?" he asked. His question wasn't about her. Like

her, he was worried about the three women. They'd already been through so much that the events of the day were the last thing they'd needed to experience. A little something inside Six broke open at his concern. Sure, he was too happy for her liking, but his worry was genuine.

"As good as can be," she answered. "We'll get to Cyn's and get everyone settled, and then we can figure out where to go from there. And you?" He'd said all was good, but that didn't necessarily mean *he* was good, just that the situation was.

A beat passed before he answered. "I'm fine, Violetta. Thank you for asking." She recognized that low rumble in his voice now. It was the tone that came out when he was thinking things about her that were best kept inside his own head.

"Gavin," she admonished with an accompanying eye roll, even though he couldn't see it.

"I hear that eye roll, love. I'm *fine*," he repeated. "I'm fifteen minutes behind you. I'll see you at the manse." And with that, he hung up, though she smiled at his parting words. Cyn did indeed live in a manse. Her seaside mansion was so over-the-top that they'd all embraced it long ago as one of Cyn's eccentricities.

The drive was mostly silent although Six did tell Abyasa—who translated for the others—a little about what to expect when they arrived at Cyn's. She wanted to prepare them for the house itself—the likes of which she was certain they'd never seen before—but also her friends. She told them about Cyn being an archaeologist and traveling all over the world, about Devil being a doctor and doing medical research, and Nora and her love of animals coming through in her work as a veterinarian. She also told them about Joe and answered the few questions they had about Gavin.

Keeping an eye on her three passengers as she navigated back to Cos Cob, she wondered at their resilience. The courage they had to reach out to Jeremy in the first place, then their willingness to leave everything familiar behind in order to stop the men perpetrating crimes, humbled Six. Sure, she'd done a lot of courageous things in her life, but she'd done it knowing she always had the safety net of Franklin and her friends. And if needed, her family. These women had none of that, and yet they'd still stepped off the ledge into the unknown. She barely knew them, but she knew they were remarkable women.

Six intentionally drove slowly, and by the time they turned off Main Street in Cos Cob and onto the oceanside road that led north to Cyn's, Gavin was behind her. A few minutes later, they were pulling through the main gate of Cyn's house and up the driveway.

Unsurprisingly, there were a lot of gasps and quiet side conversations—Cyn's house was nothing if not gasp-worthy. But by the time she brought the SUV to a stop, the women were silent. Six sensed their fear and anxiety and wished that there was something she could do to assuage it, but time, and exposure to her friends, was the only way.

Behind her, Gavin climbed out of her Tesla but remained standing at the front of the car, giving the women time to adjust without him looming over them. Six glanced at Abyasa, who was still staring at the house, as were Candra and Shinta.

"Are you ready? There will be food, clothes, showers, and, I can vouch, some of the best beds," Six said in her best Malay.

Just then, Cyn, Devil, Nora, and Joe filed from the house, though they, too, kept a respectful distance. From where Six sat in the car, she pointed to her friends and one by one, told her passengers who was who.

"And they are all friends with Jeremy?" Abyasa asked.

"Not Joe, who recently moved here, but the others, yes," Six answered.

"Did Jeremy ever come here?"

Six wasn't sure what thought was driving that question, but

she answered. "Yes, he's been a few times. Holiday parties, mostly."

"Do you have a picture?"

Without hesitation, Six pulled her phone out, logged back into her cloud account, and started hunting through her photo albums. Less than a minute later, she found a series of photos from Cyn's Fourth of July party the prior year, several of which contained Jeremy. Her eyes lingered on a photo of him with Nora. Nora had brought a litter of puppies she'd been fostering, and Jeremy and she had spent much of the afternoon playing with the little beasts. In this particular picture, Nora and Jeremy had an arm around each other and each held a little black-and-white bundle of joy in their other arm. Her friends were smiling and laughing, and the puppies were trying to lick their faces.

Six blinked away tears and handed the phone over to Abyasa, who twisted in her seat so Candra and Shinta could see the screen as well. Abyasa scrolled through several pictures. It was a paltry thing to offer. But trust was earned. If showing these women proof of her relationship with Jeremy—and his with Nora, Cyn, and Devil—helped to earn it, then that's exactly what she'd do.

All of her friends remained where they were, patiently waiting for the women to make a decision. Five minutes later, Abyasa handed Six her phone back.

"We are ready," she said.

Six nodded, then opened her door and climbed out. Circling to the passenger side, she reached it as Abyasa closed her door behind her. A few seconds later, both Shinta and Candra were standing at their side.

Six gave them a moment to look at Cyn's house. Inspired by the Breakers in Newport, Rhode Island, it wasn't a house to be ignored. "Ready to meet everyone?" Six asked.

The three women shared a look, then Abyasa nodded. Six gestured them forward, and as one, Devil, Nora, and Cyn came down the steps. Gavin joined Joe, who'd remained by the door, shaking the man's hand in greeting.

Six introduced the women to her friends and from there, Devil swiftly took over. Apparently one of the many languages she spoke was one all three women understood. Soon, her friend was ushering the women inside and through the foyer to the large kitchen at the back of the house. Six brought up the rear of the group, though Joe and Gavin trailed behind her, speaking in low voices.

It was nearing dinnertime, but Devil offered to show the women to their rooms first, and Nora assured them that there were clothes for them as well. Nodding in agreement, the women allowed Devil and Nora to usher them upstairs, while she and Cyn stayed behind to get the food ready.

When they were out of earshot, Cyn turned to Six. "Do you think Candra is one of the women in the pictures?"

Her hair and body type were the right fit, but Six didn't know and hadn't asked. "Possibly. We'll have to find out at some point, but I think we should let them settle in and talk to us when they are ready."

Cyn nodded and started pulling items out from her refrigerator. "Abyasa seems like the one they rely on to guide group decisions."

Six opened a bottle of wine as Cyn checked the oven. "Definitely. I think part of it is the language—she speaks a little English, so she probably had a different kind of connection with Jeremy. But you're right, they are all incredibly strong women to be here doing what they're doing, but Abyasa has a confidence that I think the others take comfort in."

"Are you going to introduce me?" Cyn said with a nod of her head toward where Joe and Gavin stood talking in front of the window. The two men were about the same height and, although Joe was slightly leaner, had a similar build. But that was about the extent of the similarities between them. Well, Six cocked her head and watched them. Perhaps not. They may look physically different, but they had similar intense expressions on their faces. And both men had the air of someone confident in himself and his place in the world.

She cleared her throat, and the two men looked over.

"Six," Joe said, coming forward and brushing a kiss on her cheek. "I'll admit, when Cyn told me where you'd gone this afternoon, I had my doubts it was a good idea, but I'm glad you did."

She inclined her head. "Me, too. Gavin can fill us in on what happened after I took the women away. But first, Cyn, this is Gavin Cooper, British Special Forces and paralegal extraordinaire. Gavin, this is Cyn Steele."

"It's very nice to meet you. I understand you and Six will be working...closely together," Cyn said. The words might have been polite, but Cyn had infused them with her trademark mischievous undertones. Gavin grinned, winked, and shook her hand.

"Lovely to meet you as well. I have a feeling we may be seeing more of each other after tonight."

Gavin, Cyn, and Joe all turned to look at her. "Oh, for fuck's sake," Six muttered, yanking out a single wineglass and pouring herself a healthy dose.

"None for me?" Gavin asked.

"Or me?" Cyn chimed in.

"Fuck off, both of you," she said, then took a big gulp. Cyn's wine wasn't really gulping wine, but at the moment, Six didn't care. "And you," she said, pointing to Joe. "Wipe that grin off your face."

Joe, who'd been looking down, trying to hide a smile, raised his eyes and managed to meet her gaze. "I don't know what you're talking about, Six," he said with as much innocence as he could muster. Then he cleared his throat and turned to Gavin. "We have beer, if you prefer."

Gavin nodded and walked to the fridge with Joe to see what was available. Six shot Cyn a dirty look. Just because Cyn had ended up in a relationship with Joe after Franklin's shenanigans didn't mean she and Gavin were headed down the same path. She'd traveled that road before with another operative and had no desire to ever do so again.

Yeah, there were very few secrets—other than the ones required by law—that Six had from her friends, but the events of an op eight years ago was one of them. Another time, another op, another man. It had been amazing until it wasn't and after that, Six had decided that relationships weren't for her so long as she continued to work for AISE. Especially relationships with other operatives.

"Are you going to share?" Cyn asked, pointing to the wine bottle Six still had her hand wrapped around.

"No."

Cyn arched a brow but didn't say anything. Instead, she reached into her wine refrigerator and pulled out a second bottle. "You'll need a ride home if you drink that," Cyn pointed out, unnecessarily, as she popped the cork on the second bottle.

"I'll walk," Six replied.

"He got to you, didn't he?" Cyn asked quietly. Joe and Gavin had taken their beers and were standing on the patio looking out on the ocean.

"Gavin and I aren't you and Joe," Six said, pinning her friend with a look. Cyn and Joe had one of those easy kinds of relationships that were foreign to Six. They had their spats and little fights, what couples didn't? But they also shared their lives and their space with remarkable ease. Six always hated the analogies that referred to couples as "two halves" or "pieces of a puzzle" because it made it sound like the individuals weren't whole people without the other. But in the case of Cyn and Joe, it was hard not to think of them as puzzle pieces, because they *fit*.

She and Gavin didn't fit and even if they could, she didn't

want that. Sure, a tumble or two in bed might be—would probably be—worth it, but she wasn't going to go there. Not with someone she had to work with for an unknown length of time.

Cyn studied her and looked about to say something but stopped herself when Nora walked back into the kitchen. Without a word, their friend joined them at the island. Since Six still hadn't relinquished her hold on her bottle, Nora grabbed the second bottle of wine and a glass, then poured herself a healthy dose.

"Candra and Shinta have scars," Nora said once she'd had a couple sips.

Six knew she should have expected that, but even so, the wine she'd drunk threatened to come back up. "They let you help them?" she asked instead.

Nora nodded as she took another sip. "You must have told them Devil is a doctor?" Six nodded. "Candra had an open wound on her back that wasn't healing and Abyasa convinced her to let Devil have a look. After that, Shinta admitted to having a few on her inner thighs." Nora paused and took another sip. "They looked like cigarette burns that had gotten infected."

Six released her hold on the bottle of wine and traded her glass for a tumbler of cold water. "Did they say anything about what happened to them?"

Nora shook her head. "Not yet, but they know they have to. I think we shouldn't press tonight, though."

Six and Cyn nodded.

"Abyasa said they talked to Jeremy and that he recorded their interviews. You didn't find the interviews in your files?" Nora asked.

"Find what?" Gavin asked as he and Joe joined them at the kitchen island. "Gavin Cooper, by the way," he said, holding out his hand to Nora.

Six braced herself for an inappropriate innuendo, but she

should have known better. It was *Nora*. Her friend offered a soft smile and took Gavin's hand. "It's nice to meet you, and thank you for helping today."

Gavin gave a nod of acknowledgment. "We need to compare files," he reminded Six.

She bobbed her head. "We can do that later, but my files didn't have any transcripts. At least not that I found," she said, then she filled Joe and Gavin in on what the women had told Nora.

"Definitely not in my files, either," Gavin said. "In fact, my files didn't contain anything about what he was doing regarding..." he added, with an upward gesture toward where the women were.

"Not a surprise," Cyn said. "British intelligence would have had no reason to even have Jeremy on their radar. When they pulled the file for you, it would have only been what they could get their hands on quickly."

"The women are showering and resting. They said they'd be down within the hour," Devil said, stepping into the kitchen. "Nora told you about their wounds?" Everyone nodded. Devil reached for a glass and the wine bottle. "I now have a few more people to add to my list of those I'd like to get my hands on."

"Are Candra and Shinta okay?" Six asked.

Devil's expression darkened as she relayed the results of her cursory exam of the two women's wounds. As she spoke, Gavin's expression turned to stone. Perhaps Six had been wrong about him; apparently, he did have emotions other than happy.

When Devil was done, Six turned to Gavin. "Did you learn anything from the two men?"

"I didn't give the young one a chance to talk, and the slick one had nothing to offer. I did get their fingerprints, though." He pulled his phone out of his pocket and hit a few buttons. "Hmm," he said. "Turns out Mr. Saturday Night is Anthony Alberti—which might explain why he was so confused when I called him 'Tony.' The other one is..." He pressed a few more buttons. "Albert Vecchio, goes by 'Vetch.'"

Six had no idea what Gavin meant by his reference to Tony, but before she could ask, her phone dinged. Glancing down, she saw that Gavin had already texted her the files on the two men. Picking up her phone, she automatically forwarded the information to Cyn, Devil, and Nora.

"Cyn and I can look into them," Joe offered. "It sounds like you two need to compare files." He pointed between Six and Gavin with the beer bottle he held loosely in his fingers.

"What did you find out about the people in the white SUV?" Six asked Joe, referring to the two men who'd tried to run her off the road. With the events of the last few hours, she'd all but forgotten the original intention of their get together.

"Brothers. William and Harry Oswald." He held up a hand to stop the commentary that would follow. "And yes, those are their real names. Apparently, their mother was a royal watcher."

"What else?" Gavin asked.

"Long—very long—rap sheets. They tended to operate more in the Georgia, Florida, Louisiana area. This is the first event on record for them up north," Joe answered.

"Any idea who hired them?"

Joe shook his head. "Not yet. Their accounts have been seized and because they're wanted for multiple crimes in several states, the Feds have stepped in. I assume they will be chasing the money, although they might not be inclined to share that information with me if they do find it."

Cyn waved off his concern. "Franklin can help if we need it. But other than maybe seeing if it ties to the people who hired Anthony and Albert—whom I refuse to refer to as 'Vetch'—I don't think it's going to help us. At least not straightaway."

Cyn, Nora, and Devil shared a look before Devil turned her gaze to Six. "Which begs the question, Six. What do you plan to do and how can we help?"

CHAPTER FOURTEEN

GAVIN WATCHED Violetta consider the question her friends put to her. He thought he was doing a pretty good job of winning her over. But watching how she interacted with her friends might give him some additional insight into how best to work with her. Not that he wanted to be like Devil, Nora, or Cyn, since his plans for himself and Violetta included far more than a platonic friendship. His supervisors might not be happy with him, but fuck that.

Violetta started to say something but stopped when tentative footsteps sounded on the stairs. All six of them turned to see Abyasa enter the kitchen. She halted, her eyes darting around the room, then she took a breath and continued in.

"Abyasa, is everything okay?" Cyn asked, coming around the kitchen island to greet the woman.

She nodded. "Candra and Shinta are resting, but we wondered if we might have some water to drink?"

With a small shake of her head, as if she couldn't believe she hadn't offered, Cyn hurried back behind the island as she assured Abyasa that they could have anything they wanted. Cyn was handing her a tray filled with glasses and a full jug of water when Violetta spoke.

"Abyasa, may I speak with you?" she asked.

The woman looked up, then nodded, and the two put their heads together as they walked back toward the stairs. Gavin could catch the murmur, but not make out any of the words. When they reached the stairs, they paused, spoke quietly for a few more seconds, then Violetta gave Abyasa's arm a gentle squeeze. The woman nodded, then turned and started up the stairs. Violetta watched her go and when she was out of sight, she returned to the group.

"Everything okay?" he asked.

Her eyes flitted to his before landing back on her friends. "Gavin and I are going to head back to my place and start comparing the files and filling in any missing information. The plan is to bring Shanti Joy down as Jeremy intended. *How* we do that remains to be seen, but I think we need to start by compiling our intel."

It wasn't exactly the reason he'd hoped to be invited back to Violetta's place, but he'd take it. He'd had the luxury of observing her over the past six months, of getting to see and know the woman she was. She hadn't had the same opportunity, and he was more than happy to give it to her.

Five sets of eyes swung in his direction. He glanced at his half-empty bottle of beer, then set it on the counter. "Abyasa is okay with you leaving her and the others here?" he asked.

Violetta nodded. "That's what I was talking to her about. Devil speaks better Malay than I do, and also Candra and Shinta's mother tongue. Devil's made them feel safe enough that they are okay to stay here."

Gavin wasn't the only one who let out a deep breath at that. He doubted there was a better place for the women to be, but no one standing in Cyn's ridiculously large kitchen wanted them to be uncomfortable.

"Then I think we have some things to do tonight," he said, stepping away from the kitchen island. He let his gaze drift around the room, and he murmured his "thanks" for the drink and general "nice to meet yous." Three minutes later, he was following Violetta down the drive and back to her house.

The trip was a quick one and soon, he was pulling to a stop in front of her porch as she parked in her garage. Rather than enter the house through the mudroom, Violetta walked out to join him, closing the garage door behind her.

"Everything okay?" he asked as she approached.

"I want you to go through the files Heather gave me access to and see if I missed anything," she replied. Not an answer to his question.

He nodded, but didn't drop his question and instead, repeated it. "Everything okay?"

She shot him a look as she led him to her front door. The night sky was clear, and there was a little nip in the air. He could hear the ocean lapping against the rocks on the other side of her home. Maybe some night, they could build a bonfire out back and sit around it with some wine and some of those s'more things he'd seen in movies but never tried.

But first things first.

"Seriously, Violetta, how are you doing?" They'd stepped inside her house and when she was done resetting her alarm, he reached for her arm to stop her from turning—or walking—away from him again.

"I'm *fine*, Gavin. I'm always fine," she shot back.

"Now who's the one hiding behind a chipper facade?" He only half teased. Not that her response was exactly *chipper*, but it certainly wasn't honest.

She cocked her head to the side. "You admit to hiding behind a facade, then?"

He sighed. "This isn't about me. I'm not the one who just lost a good friend and then got dropped into the middle of his life."

"That's where you're wrong, Gavin. It *is* about you. It's about you and me and my friends and this life we lead." She pulled away from him and he let her go, but only because he sensed she was going to keep talking and that she needed movement to help.

Surprising him not at all, she started pacing as she launched into a tirade in Italian about the shit things they'd all had to do and see in their line of work. About how terrible the world could be, especially when it came to those driven by greed and power. Then she moved on to calling the men who'd participated in the assaults a series of very inventive names—most of which would have made Shakespeare blush.

All the while, she paced and paced.

Then, about ten minutes into letting her steam out, she abruptly stopped and stalked to him. "And you," she said, her eyes flashing. "What the hell were you thinking staying there? Approaching those two men? You had no backup, and they were armed with Molotov cocktails and guns. Two to one aren't the worst odds in a fight, but when you don't have to fight, why take the risk? You should have followed us out."

He couldn't help it, he grinned.

She narrowed her eyes and crossed her arms over her chest. Her long hair, tied back in a ponytail, swung gently as she cocked her head and glared at him.

"You were worried about me," he said.

She continued to glare at him for a long moment. Then she threw up her hands and spun away, cursing him in such rapid Italian that even he had a hard time following. Although he did catch something about egos and big dicks and—his favorite—pretty faces.

She came to a stop in front of her big picture window and jammed her hands on her hips as she stared out into the darkness. Gavin waited a beat to see if she would remain still or resume her pacing. When it appeared she was running out of steam, he approached her. Taking a chance, he set his hands on her hips, much the same way he had that morning, only this time it was from behind and it was intentional.

He leaned down and pressed a gentle kiss to the spot where her neck met her shoulder. Her skin pricked with goose bumps at his touch, and she twitched but didn't stop him. "I trusted you would get those women safely away," he said quietly, his lips not far from her ear. She stiffened slightly at his comment, but he continued. "You need to trust that I will do my part, too. I don't take unreasonable chances, Violetta. That's not the kind of solider I am." A beat passed as his words sank in. He liked that she cared. He liked that she'd been worried about him, but she'd have to learn to trust him, and today was the first step in that.

Finally, the tension left her shoulders and though she kept her hands on her hips, she also took a deep breath and, letting it out slowly, relaxed. She didn't fully lean back against him, but she didn't move out of his hold.

They stayed that way for a moment, then he forced himself to step away and let her go. "About those files," he started. She turned and met his gaze. "What do you say we get to it? After all, love, we do have a corporation to bring down."

It was only a few hours until sunrise when Violetta sat back from her computer and let her eyes find his. She yawned, making him smile.

"Coffee?" she asked.

"I wouldn't say no." They'd had a few cups throughout the night, and she made damn good coffee. She made an even better flat white, a drink he hadn't had since leaving the UK. No one in the Boston area seemed to know quite how to make them the way he liked. Except Violetta.

Rather than stay at his computer, he rose and followed her into the kitchen. Her house was a quintessential New England seaside home—he hadn't asked, but he'd bet it had been built long ago for some wealthy sea captain and his family. It was large for one person, but not as overwhelming as Cyn's. Not even close. Especially not with the oversize furniture, colorful rugs, and gorgeous art. The house reminded him of Violetta herself, standing strong against the forces of time and nature, but filled with bursts of color and warmth. Oh, yes, she'd laugh at him if she ever heard him refer to her as being a "warm" person, but she was, in her own way. She definitely had a prickly side, but more and more, he was coming to see that her smart retorts and yes, even her temper, were two sides of the same coin. She was equally as caring—about her friends, about the women she'd ushered to safety twelve hours earlier—as she could be standoffish. In some ways, she was more balanced than most people—certainly more than he. As a tried-and-true Brit, and a soldier at that, emotional balance wasn't something he strived for. The "Keep Calm and Carry On" memes hadn't come from nothing, and no one could compartmentalize like a Brit.

"Is everyone going to come over this morning?" Gavin asked, reaching for the mug Violetta offered him. Inhaling deeply, he savored the rich scent before taking a sip.

Violetta finished making herself a latte before she answered. "They'll be by at ten. Nora has some clients later in the afternoon, but Devil took the day off, and as of yesterday, Cyn's out for the summer."

He and Violetta had a lot to share. When they'd started digging into Shanti Joy, it hadn't taken them long to discover what a shell it was. Oh, it was a legitimate company with a legitimate product. But while it sourced most of its products from what appeared to be ethical suppliers, the ethics of the company itself, and in particular its leadership, were definitely in conflict with its image.

They'd found the interviews Jeremy had done with each of

the women. The three files had been buried in his media app and had been titled as names of popular movies. The only reason Gavin had found them among the hundreds of files was because the size didn't look right for a full feature film.

The interviews had been conducted in the mother tongue of each woman. A translator had been present for each, but the recordings weren't the best, so they'd sent the files off to MI6 for a full transcript. Those weren't expected back until later that morning. Even with the low sound quality, he and Violetta had spent hours watching and rewatching the interviews. It sounded callous, even in his own head, to say that nothing they heard had come as a surprise, but that didn't make any of it easy to stomach.

The most helpful part—at least helpful to them in bringing Shanti Joy down—were the identifications the women made. Each had, independently, identified Julian Newcross as well as Austin and Kaden Fogarty. There was a fourth man there, too, but the women had each confirmed that his name was never spoken, and they didn't know who he was. The pictures Violetta had, which he'd forced himself to go through, showed only a sliver of a profile of this mystery man. Gavin had to wonder if he was just very lucky not to get caught on film or if he'd been aware of the camera all along.

"I don't think he's part of the company," Gavin said, knowing Violetta would know who he was referring to. "Not in the way the others are."

Violetta leaned against the kitchen counter and considered him as she took another sip of her drink. Around one in the morning, they'd both taken a break and showered and changed —unfortunately not together—to help wake up. Now she was dressed in a pair of black leggings and a deep yellow sweater that hung off her shoulder. The straps of her camisole were visible, and he could tell she wasn't wearing a bra. Yes, he knew he shouldn't be noticing things like that. But sue him, she had his attention at all times.

"Maybe he's the coordinator? Maybe he lives there, and this is part of what he does when the execs come to town?" she posited.

He shrugged. "Someone has to coordinate it, but I'm also wondering about blackmail. I know we only have a few pictures. But between the way he kept his back to the camera and the fact that no one spoke his name makes me think he might be doing more than just coordinating."

Violetta considered his suggestion, then frowned. "It would be a golden opportunity for someone so inclined," she said. "Those men, the ones we've identified, weren't exactly discreet about their actions."

"I can't believe I'm saying this, but I wish we had more pictures," Gavin said.

Violetta tipped her head in acknowledgment of the horrible situation that would lead them to want to have access to more visual evidence. But then she paused, catching his attention.

"What?"

"I haven't gotten into his phone yet. I can't imagine he'd keep anything on it, but we need to look," she said.

"Officially or unofficially?" he asked.

She made a face. "I don't want to wait for an official green light. We can start the official paperwork at the same time we start unofficially looking."

He nodded, then glanced down at his empty mug. Her friends would join them in five hours, and neither of them had slept all night. He wanted to get started on the phone records, but he also wanted them to be coherent when Cyn, Devil, and Nora arrived.

"We need to sleep," he said.

Her eyes came up, and she looked at him as she took another sip of her drink. He could practically hear the arguments inside her head. They had evidence to find, transcripts to review once they received them, and a plan to hatch. Not to mention that the capture of Anthony and Vetch would probably result in whoever hired them putting some other plan into motion to get at the women.

The only way to stop everything—and bring those responsible for Jeremy's murder and the abuses in Indonesia to justice —was to file the suit against Shanti Joy and bring it all out into the light. And to get it to that point, they needed all the evidence they could gather. He had no doubt that in these quiet hours of the very early morning, Violetta's mind was already cataloging the information they had and identifying the gaps.

And then there was the fact that, on principle, she tended to like to argue. She had some legitimate reasons not to want to take a break, but Gavin was waiting for her to simply say no to his suggestion just for the fun of it.

Surprising the hell out of him, she let out a deep breath. "I agree," she said, then she held out a hand for his empty cup. After setting both mugs in the dishwasher, she led them up the stairs to the second floor. For a fleeting moment—okay, for a not-so-fleeting moment—he fantasized about being invited to nap with her. Someday, that fantasy would come true, but not today, and he forced his attention away from the sway of her hips to his surroundings.

He'd showered in a full bathroom on the main floor and hadn't been to this part of her house. As they walked up the stairs and along a hallway, he absorbed this insight into Violetta's life. The wide plank floors were covered with silk carpets. The walls were painted a soft cream, and although the color itself was lifeless, it provided the right backdrop for the art hanging along her walls. All bright pictures of places and people —from the sights of Rome to the markets of Morocco to the jungles of the Amazon.

"Did you take these?" he asked, pointing to the images as

they walked. Violetta turned and looked at him over her shoulder.

"Most, not all," she answered, then she opened a door. "You can have this guest room. Sheets are clean, bathroom is stocked with fresh everything if you want to brush your teeth or shave or...whatever."

"And your room?"

It was a sign of how tired she was that she waved to a door at the end of the hall. "I'm there," was all she said.

He eyed her. "Are you going to be able to sleep?" He recognized the signs that Violetta was overfatigued. She was hovering in that weird state between exhaustion and not being exhausted enough to keep her mind from spinning with all the what-ifs the next few days would hold.

She shrugged. "We'll see. If not, I'll pick up my old corporate tax textbook and that will put me to sleep."

He barked a laugh at that, although he was nearly certain she wasn't kidding. "Let me know if you need any help. Not to brag or anything, but I bet I'd be more interesting than a textbook."

The only response he got was an eye roll and a vague wave of her hand as she turned and walked away. When her door was shut, closing her inside her room, he stepped into his own. Glancing at the bathroom, he considered brushing his teeth and shaving. But then his eyes fell on the king-size bed and before he recognized what he was doing, he was stripped down to his boxers and climbing between the cool sheets. He hoped Violetta would be able to get some rest. But as the well-trained soldier that he was, he was down for the count almost before he finished that thought.

CHAPTER FIFTEEN

SIX OPENED HER EYES, rolled over, and glanced at her clock. Then she groaned. It had taken her a while to fall asleep after leaving Gavin at the guest room. Now her friends were going to be by in less than an hour and she—they—still had so much to do.

Not giving herself any time to get overwhelmed by her lack of sleep or everything that needed to be done, she threw the blankets off and got dressed. After brushing her teeth and pulling her hair into a top bun, she made her way downstairs.

"I've started the paperwork for the filings," Gavin said, walking out of her office as she hit the landing. He was holding a piece of paper in one hand and a coffee in the other. He'd had a "go bag" in his car and changed into fresh clothes after his shower the night before. He was back in those same clothes looking better than a man had a right to with less than a few hours of sleep.

"Excuse me?" she asked, not quite processing what he'd said. It felt intimate to find him so comfortable in her house, and that thought, and that thought alone, held her attention.

He looked up from the paper he carried, and his eyes swept

over her. She was wearing a pair of jeans and a flannel shirt over a camisole. It certainly wasn't a sexy outfit. The way his eyes drank her in, though, and the small smile that flirted with his lips, made her feel as if he were seeing something entirely different from her utilitarian clothing.

He set his paper down and walked toward her. "Good morning, Violetta," he said. Damn, she hated how her name sounded coming from his lips with his rumbly voice and perfect accent. She pulled the edges of her flannel together to conceal her body's reaction to him. Judging by the way he grinned, she'd been a few seconds too late.

"Did you sleep well?" he asked as he slipped his free hand around her waist. She should move away, but she didn't. She did, however, manage to keep her arms crossed.

"No," she said. "I should have taken you up on your offer and let you orgasm me into sleep."

His arm tightened around her, and through his jeans and hers, she felt his body respond to that comment. His pupils dilated as he stared down at her. She met his gaze. His brow dipped, then his hold loosened.

"That was a joke, wasn't it?" he demanded.

She grinned back. "Maybe," she said, then spun away. "I need coffee."

"That was cruel, Salvitto," he said, following her into the kitchen.

"That's what you get when you look at me like you want to devour me," she said over her shoulder as she started up the coffee machine.

"I already know I'm playing with fire when it comes to you, Violetta," he said, taking a seat at her kitchen table. He set his coffee mug down and sprawled his legs in front of him, looking every inch the man he was.

"And that's the point, you shouldn't be playing with me at all," she retorted. He remained silent as she poured whole milk into the stainless-steel pitcher and started steaming it. By the time it was the right temperature, her two espresso shots were done, and she poured everything into her favorite cup—a pale yellow mug with an adorable little chicken on it made by a potter in England.

"Why?" Gavin asked. She didn't need any clarification on the question; she'd known it would come eventually. He wanted to know why, when they were obviously attracted to each other, she kept pushing him away.

She didn't join him at the table, and instead, she walked back out to the living room, picking up the paper he'd set down as she passed. "What paperwork?" she called out.

There was a loud sigh followed by the scrape of his chair on the kitchen floor. Appearing in the doorway, holding his coffee again, Gavin gestured to the document in her hand. "Someone will have to file the suit against Shanti Joy. I thought I'd help get the paperwork started."

Six glanced down at the sheet she held. It was the standard checklist her team used to ensure that everything was in order before filing a suit. He'd made notes in the table indicating that he'd already created a record for the case. He'd also cataloged the interview transcripts and the pictures and had started collecting past precedence on prior alien tort cases.

"Like I said, we'll need someone else to file it, but I thought it might help to start pulling things together."

She stared at him. How long had he been up? The case research alone would have taken a few hours. She cleared her throat and looked away. "Thank you," she said, then quickly continued. "Based on this, I take it the transcripts came in from MI6?"

He nodded and walked past her and back into her office. She followed behind, not used to being the person being updated on an op she was running. Sure, technically it wasn't an op in the true sense of the word, but she was treating it as one—without all the resources of AISE.

"I already emailed them to you. It's more detailed than what we could make out watching the videos of the interviews. The situation was about as bad as it could get without the women actually being killed. There's confirmation that there were more incidences than the ones in the pictures, although I'm sure that's not a surprise. And do you remember that part of Candra's interview that neither of us could quite hear no matter how high we turned the volume up?"

She nodded.

"It was her confirming that she was one of the ones in the photos."

Six sank in her chair and let the anger and revulsion flow through her—it wasn't worth fighting, nor did she wish to. "Heather will want to file the suit," she said. She was feeling much more bloodthirsty than her statement might imply. But since she couldn't do what she really wanted to do to the men involved, at least she could ensure they paid for their crimes.

"Jeremy's sister? That's fitting," Gavin said, taking a seat on the opposite side of her desk where he'd set up his own computer and makeshift workstation.

"Any chance you got started on the phone access?" She felt guilty for even asking. He'd done so much while she'd been asleep that she didn't want to make him feel as though he hadn't done enough if, in fact, he hadn't started the process. And then there was the not-so-small fact that he'd done it all *while she'd been sleeping.* She'd needed the nap, but it felt as if she'd let him down.

He didn't seem to notice her reticence and answered as if they were truly a team working together on a case. "I got Franklin's number from Cyn this morning and called him. He's started the official warrant process, but I didn't start the unofficial part. I'm very good at navigating intelligence and data, but hacking isn't my strong suit. I didn't want to start bumbling around and risk making a mistake."

"I can take care of that. I'm pretty good, but if it looks above my skill set, I have someone I can call in." Lucy James and her husband, Brian DeMarco, had become good friends with the members of the club ever since Cyn and Nora had met them on an op the year before. There was no one better in the business than those two and Brian's twin sister, Naomi.

He nodded. "I also want to look into the blackmail angle. It could be nothing, but..."

"But it's worth looking into. Are you going to run a check on the financials of Julian Newcross and Austin and Kaden Fogarty?"

"My people are doing it," he answered, bringing a smile to her face.

"You have *people* now?"

He smiled back. "It seems Franklin has a soft spot for you, and since *you* are my op, as you pointed out, I now officially have people."

She let out a small laugh at that. "Well, let me know what your people find. In the meantime, I'm going to get started on the phone records. I also want to identify that fourth man. You may be onto something with the blackmail, but even if that's not the case, he's involved, and we need to know who he is."

"While I'm waiting for the financials, I'll keep plugging away on this," he said, holding up the checklist. Normally, it would take weeks—weeks they didn't have—to pull together every-thing they needed and draft the complaint. Getting started now was efficient, but to Six, it also spoke of Gavin's commitment to the women, to doing what was right. She might be just an assignment for him, but a little something inside her was starting to accept that if she let him, there was a chance they could be more. There was a chance that they could be true part-ners. And that thought was as fascinating as it was terrifying.

Ignoring the unease bubbling inside her, Six picked up her phone and shot off a text to Heather asking who Jeremy's cell provider was. Two minutes later, she had her answer and was debating with herself the best way to gain access to the system. There were ways to get in that wouldn't trigger any alerts, but it wasn't a walk in the park, and she'd need to be careful.

"How close were you and Jeremy?" Gavin asked as she continued to puzzle out her impending hacking approach.

"If you're asking if we ever dated, the answer is no," she responded, opening a private browser. It wasn't any of Gavin's business, but for some reason she didn't feel the need to point that out.

"I wondered," he admitted. "But more to the point, instead of hacking into the system of his provider, can Heather give you access to his account? If so, you'd probably be able to see a record of all his calls. And the cloud storage associated with his account might have backups of everything else."

Her eyes shot to him. He continued to plug away at whatever he was working on and didn't look in her direction. She studied him, looking for any sign that he was gloating at her obvious oversight. Because he was right. She should be able to get all of Jeremy's login information from Heather—or guess it herself—which would be *much* easier than hacking.

She sighed and turned back to her computer, this time bringing up the home page of the maker of his phone. As part of the service that came with the purchase of the phone, they provided backup of the data. It was as good a place as any to start.

"Thank you," she said. It might have come out a little begrudgingly, but she hoped he heard the sincerity, too. She'd been so caught up in being clandestine that she'd forgotten that maybe she didn't need to be.

When he didn't respond, she picked up her phone and pinged Heather again. A few minutes later, she had Jeremy's login information to both accounts. Heather had also provided his email logins in case either site needed to send an email to authenticate the user.

"Holy fuck," Six said fifteen minutes later. She'd gone to the cloud backup of the phone data first and was glad she had. It was a fucking gold mine. A gold mine of complete shit, but a gold mine, nonetheless.

"What?" Gavin said, rising and coming to stand behind her.

Without a word, she hit Play on one of the four videos she'd found tucked away among Jeremy's other 6,436 photos and videos. The video was similar to the pictures they already had, but this time, Julian Newcross was flying solo, and it wasn't Candra, but another woman. Or possibly a girl. She looked young, very young.

"Fuck," Gavin said before turning away. He took a couple of deep breaths, and though Six kept her eyes on the screen, she was well aware of the tension radiating from his body. The four-and-half-minute video ended, and she waited for Gavin to either let her know he'd seen enough or ask to see the others. None of this was easy for her, but as he remained silent, her mind filtered through his reactions over the past twenty-four hours. He'd spun away from her at the cabin when she'd first told him of the abuse and violence. Then there'd been his stony response at Cyn's. And now this. She recognized the signs, and she'd wager *this* was the ghost from his past.

She minimized the screen and turned her chair around. Looking at her watch, she calculated she had about twenty minutes before her friends arrived. She didn't know what his story was, but looking at his rigid back and his fists jammed on his hips, she knew there *was* a story.

"Who was it?" she asked softly.

His back snapped even straighter, then his shoulders rose with a deep breath. She remained quiet, and finally, he turned to face her. "My brother," he said, not dodging the question.

She tried to keep the surprise off her face, but knew she'd failed when he gave her a sad smile. "I know," he said. "But violence and abuse doesn't just happen to women. I know statistically it's higher with women…"

"But statistics aren't people nor are people statistics," she finished.

Again, he gave her a small smile. "He was older than me by ten years. I idolized him." Gavin walked to the window and let his gaze focus on the ocean as he continued. "I was eight when he was taken in by a man who was supposed to love him. They were together for eighteen months, and while I was too young to really know what was going on, I knew my parents weren't happy with the guy Isaac was dating. I remember a lot of fights. I remember Isaac accusing my parents of being ashamed of their gay son, and I remember my parents trying to defend themselves."

He paused and shoved his hands into his pockets, his mind seemingly lost in those days, weeks, and months from years ago. "It turned out that my parents didn't care about him being gay. They just wanted him to be happy, but they knew he wouldn't be happy with the man he insisted he was in love with. They saw through Wesley Penwright in a way my brother hadn't."

Again, he paused. Reaching up, he placed a palm on the window. Six fought the urge to go to him. She wanted to. She wanted to offer human comfort, but she sensed that right now, as he was back in that time, he needed, and wanted, to be there alone. She remained in her seat, waiting. Her heart beating for what she knew was about to come.

"Wesley Penwright was a user, a dealer, and a pimp. A well-heeled one, but one all the same. He turned my brother into an addict and then started pimping him out, telling him he needed to earn his next fix. I suspect it wasn't just the drugs that Isaac wanted. Even after everything he'd done, I suspect Isaac wanted to *earn* Wesley's attention—and love—too."

His palm left the window, but he traced a line with his finger down the pane. "He'd stopped calling and coming around. Then one day he called home. I was nine by then and I still didn't understand anything other than that he wasn't around anymore and I missed him. My parents had popped out to the shop, and I answered the phone. Isaac was crying, it was...it was like nothing I'd ever experienced. I was *nine*, I didn't know what to do with his emotions. But he kept crying, saying he was sorry and that he wanted to come home. I asked him where he was and told him I'd get help. He gave me an address and when I hung up, I ran. I ran as fast as I could to where he told me he'd be."

Suddenly, he spun away from the window and started pacing. "I remember running up the three flights of stairs of the apartment complex. It was one of those estate complexes," he said, referring to the government-assisted housing. "Without any thought, I burst into the apartment, all full of nine-year-old fear and righteousness. It never occurred to me to wonder why the door wasn't locked. To this day, I still don't know why, other than maybe it was some sort of sick joke Penwright played with my brother—leaving an easy escape so each time Isaac *didn't* take it, Penwright had a little more power over him.

"Isaac was there, on the bed, bloodied and beaten. It was a studio apartment, and I could see him right away. His hair had been shaved, and I almost didn't recognize him. But then he looked at me and I knew—he wasn't who I remembered, but I still remembered him."

Gavin returned to the window and took a few moments before he continued. "I panicked. I didn't know what to do."

Six thought about pointing out that he was nine and there was no way he'd been equipped to handle that situation, but decided not to interrupt. Gavin didn't need to hear her platitudes.

"I ended up banging on the neighbor's door. They'd had

issues with what had been going on in the apartment next door, but they weren't so jaded as to turn away a kid. It was all a blur after that. The police came, then we were at the hospital. My parents were summoned. In the end, my brother refused to press charges, but he also refused to go back. He wanted to wash Penwright out of his life forever, which included not pressing charges because he didn't want to have to testify."

Six had seen that reaction from several crime victims. But while she didn't understand it, she understood enough to know that her ignorance was a privilege. She'd never been in the position the victims had. She didn't really *know* what she'd do in their place. And she had no right to judge. She also wasn't about to ask what happened next. She hadn't heard the end of his and Isaac's story yet.

Finally, Gavin spoke again. "He came home and when he was healed, my parents got him into rehab for the addiction and into therapy for the months of abuse he'd suffered. It took a while and every now and then, I'd get a glimpse of my brother, of the brother I'd had before Penwright came into our lives." He paused and cleared his throat. "But it wasn't enough. Eight months after getting out of that hellhole, Isaac couldn't take the pain—and shame—anymore, and he stepped in front of a train."

A tear tracked its way down Six's cheek and fell on her chest. Quickly, she reached up to wipe away the evidence only to find she'd shed more than one for Gavin's loss.

Again, his finger came up and he traced an invisible pattern on the windowpane. "I was there," he said quietly. "I tried to stop him, but he was convinced that dying was the only way to stop the pain. He smiled and told me it would be for the best and that I should take care of Mum and Dad and make sure they didn't mourn him too much because he wasn't worth it. And then he waved and stepped in front of the train."

And with that, Six understood so much more than what he'd told her. He'd been tasked by a brother he loved with taking care of his parents. In his nine-year-old mind that probably meant trying to keep them from being sad. There was no way he could do that, but if the boy he'd been was anything like the man he was, then he would have tried. Which explained his near-perpetual cheer. It may be a part of who he was now as a man, but it had started as a promise and a coping mechanism in the boy he'd once been.

"I'm sorry," Six said, her voice quiet in the room. Gavin looked over his shoulder at her. Their gazes locked and held. There was so much more to this man than she'd given him credit for. No, that wasn't quite true. Someone like Gavin didn't lead the life he'd led without having substance and depth. He was far more than the average foot soldier, and he was well beyond just following orders. She just hadn't let herself consider, really consider, *him*. Him as a person, him as a man with a past, with ghosts, with loves and losses. It had been much easier to see him as someone assigned to her.

Being honest with herself, she wasn't sure she *wanted* to know much more about him. Because with that came complications. But that horse had left the barn, and it wasn't going to be led back in and forgotten anytime soon. Or ever. In fact, she was pretty sure the image of a nine-year-old Gavin watching his brother commit suicide would remain with her for a long time.

His eyes were still locked on hers when the first car drove up, her phone alerting her to the arrival.

"Cyn," she said, recognizing the sound of the engine. "Devil and Nora will be here soon, too. If you need some time, take it. I'll catch them up on what we both already know, and I'll wait until you're back to go over what else I found in Jeremy's account."

He gave her a conflicted look. She rose from her seat and walked over to him. "Go," she said, placing a hand on his arm and brushing a kiss on his cheek. He closed his eyes and took a deep breath. "We all need space every now and then. Take it.

Trust me," she said, pulling his words from the night before into their conversation. She wanted him to trust her to take his words and his grief and hold them safely, to trust her to let him be human and feel pain without judgment.

His dark eyes searched hers, then finally he nodded. "Just a few minutes."

She let a smile touch her lips. "If you head south along the water, sometimes the seals come out to play. They won't fix everything wrong in the world, but they are pretty damn cute."

At that, he smiled. A real smile. "Thanks," he said, then he took his leave, walking out the back door as Cyn walked in the front.

CHAPTER SIXTEEN

"HIS NAME IS VICTOR DEPALMA," Violetta said when Gavin returned to her house after his walk. She'd been right—the seals were what he'd needed to bring his mind back from those dark memories. The animals really did have adorable doglike faces. He knew that despite their appearance, they were kind of assholes, but that didn't make them any less fun to watch. They barked at each other, rolled over a lot, and generally looked like drunken blobs of sausage with flippers and cute eyes.

"The fourth man?" he clarified. Cyn, Devil, and Nora were all standing behind Violetta as she sat at her desk, intently reading something on her screen.

"Yes," she confirmed.

"We all know Julia Newcross's story," Cyn said.

"Raised by her mom until her mom died of cancer," Nora started.

"Then into the foster care system until she aged out," Cyn chimed in.

"Then clawed her way into college on a scholarship," Devil said.

"Where she learned all the science that she needed to start her company," Violetta finished.

Now that he was sure a video was no longer playing on her computer, Gavin walked over and joined them. His eyes skimmed the report and though he shouldn't be surprised, he was.

"Well, imagine that, she lied about her background," he said.

Violetta cocked her head. "Technically, it's all true. She just never mentioned that the foster home she went into was a family friend. Or, with the exception of losing her mother, that her life was hardly a hardship." As Violetta spoke, she flicked through a few pictures of a young Julia with, presumably, her foster family. She paused on one—a family picture. The five people in the photo were standing on a manicured lawn in front of a huge house. Julia wore a cap and gown and judging by her age, he guessed it to be a photo of her high school graduation. The older woman in the picture wore a sundress, heels, and plenty of diamonds while the man—Gavin assumed he was the father—and the two teenage boys wore suits and ties. A Mercedes was visible in the driveway.

"Her foster family?" he asked.

Violetta nodded. "And that," she said, pointing to the older of the two boys, "is Victor DePalma. Her foster brother."

"Anything we should know about the family?" he asked. "They look like a country club set to me, but of course, dark things can hide under a glossy sheen."

Violetta glanced up at him, then returned her attention to the screen and opened a document. He leaned forward and scanned the contents. "Where did you get this?" he asked. It was an active file from an ongoing investigation into the entire DePalma family. If the FBI was on the right trail, it looked as if Victor's activities in Indonesia were the tip of the iceberg.

Cyn cleared her throat. "From a friend."

Gavin looked over at her. She cocked a brow and grinned.

"Well, needs must sometimes," she said, confirming his suspicion that he didn't want to know how they got the FBI file.

"Does he work for Shanti Joy?" he asked.

Violetta shook her head. "Not officially. Officially, and conveniently, he works for a security firm tasked with accompanying precious cargo while in transit."

"Such as?" he asked.

"Art," Devil said.

"Jewels," Nora added.

"Horses," Cyn said, drawing his attention to her.

"Horses?" he asked.

She lifted a shoulder. "When you spend millions of dollars on a horse, you want to be sure it stays safe in transit."

He stared at her. He was from England, the land of horses. But still... "People actually pay millions of dollars for horses?"

Cyn's cheeks went a little pink, a look he'd never thought he'd see on her based on the file he'd read. "Um, yes," she said.

His eyes narrowed. "*You've* spent millions on a horse, haven't you?"

"Maybe."

He held her gaze.

She threw up her hands in a motion that reminded him of Violetta. "Fine, yes. I have. I *love* horses."

"And to be fair," Nora said, joining the conversation, "you have a good eye for them." Then turning to Gavin, she added, "She's had several horses win some big-name races, including a Kentucky Derby winner, one who won the Epsom Derby in England, and two Breeders' Cup champions." While Cyn might be a little uneasy discussing her four-legged spending habits, Nora was clearly proud of her friend. As she well should be. He might not know the first thing about how much horses cost, but he knew statistics, and statistically, winning those kinds of races took a keen eye for horseflesh and some excellent training.

"Right. Okay," he said, turning back to the task at hand. "So,

Victor DePalma… If he's still tight with his foster sister, then I doubt he's also into blackmail. All the men involved work for—or, in Julian's case, is married to—her." Violetta made a sound in the back of her throat. "What?" he asked.

"I don't know that I'd ditch your idea altogether," she said. He gestured for her to continue. "He has gambling debts. A lot of them. The kinds of debts he wouldn't want to go running to Mommy and Daddy to for help with their dirty money."

"And how did you find this out?" he asked.

She brought up another picture. "This was on Jeremy's phone." Gavin looked at the screen and saw a picture of Victor talking to some man. "That's Rodrigo DeSpaio," she said. "He's a loan shark. A high-end one, but a loan shark nonetheless. You know how in books, loan sharks always say they'd never kill people who owe them money because then they'd never get paid?"

Gavin nodded.

"Well, DeSpaio doesn't subscribe to that," Devil said. "He's more of the 'if I make a statement by killing people who don't pay me, then people will pay me' kind of guy."

"How many kills?" Gavin asked.

"No one knows for certain, but there are seven cases the FBI is tracking," Nora answered.

"Okay, so blackmail is still on the table for DePalma. I'll check my email to see if the financials on Newcross and the Fogartys have come in," he said, moving around to the other side of the desk.

"And I'll look into DePalma's financials," Cyn said, pulling out a laptop from a bag that he hadn't seen by the door to the office. "We came prepared," Cyn said, holding the device up with a smile.

Franklin had told him that these four women were close, but it hadn't been until the past few days that he understood what that meant. They might not be able to work together officially, but they were tied at the hip in every other respect. He had a few army buddies like that—men and women he'd move mountains for and vice versa. Even so, he suspected it was still a different bond than what these women had. They'd grown up together, gone to school together, lived within ten minutes of one another, and of course, they shared one hell of a secret.

He didn't know the specifics of each of their careers, nor would he ever know, but he liked their unfailing support of one another. He'd even wager that on some days, the bad ones, their friendships were the only thing that got them through to the next day.

He smiled at Cyn and took a seat behind his own computer. A few minutes later, Devil and Nora were side by side on the couch, their feet up on the coffee table and their laptops open on their laps. He didn't know what they were working on, but they had their heads together and were talking softly.

After logging into the secure server and opening his email, he was relieved to see the message at the top of his inbox. "I have the financials of Julian Newcross as well as Kaden and Austin Fogarty," he said.

"You take Julian and send Kaden and Austin's to us," Devil said. "We're just going over the videos to see if we can pick up anything new, but we can do that later."

She rattled off their addresses, and he attached the reports to an email and hit Send before digging into the state of Julian Newcross's affairs. Not surprisingly, Julian and Julia had a complex set of financials. There were numerous joint accounts, but Julian had a few just in his name, too. Gavin scanned, then dismissed the joint accounts. The transactions looked normal for the kind of lives the couple led. He also thought that while Julian's moral compass might be lacking, he wouldn't be stupid enough to pay any blackmail—if there was any blackmail—from an account he shared with his wife.

Closing those files out, he focused on the four bank accounts in Julian's name and the six accounts he had with a money manager based out of New York. Gavin had gone through the bank accounts and was about to open the second of the managed accounts when Violetta started, her chair jumping back on its wheels. Everyone in the room looked at her.

"What did you find?" Gavin asked, rising and circling the desk to stand behind her.

"That," Violetta said, pointing to a series of lines on a phone log. Cyn, Devil, and Nora joined them.

"Is that Jeremy's call record?" Nora asked.

"It is," Violetta confirmed. "And he had two conversations with this number the morning before he died." She pointed to a Boston area number. "But before that, there was this." She pointed to another number, a call that Jeremy had received in the very early hours of the morning before he'd been killed. It was an international call, and although Gavin didn't have his country codes memorized, it didn't take a genius to guess the call had come from Indonesia.

"Do you know whose number that is?" Cyn asked, pointing to the international number.

Violetta shook her head. "Not yet. But I do know whose number this is," she said, pointing to the Boston number.

Something niggled in the back of Gavin's mind. Something he'd seen on another document. Quickly, he sifted through his memory and when it hit him, it hit him with the subtlety of a sledgehammer.

He squeezed Violetta's shoulder, and she looked up at him. With his eyes locked on hers, he nodded to the screen. "That's Julian Newcross's number, isn't it?"

Cyn, Devil, and Nora all shifted. Cyn even leaned down to look more closely at the screen as if the numbers themselves might divulge a secret. He kept his eyes on Violetta as she nodded.

"Any text messages or anything?" he asked. The phone log

only showed the two men had spoken. The first time for six minutes and thirty-two seconds, and then again for two minutes and twenty-six seconds. A log of any text messages might give them some context.

Violetta shook her head. "I went through those first. There's very little there other than a few conversations with his sister and a couple with friends. He has the same app we do on our work phones, though, so it's possible they communicated over that."

The app she was referring to was a texting app where the messages disappeared after a certain amount of time. Everyone in the office had it, and it allowed the staff to shoot off sensitive questions to each other without worrying that they might be discoverable by other lawyers later.

"I want to know about this call," Devil said, leaning forward and pointing to the one from Indonesia.

"I backtracked the number," Cyn said, drawing everyone's attention. "Give me one second," she muttered as her fingers flew across the keyboard. Cyn Steele was a tiny ball of energy, and Gavin wondered if Joe ever got her to slow down. Then he smiled to himself; he'd seen the way the couple tracked each other when they were in the same room. Yeah, Gavin would bet Joe Harris had a way of slowing Cyn down.

"Anyone know this man?" Cyn asked, moving her computer so everyone could see the screen.

In sync, Devil, Nora, and Violetta all tipped their heads to the side as they studied the image.

"He looks familiar," Nora said.

"It's the eyes. I recognize the eyes," Devil said.

"Oh my god, it's Bernie Macauley," Violetta burst out.

Nora and Devil leaned forward, then both jerked back. "Oh my god, you're right," Devil said.

"Uh, who's Bernie Macauley?" Gavin asked.

"We went to college with him," Nora said.

"And he started law school with me and Jeremy, but then decided to join the Navy and dropped out after the first year. I haven't seen or heard from him since," Violetta said.

"Apparently, he now lives in Indonesia?" Gavin pondered, wondering about the connection between Bernie and Jeremy.

"He does," Cyn confirmed, having taken her computer back and continued doing whatever it was she'd been doing. "He's still Navy, but he's been assigned as the military liaison at the US embassy. There's been enough instability in the region that they have a dedicated post for him."

"If he was only in law school with you for a year, would he and Jeremy have known each other well enough to stay in touch?" Gavin asked.

Violetta raised a shoulder and shook her head. "I don't know. Jeremy never mentioned they'd stayed in touch, but maybe they reconnected when he started traveling to Indonesia."

"Are you going to call him?" Gavin asked.

Violetta mulled this over. He could understand her reticence. They had no context for how—or why—Bernie and Jeremy were connected. If it was because Bernie was involved in the Shanti Joy activities, she wouldn't want to tip him off to her investigation. On the other hand, if he wasn't involved, and had been providing help to Jeremy, then connecting with him might be invaluable.

"Call him," Cyn said. Violetta looked at her friend. "Trust me, call him," Cyn said. Some unspoken communication passed between the friends, then Violetta nodded.

"It's a little late at night, but if he doesn't answer, I'll leave a message," she said. Rising from her seat, she then walked out to the living room where she'd have room to pace while she called her former classmate.

Gavin watched her leave, then retook his seat. If something had been set in motion by the call between Macauley and

Jeremy, Gavin wondered if the financials might reflect that as well. He didn't know for certain if there was *any* financial angle to the situation. It was a lead they needed to follow, though. And looking at transactions from the day Jeremy had been killed seemed as good a place to start as any.

It was only a matter of a few minutes before he discovered an anomaly. Only what he'd found wasn't what he'd thought he'd find. He couldn't explain it, not right away, and he kept digging while Violetta continued her call.

He'd just discovered another piece of the puzzle when Violetta walked back into the room. Everyone looked at her expectantly. She tapped her phone against her thigh, her eyes fixed on some point across the room. Then, with a deep breath, she looked at him and spoke.

"I know why Bernie called Jeremy, and I have my suspicions about why Jeremy called Julian. If I'm right, then I know exactly why Jeremy was killed."

CHAPTER SEVENTEEN

"Talk to us," Cyn said. Six pulled her gaze from Gavin and looked at her friends. She didn't have all the answers, but at least she had one—one important one.

"We all believe that Jeremy was planning on bringing a lawsuit against Shanti Joy for their actions in Indonesia. And we believe he was killed to stop him from doing that. But one of the questions I've had since all this started was how Shanti Joy —or whoever hired those two men to kill Jeremy—even knew about the suit. It wouldn't be something Jeremy would have talked about. Hell, his own sister didn't know what he was doing."

"What changed that?" Gavin asked.

She glanced down at him, then walked to the couch. Sinking into the comforting upholstery, she told them. "It wasn't Bernie who called Jeremy. Not really. When Jeremy managed to get Abyasa, Candra, and Shinta out of the country, he gave Abyasa's mother Bernie's name. He couldn't leave a phone with her since she didn't have consistent enough electricity to keep it charged. Nor, for that matter, did he want to leave anything that might tie back to him and get Abyasa's mother in trouble. But he told her that if she needed to reach him or her daughter, to go through Bernie."

"But isn't Bernie based in Jakarta at the main embassy?" Devil asked.

Six nodded. "He is, but he travels around to the other islands, and at least once a month, he visits the consulate on the island where the plantation is."

"What drove Abyasa's mother to reach out to him?" Gavin asked.

"An auction," Six said, her stomach roiling as she spoke. "And yes, it's as bad as you think it is. She'd heard a rumor that DePalma was planning to auction off two young women and a young man."

Six closed her eyes and let her head fall back against the couch as her friends filled her office with all sorts of inventive swear words in several different languages. When they quieted down, she continued. "Jeremy received the call early that morning and was then stuck between a rock and a hard place."

"Say nothing to tip Shanti Joy off, and the auction moves ahead," Gavin said.

"Or say something to Shanti Joy in the hopes of scaring them enough to stop it, but tip his hand in the process," Nora finished, her voice tinged with pain for the decision Jeremy had had to make. A decision that had ultimately cost him his life, although it might have saved three others.

Silence fell across the room, then Cyn spoke. "We all know what choice Jeremy made," she said. "Do we know if it stopped the auction?"

Six opened her eyes and drew strength from the presence of her friends and, oddly, Gavin. "Bernie went out to the plantation to check on things and dropped a few hints that he'd heard rumors about their operations and now had eyes on them. There's no guarantee it didn't, or won't, go forward, but he said he has people looking into it."

The room fell into a deep silence. Six had no idea what everyone else was thinking, but her thoughts flitted between the agonizing decision Jeremy had been forced to make, and the strength of the woman who tracked Bernie down because she didn't want what had happened to her daughter to happen to any more young people.

"I found an oddity in Julian Newcross's finances that I can't explain," Gavin said, interrupting a moment that was close to turning maudlin. Six rolled her head to look at him and he continued. "The day Jeremy was murdered, Julian *deposited* a total of $1,200,000, spread across three of his managed accounts. In fact, the funds were deposited about two hours after Jeremy was killed."

Six frowned. "Was Julian paid to kill Jeremy? If he was, I guess he could have hired those two men to do it for him."

Gavin shook his head. "No, I don't think he had anything to do with Jeremy's death. Not directly. A few days before the deposits, he withdrew the money from those same accounts."

Six sat up, and her friends straightened in their seats as well. "So he deposited the same money he'd withdrawn from his own accounts a few days earlier?" she clarified.

Gavin gave a sharp nod. "That's what it looks like."

"But why would he do that?" Cyn asked.

"And what does that have to do with Jeremy?" Nora asked.

Gavin met Six's gaze, and in his eyes, she could read the conclusion he'd come to. "He *was* being blackmailed," Six said.

"And then something happened to change his mind about paying out," Gavin finished.

"Wait, what?" Cyn said, rising from her seat and coming around the desk. Leaning against it, she crossed her arms and demanded more intel. "I know we've established that DePalma has a reason to blackmail, but why would you think Newcross was his victim if there wasn't any payout?"

"And more to the point, if Newcross was his victim, why

would he have changed his mind? He had a lot to lose," Devil chimed in.

Six looked to Gavin, who gestured for her to explain. She nodded and turned to her friends. "He did have a lot to lose, but what if he was going to lose it anyway?" She paused, organizing her thoughts, then continued. "What if he withdrew the money, intending to pay. But then Jeremy called and, rather than reach Julia, he spoke to Julian and told *him* about the lawsuit he was planning to file. Maybe even mentioned the videos."

"Ah," Nora said, catching on. "He realized he was going to lose everything anyway. The videos alone would see to that."

"So why bother paying a blackmailer," Cyn said, coming to the same conclusion Six had.

Six nodded. "It's conjecture, of course. But I suspect after the first call between Jeremy and Julian, Julian called DePalma, told him he wasn't paying, and why."

"At which point, *DePalma* is the one who took action and decided to have Jeremy killed in order to silence him," Devil said. Six gave a small nod of agreement.

"But after Jeremy was killed, don't you think DePalma would be back on Newcross's case?" Nora asked.

Six looked at Gavin, and he seemed to be considering the idea. After a beat, he spoke. "It's a good point, Nora. If I were DePalma, I'd certainly be pushing to get my payout. I'd maybe even use Jeremy's murder as an incentive to comply."

"I assume he hasn't withdrawn any more money, though, or you would have said as much," Six said.

Gavin nodded. "He hasn't, but that could also be because he sees the house of cards for what it is and knows it's futile to try to stop what's going to come next," Gavin said. "Jeremy may be dead, but there are videos out there somewhere."

"Or maybe there's something else going on," Devil said. She'd been typing away on her laptop as they'd been talking, and Six nudged her with her toe to continue when she didn't immediately explain her statement.

"I gained access to the servers at Shanti Joy. Not the top-secret stuff, but enough to look at calendars. It appears that Julia Newcross left the country on an *emergency* trip to Paris the day after Jeremy was killed."

"Her husband didn't go with her?" Gavin asked.

Devil shook her head. "No, he had one charge on his company card for dinner the night she left, but it hasn't been active since."

"That was only a few days ago," Nora pointed out.

"And he's not an employee so he may not use that card very often," Cyn added.

"All true," Devil conceded. "But there hasn't been any activity on any of his four personal cards, either. I know it's only been a few days, but his usual spending habits include several charges a day, including a consistent one for lunch at the gym he goes to."

"This better not be another fucking Kevin Bartlett," Cyn muttered, returning to her seat behind her computer.

"Kevin Bartlett?" Gavin asked.

"A hacker who helped a bunch of white supremacists access things that they shouldn't," Six said. "We were investigating the group when his name cropped up. Joe and Cyn went to talk to him. It didn't turn out well."

"And by not well, she means he'd been murdered," Nora added.

"And you think that's what's happened to Julian Newcross?" Gavin asked.

Six didn't answer, but one by one, she met the gaze of her friends. Yeah, that's exactly what they thought had happened, even if they weren't going to say it.

"Any leads on where he could be if he isn't dead?" Six asked, dragging her body off the couch.

"Are we going on a road trip?" Gavin asked, joining her.

"His phone's at his home in Beacon Hill," Devil said.

"But his car—which has one of those emergency locator things on it—is somewhere near Keene, New Hampshire," Cyn said. "Any chance they have a second home there?"

"They have five homes throughout the world, but yes," Nora said. "One is in Keene."

Six looked to Gavin. She should make the call; Jeremy was her friend, and she'd been the one to bring everyone into this. But just once, it would be nice to have someone else decide. Someone she trusted. And as shocking as that thought should have been, it wasn't.

"Let's head to Keene. It's, what, about two hours away? Or I could go on my own if you want to stay here," he offered.

She was shaking her head before he even finished the sentence. "No one goes alone unless we have to. I think we've all learned our lesson on that."

"And we'll hold the fort here," Devil said.

Nora and Cyn nodded. "We'll finish with the financials and if anything comes up, we're a phone call away," Cyn said.

"What about Abyasa, Candra, and Shinta?" Six asked.

Cyn waved her off. "They'll be fine. Michaela was teaching them self-defense when I left, and Dan was going to have them show him how to cook some of their favorite meals."

Michaela was Cyn's groundskeeper and personal trainer, and Dan was her house manager and chef. Six, Devil, and Nora all had people that came in to cook and clean, but Cyn, with her ginormous house, was the only one with *staff*.

Six cast her friends one more questioning look. Had the tables been turned, as they had been in January when Cyn was in the thick of stopping a terrorist attack, Six wouldn't give a second thought to helping. In fact, there'd be nothing else she'd want to do other than to help her friends—it's what they'd been doing for one another since the day they'd met. But this somehow felt different, and she didn't like leaving them with all sorts of unanswered questions while she and Gavin went off on a road trip. No matter how important that road trip might turn out to be.

"Go," Nora said. Her voice was gentle, but there was no mistaking the steel in it. Cyn and Devil nodded their agreement.

Her gaze lingered on her friends, then shifted to Gavin. "I guess we're going on a road trip. My car or yours?"

CHAPTER EIGHTEEN

"THEY MUST KNOW that Jeremy's records didn't die with him," Gavin said as they wound through the hills toward Keene, New Hampshire. Both he and Violetta had been quiet for the past thirty minutes, but it was a comfortable silence.

"I agree," she said after a beat. She was driving, and he was enjoying the luxury of watching her. And the countryside. He hadn't gotten out and around New England much since he'd moved. The variety of greens reminded him of England, but everything was just a little wilder in America. And he kind of liked it.

"They are a modern company with the sophisticated technology needed to protect their product. They'd know that the odds of Jeremy having backups and a storage service and similar technology are high," she continued. "Do you think Julia is doing a runner by going to Paris?"

He didn't, and he didn't think Violetta did either if the tone of her voice was any indication. "There was no unusual activity in her accounts—at least not the ones I looked at. I think she's hiding out while DePalma cleans up the mess. It gives her some distance from whatever he's doing if she's out of the country."

"But he can't possibly clean everything up," she reiterated. "He might be able to find someone to hack into Jeremy's accounts, and if he could do that, he could wipe them. In fact, he probably did and hacking in is probably how they found out about the women. But even if they wiped the data after I accessed it, backups of backups exist and can almost always be reconstructed."

They crested a small hill, and a lush valley spread out below them. "It's bothering you, isn't it?"

She nodded. "Assuming Julian told DePalma he wasn't going to pay and why, DePalma has to be feeling like an animal backed into a corner, and that's never a good thing."

Gavin agreed. DePalma was a first-class douche of a human, but he wasn't stupid. He'd know that everything was about to come crashing down around him. And a person who has nothing to lose could be, well, unpredictable.

Which made him worry about Violetta. Not that he hadn't been worried about her before, especially when she'd guided the women through the woods on her own with no backup. But that had been a low-grade kind of worry since the situation was well in hand, and he'd had his eyes on the two killers the entire time. This was different.

Assuming DePalma was behind Jeremy's murder, the attempt to run Violetta off the road, and the two hitmen sent for the women, Gavin had a hard time believing the man *wouldn't* come after Violetta again. Because if DePalma had even a modicum of intelligence, he'd be able to figure out that she was behind the escape of Abyasa, Candra, and Shinta. And if she knew about them, then he'd be crazy not to think she knew about everything else.

"I think we need to get Heather to file the suit soon," Gavin said. The best way to protect Violetta was to get the complaint into the system and out to the public.

Oblivious to the specific direction of his thoughts, Violetta nodded. "Do we know where DePalma is right now? He's the loose cannon."

"I suspect your friends are already tracking his movements, as well as the Fogartys, but I'll text Cyn and see if they can get a bead on DePalma."

He sent the text, and they fell back into silence waiting for Cyn's reply. According to the map on Violetta's dashboard screen, they were an hour out from the coordinates Nora had given them for the Newcrosses' Keene home. As the minutes ticked by, Gavin replayed in his mind everything that had happened in a few short days.

He'd hated keeping his role in her life from her, and when he'd first been given the assignment, he'd argued that she should be told. Franklin was equally adamant that the information be kept from her. In retrospect, having his assignment come to light in the way it had—in a moment when his assistance could be appreciated—was far better. She still hadn't welcomed him with open arms, but at least he'd been able to demonstrate that he was worthy of her respect.

And he had it. He knew he did. He could see it in her eyes and in the easy way she was now working with him. She'd had his from the first time he'd read her file. But again, that had been part of the problem. He'd known so much about her before he'd even arrived, while she'd been kept in the dark about him for months.

"What are you thinking?" Violetta asked, breaking into the silence.

He had no desire for Violetta to know how often he thought of her and so a lie—or at least a fudge of the truth—fell easily from his lips. "I was thinking that this investigation reminds me a little bit of hunting a terrorist."

She glanced over and arched a brow at him, making him smile.

"It's not a classic whodunit investigation like on all those

American crime shows. We know who the perpetrators of the crimes are. And we have a pretty good idea of the breadth of those crimes thanks to the interviews with Abyasa, Candra, and Shinta. Like hunting a terrorist, we know who they are, and we know what they've done, and our job is to bring them to ground. When I was in the field, usually that meant capture or kill. But here, it means bringing them to justice. I kind of feel like we stepped into the second half of an episode of *Law & Order.*"

Violetta snorted. "You know how bad that show is, right? I mean it's great, I love it, who doesn't? But it's terrible in how it portrays investigations and trials."

He made a face at her. "Spoilsport."

She laughed. "Maybe, but I see your point. I hadn't thought of it like that. The phrase 'hunting terrorists' is so closely associated with warfare, and it's hard to think of something that's happening in your own backyard—when you live here in the US —as being warfare. You're right, though, and I guess that puts us a little ahead of the game. We don't have to look for *who*, we just need to focus on how to stop DePalma and the others. Although frankly, in my mind, the Fogartys, Julian Newcross, and DePalma *are* terrorists, just maybe not in the common parlance of the word."

"Any suggestions on *how* we stop them?" he asked as his phone dinged with a text from Cyn. He opened the app and read. "DePalma was in Indonesia earlier this week but returned to Boston the day after Jeremy was killed. Cyn and the others are working on getting an exact location for him, but he hasn't left the country again. At least not legally," he added.

"If Jeremy talked to Julian the morning before he died and Julian then called DePalma, DePalma worked fast. He had two hitmen on Jeremy by the middle of the afternoon," Violetta said.

"Which tells us he's well connected to the wrong kind of people."

Violetta nodded. "And when he lost those two men the night they came after me, he had two more on tap to send after the women."

"We need eyes on him," he muttered, considering whether to send Cyn a text to that effect. In the end, he set his phone down. They'd just discovered who DePalma was a few hours ago. Cyn, Nora, and Devil would do their best, and they didn't need him telling them how to do their jobs. Hell, with their secret spy schooling, they'd been doing this kind of shit a lot longer than he had.

"If you ever have a daughter, would you send her to St. Josue?" he asked. The question was a bit apropos of nothing, but thinking about the school—and picturing Violetta, Cyn, Nora, and Devil there—made him wonder.

The question caught Violetta off guard, and her head whipped around. "Pardon?"

He fought a grin. Her Italian accent was much heavier when she was surprised. "If you ever have a daughter, would you send her to the school you attended?"

She made a face at him. "I'm thirty-eight and not likely to ever have kids. I know women in their forties have kids all the time, but I don't have the kind of life that is conducive to being a parent. Not a good one, anyway."

"What if you had help?" he asked, then immediately wondered why he'd asked. No, that wasn't quite true; he'd definitely conjured up a few fantasies about him and Violetta being more than colleagues. But to ask a question that implied he might be the one to help raise any fictional kids they might have was a bit of a reach.

The flash of confusion he felt must have shown on his face, because Violetta laughed. "Don't worry," she said. "I won't think you're offering. Besides, even if you were, I'm not sure I want kids. Maybe I do, but it's not something I've ever contemplated, so I don't know what I think about it." She paused as she passed a slow-moving truck. "That said, if I ever did have a daughter, I'd offer her the opportunity if I could."

"What do you mean, if you could?"

Violetta bobbed her head. "St. Josue isn't like a regular boarding school. I don't just mean in what they teach. It's by invitation only, and only one girl from each of the participating countries gets offered a place. If I ever had a daughter and if I wanted her to attend, I might not have the choice, if she's not offered the place."

He'd known it was exclusive. For some reason, though, he'd assumed that someone like Violetta, someone who'd been through the school and had an exemplary career, would get preference if she had a daughter who wanted to attend. Then again, maybe it made sense that she didn't. One of the goals of the school was building community. If Violetta ever had kids, those kids would already have an international community in Cyn, Devil, and Nora and their respective contacts. Not to mention, if Cyn, Devil, or Nora ever had kids, too, then the kids would grow up together in much the same way their mothers had.

His phone dinged again, and he picked it up. Another message from Cyn. "Fuck," he grumbled after reading it.

"What?"

"Guess who else is in Keene?"

"*Fanculo*," she muttered. "Confirmed sighting or just location tracking?"

"Tracking," he answered. "DePalma's phone and car. Cyn is working on exact coordinates."

"Fun," Violetta said under her breath, mirroring his own sentiments.

"What's our story going to be with Newcross?" Gavin asked. "I assume we're not going to knock on his door and ask him about Jeremy and Victor?"

Violetta pursed her lips as she considered the question. Then after a beat, she answered, "I actually wonder if we should."

He chuckled. "That was not the answer I was anticipating."

She flashed him a grin that hit him right in the chest. "We have records and backup records of everything Jeremy discovered. There's no point in killing us, because it will all get out anyway. We have no reason for knocking on his door other than our connection to Jeremy. And I don't know about you, but I don't feel like going all superspy and breaking in. If we wanted intel on his computers or devices, that might be a better option, but we came up here to talk to him. Assuming DePalma hasn't decided to tie off that particular loose end and he's still alive, of course."

Gavin tipped his head. "With DePalma in the area, I'd say Newcross is either dead or will be in the near future. What if Newcross isn't home?"

"Then we wait to see if my friends can find him." She paused, then added, "And maybe ask Joe to call in a favor and send the local police chief up to make a wellness check in case he's dead in his home."

"If nothing else, this afternoon will prove to be an interesting one," Gavin replied, then turned his head to look at the lush scenery. "You ever think of moving back to Italy?"

Again, his question surprised Violetta, and she shot him a quick look. When her eyes were back on the road, she answered. "No, I don't, actually. I love Italy and I love visiting my family. But I don't have a lot of friends there since I was so young when I left. I've lived far more of my life here than there. Are you looking forward to getting back to England once this assignment is over? When is this assignment over?" She turned and gave him another look. This time her brow was furrowed as if she couldn't believe she hadn't asked the question before now.

He lifted a shoulder. "I don't know," he answered honestly.

He'd asked, but the only response he'd received was that he'd be on this assignment until the government decided otherwise.

"But you have family at home, right? Friends, maybe even a girlfriend or a kid?"

He would have smiled if he'd thought she was fishing for information on his life, but what he heard in her voice stopped him. *Guilt* infused her every word. She didn't want to be responsible for taking him away from people he cared about, from his life before this assignment. She didn't like the idea that he might have to give those things, and those people, up for this assignment that neither of them really understood. She might be a bit brash and tempestuous at times, but she cared. He wanted to think she cared *about him*, and she probably did. But he didn't doubt her current dismay was of a more general sort.

"My parents passed away last year within three months of each other. They were older when they had Isaac and even older when they had me. Their deaths were peaceful, though I'll admit, it wasn't the easiest few months. I'm officially an orphan now." The smile he shot her was intended to be wry, but by the way her eyes softened, he thought it had come across more as sad.

"I have friends, but most are in the army or recently retired, and they're scattered all over the place. No girlfriend or kids," he added, hiding the annoyance he felt at her even considering that an option. He never would have done or said the things he'd done and said to her if he had someone else at home.

"Still, you aren't like me in that I lived in Italy for such a small amount of time. Surely you miss it?"

He considered her question. There were things he did miss, sure. He missed pubs and cobblestoned streets. He missed chip shops and the wry, dry British sense of humor. He missed being able to rely on trains for travel, and he missed being able to pop to places like Paris or Rome for a weekend. But did he really miss it? Did he miss the regimented life he led because of his work? Did he miss the dreary weather and five days of summer they had each year?

It was a complicated question, and in his gut, he knew that for the right reason, he'd be happy to leave it all behind. But that wasn't something he was going to say to Violetta.

"I missed it until I tasted your flat white. Now I'm good and have no reason to ever go back provided you keep making them for me," he added with a grin and a wink.

Violetta rolled her eyes but laughed at him. "Maybe I'll buy you your own machine."

"I'm positive anything I made wouldn't be nearly as good. So if you want me to stay, which I know the jury is still out on for you, you will have to keep making me flat whites."

"You are ridiculous," she said, but she was still smiling. "And by the way, we're only fifteen minutes out. Can you check with Cyn on the security at the Newcross house? The driveway is a long one so hopefully they don't have a gate, but I didn't ask before we left."

Gavin started typing out a message as he spoke. "If there is a gate, I bet if you mention Jeremy's name, we'll be let through."

Violetta inclined her head. "Yes, but I'd rather not be locked *in* if things go sideways."

"Fair point. I guess it's a good thing there's no gate then," he said, holding up his phone with Cyn's reply. Not that Violetta could read it while she was driving.

"Any other details?" she asked.

He read through the message and then through a second one that popped up. "Looks like run-of-the-mill security. They are rich, *very* rich by global standards. But not the kind of rich that would make them high value targets, so they seem to be relying on a system alone. A good one and a very high-end one, but just the one." He paused and considered what he'd said. Violetta, Cyn, Devil, and Nora all came from some of the wealthiest families in their countries; hadn't they ever worried about kidnappings? Other than their work for their governments, they all led relatively quiet lives. Maybe they'd been out of the country for so long that people had more or less forgotten about them? That thought added another twist to the concept of St. Josue. Not all the girls who were invited to attend came from families like Violetta's. But for those who did, it had probably been an exceptionally secure place for them to grow up and go to school. And even though they left at eighteen, they'd left with skills that would help protect them.

Hmm, maybe Violetta's parents had had reasons for agreeing to send her there other than the honor it was to be invited.

"You're awfully quiet over there," Violetta said.

"Just woolgathering," he replied, suddenly grateful for the odd little school tucked up in the mountains of Switzerland that he hadn't, at first, even believed was a real thing. Unlike the Newcrosses, Violetta, Cyn, Devil, and Nora *were* extremely high-value targets. Especially as children. That they'd had a chance to grow up relatively free from that worry, and free from constantly having personal bodyguards, must have been a blessing.

She glanced over at him as she flicked her blinker on. He could read the curiosity on her face, but she dropped the topic and nodded to the road. "The driveway is off this road, three hundred meters up."

They'd done a quick scan of the property using Google Maps, and the house sat on the back side of the one hundred eighty acres the Newcrosses owned. The property started at the road, and a driveway wound through dense woods as it climbed a steep hill before leveling out at an open field. The house was situated in the middle of the field. The grounds behind it rose a touch more before reaching the peak of the mountain, then descended back down the other side.

"There's been no movement?" Violetta asked, slowing to make the turn onto the driveway.

Gavin shook his head. "None at all according to Cyn."

They turned onto the drive and about twenty meters in, they passed by a well-hidden—though not hidden enough—sensor. "I know the make and model of this system," he said. "Julian will know someone is coming, but he won't know who. Not yet, anyway. According to Cyn, there are cameras, but they are farther up, tucked into the trees right as the woods give way to the clearing."

Violetta nodded and continued navigating up the drive. Five minutes later, the woods ended abruptly, and they broke into a wide, lush field. The grass was a rich, deep green and May wildflowers dotted the landscape, bringing a shot of color. To their right, a fenced field housed two horses who were lazily grazing away on this picture-perfect day. A small barn could be seen on the other side of the pasture.

Less than a minute later the Newcrosses' home came into view. For some reason, he'd expected a large New England-style farmhouse, or at least a house that honored that tradition even if newly built. What he had not expected was the Tudor-style behemoth in front of them. Yes, with its multiple peaks, pitched roof, and tower, it was beautiful. And it was definitely large enough to rival some of those in England. But it fit oddly into the landscape. Some houses were built to pay no mind to their surroundings and were unapologetic about the mismatch. This house wasn't that. It was as if it wanted to fit in, but instead, sat awkwardly on the fringes of acceptance.

"If I ever build a house, remind me not to hire whomever the architect was for this," Violetta muttered, leaning forward to look at the building as they approached.

"Oh, look, they do have a security guard," Gavin said, gesturing with his head to the man who'd walked out of the house through a small door on the far left side. "You ready?" he asked, not altogether sure what Violetta was planning other than being direct with Julian.

"I'm ready," she said. Then, as she rolled her window down to greet the man, she added, "Play along."

He couldn't help it, he brushed a finger along her arm and grinned. "Whatever games you want, I'm happy to play."

That surprised a laugh out of her, and she was smiling when the guard approached them.

"You're on private property," he said, full of swagger. He even had his hand resting on the gun at his hip.

Violetta laughed again. "I'm Violetta Salvitto and I met Julia and Julian at Cannes last year. As you can imagine, I'm well acquainted with their products as so many of the actresses and models my family's business works with use them. Anyway, we hit it off and they said I should stop by next time I was in New Hampshire."

The guard eyed her, and Gavin wasn't surprised he didn't know the Salvitto name. They were royalty when it came to media and entertainment, but like so many in that business, the spotlight always fell on the more public faces.

"This is my boyfriend, Gavin," she said, waving to him. Gavin smiled and waved. "I tried calling Julian this morning," she continued, "but he wasn't answering his phone. We're heading up to Quebec tonight, so I thought I'd try my luck and pop by."

Something about what she'd said must have resonated, because the man dropped his hand and pulled out a phone. "Let me check to see if Mr. Newcross is available. Mrs. Newcross—"

"Is in Paris, I know," Violetta said. "I'd heard she needed to make the unexpected trip." The fact that she already seemed to know his employers well enough to know their schedules relaxed him enough to bring a smile to his face. He nodded and walked a few steps away, turning his back to them.

"Did you really meet them at Cannes?" Gavin asked quietly.

She shook her head. "No, I hate going to those things. Some are okay, but they aren't my thing. Chances are, they would have met my mother or father, though. And there's no way someone from Shanti Joy—a company that makes millions from the entertainment industry—is going to say no to meeting a Salvitto. The guard might not recognize my name, but Julian sure as shit will."

Gavin's lips twitched. "You sound so very American at times, you know, love."

She smiled back. "Americans have the best idioms. A few years after I moved here, I tried to go a week just speaking with idioms, colloquialisms, and sayings. I got through a day and a half and then I kept cracking myself up so had to stop, since my professors didn't find it nearly as amusing as I did."

"Mr. Newcross said to head on up," the guard said, then he pointed to a pullout on the driveway. "You can park there."

Violetta flashed the man a smile and he blinked. Then he smiled back before returning to the door through which he'd come.

"Ready?" Violetta asked as she pulled into the indicated spot.

"As I'll ever be," Gavin replied. And a not-so-little part of him was truly looking forward to seeing Violetta Salvitto—billionaire, federal prosecutor, Italian spy—in action.

CHAPTER NINETEEN

"JULIAN!" Six exclaimed when the man himself opened the door. It was near impossible to not punch him in the face for everything that he'd done. But she kept a firm image of Abyasa, Candra, and Shinta in her mind as she leaned forward and brushed her cheek against the disgusting lump of human flesh. She was here for the women and all the others that he and his friends and colleagues had abused. She was here for Jeremy.

"Lovely to see you again," she said, pushing into the house with Gavin on her heels. "I tried to call earlier, but you weren't answering your phone and I'm *so* sorry to miss Julia but understand when business calls. How have you been?" She didn't wait for an answer as she continued through the foyer to a sitting room she'd spotted off to the right. "I heard you were getting ready to release something in time for the fall fashion week in Milan? Whatever it is, I'm sure we'll be hearing a lot more about it."

The man followed her and Gavin into the sitting room. Once they were all seated, she looked at Julian Newcross, expectantly.

He had a few days' worth of beard growth, his eyes were

bloodshot, and his hair was sticking up at all angles. And if she wasn't mistaken, there was a stain on his shirt and one on his shorts.

He blinked at her, then gave a little shake of his head. "I'm sorry, would you both like something to drink?" he offered.

Six smiled. "No, thank you. We won't trouble you too much seeing as we dropped in without notice. I was wondering if Victor is around?" she asked.

Julian started and may have turned a little green. He gave a quick shake of his head. "No, he's not. How do you know Victor?"

She gave an airy wave. "Oh, you know. From here and there. I never got his number when we last met and I was hoping to meet up with him."

"Uh, why?" Julian asked, then seemed to think better of his comment and straightened in his chair in an effort to pull himself together. "I mean, I'm sure he'll be disappointed. I think he may be on a job for his father. Maybe somewhere in the Caribbean."

She made a face. "That's too bad. I wanted to ask both of you about Jeremy Wheaton and the activities taking place in Indonesia."

Julian blinked again, then all color drained from his face. He opened his mouth to say something but didn't get very far. No, instead, his eyes rolled into the back of his head, and he fainted, slumping onto the couch, then sliding forward onto the ground.

Both she and Gavin watched.

"Well, once again, that was not what I was expecting," Gavin said as they remained in their seats. Six glanced at the coffee table and wished Julian had hit his head on it on the way down. Or maybe she could arrange that for him and blame it on his fall when he came to.

"Don't do it, Violetta," Gavin said from beside her, wrapping his hand around hers to anchor her to her spot. How he knew what she'd been thinking she couldn't guess. Then again, he might have been thinking the same thing.

"So we sit here and wait?" she complained.

"Unless you want to go riffling through his house, but you said yourself, we're here to talk to him, not surveil the house."

She let out a huff and Gavin chuckled.

"Any interest in helping him?" Gavin asked, though his tone made it clear that he offered only because he thought he should. She didn't deign to answer. Five minutes later, Julian's eyes fluttered, and he woke with a start. He jerked upright and hit his head on the coffee table. It was satisfying. Perhaps not as satisfying as being the cause of his pain, but she'd take what she could get. Especially since Gavin hadn't yet let go of her hand, and although she was damn good at hand-to-hand combat, she wasn't confident she could take him.

Julian rose to a sitting position, rubbing his head, his expression one of confusion. Six and Gavin continued to watch him. A few seconds later, Julian's eyes lifted, and he caught sight of them. His brow furrowed, then his eyes widened and the color—what was left of it—drained from his face once again.

"You," he breathed, hefting himself up from the floor and onto the couch.

Six grinned. "Yes, us. We're still here. So," she said, once he was seated, "Jeremy Wheaton?"

He blinked several times. "I don't know who you're talking about."

Six raised an eyebrow. "For a serial rapist and criminal, you are a remarkably bad liar." It was a struggle for Julian to try to remain detached, but at least he didn't pass out again.

"Again, I don't know what you're talking about." His voice came out something between a whisper and a croak.

Six considered showing him the video she'd uploaded to her phone but decided against it. The lawyer in her took over and the idea of burying him in a hole of his own making held far more appeal.

"Jeremy called you on Monday. You had two conversations with him. The first was over six minutes and the second, just over two. I want to know what you talked about," she said.

Again, Julian blinked at her. Multiple times. Like someone who had something in their eye. "I, uh, I lost my phone."

Six didn't have any love for Julia Newcross, as she assumed the CEO of Shanti Joy knew about her husband's proclivities. Still, she wondered how the two had ended up together in the first place. Despite everything, or maybe because of it, Six 100 percent believed that Julia was a bright woman. To have built the business she had—and to have maintained the charade as long as she had—spoke of intelligence. It also spoke of socio-pathic tendencies, but those two traits weren't mutually exclusive. How she'd ended up with man like Julian was a mystery to Six.

"Really?" Six asked. He nodded. "When did that happen?" she asked.

"Uh, Sunday?"

Six cast a glance at Gavin, whose gaze was fixed on Julian.

"How long have you been up here? In Keene?" she asked.

His gaze darted to Gavin before he answered. "Um, I don't need to answer that. In fact, I think you should leave?"

Six laughed. It wasn't appropriate, but she didn't care.

"How long have you been in Keene?" she repeated.

Again, Julian's gaze drifted to Gavin. "I, you...I mean, I think you should leave."

"That's not happening, Mr. Newcross," Gavin said. "I suggest you answer Ms. Salvitto's questions."

Julian swallowed, his attention darting between the two. Then it shot to the foyer, visible from where they sat.

"Your security isn't coming. And if you think we will let you make a move to call him, you are sorely mistaken," Gavin said.

His tone was one Six hadn't heard before. His no-bullshit approach drew her attention in a way that maybe it shouldn't have. At least not at that moment.

"We know everything, Julian...the videos, the girls, the auctions," Six said. "We just want to hear it in your words."

"What auction? I don't know anything about an auction!" Julian jerked back in his seat as he answered.

Six ignored his response. It was entirely possible that Julian didn't know about DePalma's other activities. If she were DePalma, she would *definitely* keep Julian Newcross in the dark.

"Tell me about Jeremy Wheaton," Six pressed.

Julian's gaze darted between the two, then something caved inside him. His shoulders slumped, and his eyes shifted down and took on a vacant, defeated look. "DePalma killed him. Or had someone kill him," Julian started. Six made a gesture with her hand for him to continue. Julian took a deep breath, leaned against the back of the couch, and shut his eyes.

"I don't know how it happened, but he, Jeremy, learned about what...about what happened in Indonesia. He called to tell me he knew all about it. He wanted to stop some auction. I don't know what auction he was talking about but...I knew what else he was referring to.

"I called Victor after the first call. I told him Jeremy knew everything. I don't actually know that Jeremy knew everything, but he knew enough for me to believe him when he said there'd be consequences for our actions."

"What did Victor say?" Six asked.

Julian snorted. "What Victor always says. That I'm an idiot and he'll take care of everything and not to say anything to anyone. You know he's having an affair with my wife, right? I think they've been sleeping together since she moved in with him and his family when she was a kid. Kind of sick since he's like ten years older and I think she was maybe thirteen when she moved in."

The irony of that statement had Gavin gripping her hand to keep her in place.

"What happened next?" Gavin asked, because she was unable to.

"He told me to call Jeremy back and agree to meet him somewhere. I did and then I left Boston. I may not be the sharpest knife in the drawer, but I could see where things were going. If this Jeremy person knew—someone I never knew even existed until he called—then chances were someone else, or a whole lot of someone elses, knew. Victor tried to convince me Jeremy was the only problem, but I think he was trying to lull me into a sense of security." He paused, and his attention shifted to the window beside him. "I'm pretty sure Victor means to kill me. That's why I came up here. I'm not surrounded by guards or anything, but this house has decent security and because of the field, it's pretty hard to sneak into. I haven't left since I arrived here on Monday night."

"What, specifically, did Victor say when you told him about Jeremy?" Six asked.

Julian's gaze remained on the window, but he lifted a shoulder. "He told me to arrange the meetup but not to say anything else."

"You've already told us what he said in relation to Jeremy, but what did he say to you about the situation?" Gavin asked.

Julian remained silent for a long moment. "He said he'd take care of everything. That everything would be fine."

"You didn't believe him?" Gavin asked.

For the first time, Julian showed a truly human reaction and gave them a smile that was half rueful and half sad. "Of course not. Jeremy said he had videos and described one of the nights in enough detail that I knew he wasn't bluffing. Victor tried to convince me he *was* bluffing, but I knew better. And now I think Victor wants to kill me."

That was the second time Julian had alluded to Victor having it out for him. Six didn't disagree. If she were Victor, she'd want to take Julian—and his propensity to faint when asked hard questions—out as well. But she was curious as to why he thought so, and so she asked.

That same smile appeared. "I'm the weak link," he said, surprising Six. "I know...I know you probably don't believe me, but I love them. All the women, the girls, I'm with. I want to protect them, to show them what it's like to be with someone who cares about them. I'm not like the others. I don't want power and I don't want to hurt them. God no. I want them to know what it's like to be with a man who loves them."

"And so you force yourself on them," Six said, not bothering to hide the disgust and disbelief in her voice.

Julian's guileless gaze met hers. "I want them to *know* what it's like to be with a man who cares for them. I care for them."

Bile rose in Six's throat and involuntarily, she gripped Gavin's hand. In response, he rubbed his thumb over her skin, and something about the rough texture grounded her. Not enough to be able to speak to the sociopath without screaming, but enough to keep her quiet and let Gavin take over.

"Why does Victor think you're the weak link?" Gavin asked.

"Because Jeremy Wheaton made what I did sound *bad*," he answered. "I mean, I know by societal standards, it's not right. But you know, ancient civilizations did it all the time. It wasn't until modern times that such things were considered taboo, that they were considered wrong. It's all a social construct created to make people feel superior. Love, physical love, between an adult and a child, is normal."

"Can I kill him myself?" Six said, directing her question to Gavin.

Gavin considered the man sitting across from them before answering. "No, but only because I think Victor will do it for us. Because DePalma is right, Julian *is* a weak link. He thinks what he did was the right thing and will defend it. That puts everyone else in jeopardy. And if DePalma kills him, well, that's one less thing we have to worry about."

Gavin's reasoning might sound trite, but he was right. *If* DePalma took Julian out, Julian wouldn't be brought to justice, but he also wouldn't ever harm another child. Her years of working for AISE had inured her to the idea that the killing of another human was always wrong. And while she'd like to see Julian made an example of, she also didn't care one whit if he didn't live to see the sunset. But if she didn't have to be the one to do the job, then all the better considering she wasn't supposed to be operating on US soil. There was also the added bonus that if DePalma killed him, that might be one more charge they could get DePalma on. And unlike the civil case Jeremy had been preparing, murder would be a criminal suit.

"Where's DePalma now?" Six asked.

Julian's eyes jerked from the window to the foyer as if by asking, they might suddenly conjure him.

"I don't...know," Julian answered.

"You don't know, or you won't say?" Gavin asked.

Julian frowned. "He's out to kill me. I know it. If I knew where he was, I'd tell you, because then maybe he'd believe that everything Jeremy knew hasn't been kept a secret and then there'd be no point in killing me."

"He might kill you because you're a prat," Gavin said, surprising a huff of laughter out of Six.

Julian blinked rapidly at them again, and Six wondered if it was a nervous tic or a sign of something else, like an addiction of some sort. "Um, what are you going to do now? Are you even a Salvitto? Just who are you? Can you protect me?" Julian wasn't gaining a spine; his questions were more bewildered than aggressive.

"Would you be willing to testify against DePalma, the Fogartys, and most likely your wife?" Six countered. If he was, she could arrange for protection. The Feds wouldn't do it because he wouldn't qualify for the Witness Security Program, but *she* could arrange it.

Julian started breathing hard. A bead of sweat that had been hovering near his hairline dripped down his temple, then flew off as he rapidly shook his head. "I won't do that. I'd rather die or, I don't know, take my chances."

Six sighed. At least she'd tried. "Then it doesn't matter who I am," she said, rising from her seat. Gavin rose, too, keeping her hand in his. "What does matter is that you're right. You may not be the sharpest tool in the shed, but the days of Shanti Joy are limited, and DePalma probably *is* out to kill you. In fact, we happen to know he's in Keene right now." She paused and watched Julian. More beads of sweat appeared on his forehead, and he started rocking back and forth in his seat. He didn't look as if he was going to pass out again, though, so she continued. "The only thing you need to know about who I am, is that I am the person who will burn the whole operation—including the company your wife built—to the ground. And I will make you all pay for what you've done."

Julian's attention shot to Gavin, but Gavin just grinned down at the man. "And she's Italian," Gavin said. "When she's says she's going to burn it to the ground, there won't even be any ashes left." Julian swallowed, and Gavin's grin turned into a feral smile. "No need to get up, mate, we'll show ourselves out."

CHAPTER TWENTY

Six LED them out the door, then to her car. Rather than get into the driver's seat, she circled to the passenger side. "I want to check in with everyone and make a few calls," she said by way of explanation. With a nod, Gavin climbed in behind the steering wheel and adjusted the seat.

"I honestly don't give a shit if DePalma kills Julian, but as an officer of the court, are you bound to report this to someone?" he asked, starting the Tesla.

"It's a gray line," she replied as she started a text. "We have a pretty damn good guess about what might happen, but I have no *actual* knowledge of an impending crime or harm. Arguably, we don't even meet the burden of reasonable belief since we have no hard proof that DePalma was involved in Jeremy's death. Still, you're right, and that's why I want to get the name of the FBI agent, or team, that was already looking into the DePalma family. Once I have that, I'll send them an email."

Gavin chuckled as they made their way back down the winding driveway. "And by the time you get the name, send the email, the agent reads it, then investigates whether to respond, it will likely be too late."

Six flashed him a smile as she finished her text to Devil asking for her to identify the best FBI contact. "Bureaucracy can be such a bitch."

He started to laugh, but when the sound abruptly cut off, Six looked up. "Get down!" Gavin barked.

Ignoring him, she kept her eyes on the road and the black Escalade making its way toward them. "Is that DePalma?" she asked. The car was too far away to allow them to see inside. But even if they'd been closer, the windows were tinted dark enough that they wouldn't be able to see the driver.

"Wasn't Cyn going to send you coordinates for him?" Gavin asked. She didn't miss the way he scanned the road and the area around it. There were woods on both sides, but the driveway was wide enough for the two cars to pass. With the size of the Escalade, it would be tight, but they could make it. Glancing down at her phone and letting Gavin navigate the passing, she saw a text from Cyn that had come in while they'd been talking to Julian. She read the message, then looked up at the black SUV forty feet in front of them and its visible license plate.

"Yeah, that's him," she said.

"You need to get down," Gavin said.

"Why on earth would I do that?" she shot back, pulling a small but very powerful gun from her ankle holster. She wasn't anticipating trouble—she firmly believed DePalma was there to take care of Julian—but it never hurt to be prepared.

"Because he knows who you are. Remember, he had his goons follow you from Jeremy's apartment?" Gavin shot back. "Our best chance of getting away without engaging with him right now is for him to think I'm on my own. If we want to engage with him later, that's fine, we can decide to do that, but I'd rather do it on our terms and not his."

Six frowned. As much as she hated to admit it, Gavin had a point. Not that she wanted to begrudge him good ideas, she just didn't like the idea of hiding. Then again, if that meant that she could then set the rules for their next encounter, maybe that wasn't such a bad thing.

Sliding down into the space in front of her seat, she contorted her body in a way that would keep her from DePalma's line of sight but still allowed her to use her phone. As she ducked down, she handed Gavin the gun. "Just in case," she said. Without a word, he took the weapon and rested it on the top of his thigh, his large hand completely covering it.

Leaving Gavin to deal with DePalma, she shot off a few texts to her friends. She had a plan, but they'd all have to act fast. Once the messages were sent, she pulled up her email app and started composing a message to Heather.

It had only been four days since Jeremy's murder. Six hated having to ask Heather to focus on anything other than the funeral in two days, but she trusted that not only would Heather understand, but that she'd be grateful for the opportunity. With the courts closed over the weekend, they'd have two and a half days to get everything together to file the suit Jeremy had planned all along. They'd need every hour of those two and a half days to get it done, but with Six, Gavin, and Heather all working on it, she believed they could do it. And if they could get the suit filed on Monday, a spotlight like nothing Shanti Joy had ever experienced would shine on the corrupt company and its behavior. Six wondered if more women—and more stories of horror—would arise once everything was out in the open. But even if they didn't, going public with the information they had was the best way to protect everyone involved.

"You can get up now," Gavin said.

"Anything interesting?" she asked as she unfolded from her position.

"I'm pretty sure he recognized your car. The guys who tried to run you off the road probably gave him the description, and he looked closely but didn't stop. He did slow down enough to make sure I continued on my way, though. You okay?"

She nodded as she stretched a kink from her hip, then buckled her seat belt. "Head into town," she said. "We have a car to pick up."

"A car?" Gavin asked but did as she directed when they came to the end of the driveway.

"I figured he'd recognize this one, and you confirmed that. You also said we need to engage on our terms, and so that's what we're going to do. Cyn is tapping into the security feeds to get a bead on DePalma's movements around the property. She won't be able to see inside the house itself, of course, but when he leaves, she'll know. In the meantime, we're going to pick up a car that DePalma won't recognize."

"And the plan is?"

The Newcrosses didn't live far from town, and they were already coming up on the outskirts. "Turn here," she said, pointing to the road on her left. "The place is a mile down the way. And as to the plan, we're going to follow him. If possible, I'd like to put a tracker on his car and, if we can get close enough, a bug inside it."

Gavin slid her a look but to his credit, he didn't say anything. Yeah, she wasn't sure yet how they were going to do either of those things, but a woman had to have goals.

"There," she said, pointing to a Subaru dealer.

Again, he shot her a look. "We're going to *buy* a new car?" he clarified as he turned into the lot.

She tipped her head in acknowledgment of the absurdity. "Believe me, with the kind of money my friends and I have, this is a lot easier than renting. Besides, I'll donate it when we're done, or if Abyasa, Candra, or Shinta want to stay once this is all over, I'll give it to them."

Gavin made a noise that was something between a grunt and a laugh and pulled into a spot. "If that's the case, why a Subaru? Why not something more fun, like Devil's Cayenne?"

"We're going for generic here, Gavin," she said, popping her door open and sliding from her seat. "How many Cayennes do you see on the road versus Subarus?" She shut the door behind her and missed his reply. She'd barely started walking to the showroom when a man approached her.

"Ms. Salvitto?" he asked. Six smiled at her ever-efficient friends; he was already carrying a key and had some paperwork on a clipboard.

"Yes, that's me," she answered, and held out her hand. He shifted the key to his other hand and shook hers.

"David Holland," he said, his eyes flitting to Gavin, who'd also exited her Tesla and now stood, arms crossed, watching them. "I'll need to check your driver's license, and I have someone inside finishing up the paperwork, but it shouldn't take more than five minutes. In the meantime, let me show you to your new car."

"I'll stay here and get our things together," Gavin offered. Six nodded. She wasn't sure where he'd put the gun she'd given him earlier, but it wasn't the only weapon they'd need to retrieve and transfer to their new transport.

"There are a few things in the trunk," she said.

He nodded. "I know. Franklin mentioned it."

That comment gave her pause for about three seconds—she hadn't known Franklin knew about her secret compartment, though she should have. But then she pulled her license from her wallet and followed David Holland to a dark green WRX STI Limited. She paid no attention to the salesman as he spouted the features of the vehicle and instead, she turned her mind to their next steps. Despite her earlier words, she'd much prefer it if Julian lived to pay for his sins. If he didn't, she wouldn't mourn him, but if she had her way, she wanted to bring him—and everyone involved in the actions at the plantation—to their knees. She wanted to strip them of their arrogance and entitlement. She wanted to rip away their money and the insular bubble they'd built around themselves. She wanted the world to know that sometimes, the biggest monsters hid behind suits and luxury homes. Knowing that wolves sometimes dressed in sheep's clothing wasn't a new concept. And the men involved weren't the first, nor, unfortunately, would they be the last. But they were the ones Six could bring down.

"Do you have any questions?" David Holland asked, having finished his spiel that she'd heard none of.

Six shook her head and handed over her driver's license. David took it and wrote a few things down on the clipboard he carried. Then he pulled out a small tablet, a little larger than a phone, and took a picture of it. He was sliding the device back into his pocket when a phone dinged. Pulling *that* device from his other pocket, he read a message, then smiled.

"Everything okay?" Six asked.

"Of course, Ms. Salvitto. Thank you for doing business with us, and if you ever need another car, I hope you'll keep us in mind." And with that he handed her the key and opened the driver's door.

She murmured a platitude and a thank you, then slid onto the leather seat. Glancing at the unfamiliar dashboard and controls, she considered that it might have been good to listen to the salesman describe all the features and functionality. Finally, her eye caught on the start button and once she adjusted her seat, she brought the engine to life. David smiled at her, then shut the door and stepped away.

Taking a moment to assess the controls, she was pleased to find it a manual transmission. She loved her automatics, but there was nothing quite like a manual for harnessing speed and power. Shifting into first gear, she pulled the car out of the spot and headed back to where Gavin stood beside her Tesla, a duffel bag slung over his shoulder. She had no idea where the bag had come from, but since she used her car like a closet, its presence didn't surprise her.

"Hey, sexy, want a ride?" she teased after pulling up in front of him and rolling her window down.

He shook his head and smiled, then rounded the car and took a seat beside her, tossing the bag at his feet. "What about your car?" he asked.

"I'll have Javier come get it over the weekend."

"And who is Javier?" Gavin asked, buckling his seat belt.

"My cleaner. His mom cooks for me, too. She's Spanish but married an Italian and learned all the best Italian dishes. She's amazing, and her son is a cleaner extraordinaire. He's a little more like a house manager than just a cleaner, but he's the best."

"Right, fine," Gavin said. "So, what is the plan?" he asked again as she turned onto the road and tested the acceleration.

"Can you set this up?" she asked, handing him her phone and nodding to the small in-dash screen. He took the device and when he started connecting it to the Bluetooth, she continued. "As much as I think the world would be a better place without Julian Newcross, we need to protect him from DePalma. He might not testify against anyone, but I want Abyasa, Candra, and Shinta to have the opportunity to face him in court."

"You want to humiliate him," Gavin said, handing her phone back. He'd connected it to the system in less time than it took her to pull her shoes on.

"That too, yes," she admitted. "I think that's almost a worse punishment than the swift death DePalma likely has planned."

"So back to the house?" he asked.

She was about to nod when the phone rang, startlingly loud in the cab of the car. Nora's name appeared on the screen, and Gavin quickly adjusted the volume, then hit the Answer button.

"DePalma is getting ready to leave," she said without preamble. "He's outside, talking to the guard. Devil is trying to lip-read, but she can only see the guard. From what we can tell, DePalma must have asked about you, because the guard definitely said your name."

"Not a surprise," Gavin said. "Thankfully, we now have a brand new car to follow him with that he won't recognize."

"Did I sense a little bit of sarcasm there, Gavin?" Nora asked, her response lit with humor.

"You all bought a car in less time than it takes me to go to the grocery store and buy ice cream. I'm equal parts in awe and disappointed that I wasn't given this assignment years ago," he responded. Then, after casting a quick glance at Six, he added, "Then again, I don't think I would have been ready for this assignment if it'd come along any earlier."

Six shot him a quick look, then returned her eyes to the road. They didn't know which direction DePalma would take when he left the Newcrosses', so she needed to find a place with a view of the driveway to lie in wait.

"Any signs of Julian?" she asked, spotting a small road almost directly across from where DePalma would emerge. She hadn't noticed it on their way in as it was narrow and bordered by thick trees, but it would do.

"None," Nora answered as Six pulled onto the small road. "Should we ask Joe to send someone up to check on him?"

Six executed a six-point turn, inching between a ditch on one side of the road and trees on the other. "Yes. It's probably too late to save Julian, but we need to preserve any evidence we can."

"Will do," Nora confirmed. "DePalma is getting into his car now so should be down the drive in about five minutes. You good?"

Six glanced at Gavin, who nodded. "Yeah, we're good," she answered.

"We'll be tracking you, but let us know if you need anything," Nora said.

Six was about to thank her and end the call but stopped short when she realized there was more her friends could do. Knowing DePalma was minutes away, she quickly updated

Nora on her email to Heather and asked Nora to reach out to Jeremy's sister and fill her in on everything they'd discovered. She also requested they forward Heather all the files and invite her to the house to work on the complaint together if she felt up to making the trip to Cos Cob.

Nora assured her she'd take care of everything, and they'd just ended the call when DePalma's SUV appeared on the driveway. Tucked far enough back that they didn't have to worry about him seeing them unless he drove by and made an effort to look, Six and Gavin watched.

DePalma paused at the end of the drive and a minute passed, then another. Finally, he inched forward and turned left, away from them. Six waited thirty seconds, then pulled out onto the road.

"Anything you want me to do while you drive?" Gavin asked.

"What did you throw in that bag?" Six countered, realizing she should have given him some direction as to what to take from her car. Aside from the gun she'd handed him earlier, there were a number of things that could come in handy, including her trusty switchblade, a pair of nunchucks, a second gun with a silencer, and her small appliance kit that had everything from a tracking device to a bug to a small dose of poison. The second gun and the kit had been tucked into the hidden compartment.

"I grabbed everything, including the contents of the compartment," he responded.

Six wasn't quite sure *how* to respond to the reminder that he'd been told about the secret compartment and so she stayed silent. She wasn't so much bothered by Gavin knowing, but it pissed her off that the information had come from Franklin. It was another reminder of all the intel Gavin had been gifted with pertaining to her. And *that* didn't sit well with her. On the other hand, if he was truly going to be a partner, then she was glad he had the intelligence to remember the minor detail Franklin had imparted at some point.

"So, the plan?" he asked for the third time.

"We'll follow him and see where he goes. If we're lucky, he'll stop for gas or a piece of pie or something and we place the tracker and bug then."

"If not?"

"He has to stop at some point. We follow him until he does." Gavin didn't respond, and they drove in silence for thirty minutes as DePalma headed northeast toward Concord. As the miles ticked by, it wasn't hard to admit that this wasn't her greatest plan, but it was the best option they had given the circumstances. And she assumed Gavin agreed, or he would have said otherwise.

Forty minutes into the drive, a text came in from Nora saying Heather was on board. She planned to review all the files Nora had sent, then she'd come to Cos Cob Saturday morning so they could strategize. Six was grateful Heather hadn't hesitated, but she'd be lying if she said Heather's involvement didn't make her nervous—too many people had died already.

On a whim, she called Cyn and asked her to reach out to their friends Lucy James and Brian DeMarco. Brian's family was filled with men and women in all sorts of law enforcement agencies. On occasion, and for the right people, some of the retired ones provided personal security. Another ten minutes later, a text from Cyn came in assuring Six that the DeMarcos now had two people watching over Heather.

"Where do you think he's going?" Gavin asked as they passed through Concord, New Hampshire.

Six shook her head. "No idea. Why don't we see if he has any properties or ties to the area? The club can help."

Gavin pulled his phone out and sent a text. A few minutes later, the device dinged. "That was fast," he muttered, reading the message. "Well, fuck," he added after a beat.

"Not good?" she asked, perhaps unnecessarily.

"Depends on how you look at it," he answered. "Cyn thinks he's headed to the Stanley Rose quarry."

Six frowned. "An active quarry or an old one?"

"Old," he said on a sigh. "They stopped cutting there in the early sixties."

Six let out a rueful laugh. "Great, just what we need...a man who most likely just murdered Julian Newcross headed to an abandoned quarry."

CHAPTER TWENTY-ONE

GAVIN KEPT a discreet eye on Violetta. Not because he was worried about her, but because never in his life had he wanted a woman in the way, and with the intensity, that he wanted Violetta. They had things to do, a murderer to catch, and a massive court case to file. But watching her operate—both on her own and seamlessly with her friends—was about the sexiest thing he'd ever seen. Then again, watching Violetta walk into the office every day tended to do it for him, too.

He turned and looked out the window, not wanting her to catch him staring. Aside from it not being a good time to do any of the things his mind—and his body—were encouraging him to do, he still wasn't sure where he sat with her. Clearly, she was starting to trust him, and she was attracted to him, but that didn't necessarily mean she was ready to go in the same direction he wanted to go.

"And here we go," Violetta said, quietly. He shifted his attention to see DePalma turning onto the road that would lead him to the entrance of the quarry. "How did Cyn figure this out?"

"There's a gas station about a mile past the quarry on the way to Chichester. In the last two months, he's had four credit card charges there," he answered as she drove past the road where DePalma had turned.

"Other than the entrance DePalma will take, are there any other ways in?" She guided the car to a small pullout, then turned to him.

"Cyn didn't say, but let's call her. I don't know her well, but I suspect she and the others have been researching that very question."

Violetta nodded and hit a few buttons. A few seconds later, the car filled with the sound of the phone ringing and two rings in, Cyn answered. "He's at the quarry, isn't he?" she asked by way of answering.

"Presumably," Violetta answered. "We pulled over so as not to follow right behind him. Assuming he takes the main entrance, is there another way in?"

Cyn didn't hesitate, confirming what Gavin had suspected. "There are two other access roads. One isn't suitable, as it's on the other side of the quarry. The other isn't great either but is the better of the two. Looking at the quarry from the top and like a clock, DePalma will come in at six o'clock and the entrance we think you should take will bring you in at nine o'clock. The catch is, that entrance doesn't go all the way to the quarry, and you'll have to walk the rest of the way. It isn't far, maybe a mile, but it doesn't look like there are any discernable trails. I'm sending you the data now."

Gavin glanced down at Violetta's shoes. She wore tennis shoes, and he had a pair of boots on. They'd be fine.

Violetta's phone dinged, and she pulled a map up on the screen in the car. They both leaned forward to study it. The entrance Cyn had marked lay two miles past the main one. "Why build a road to nothing?" she asked as she sat back, then pulled out onto the road.

"I think the work camp was there in the twenties and thirties," Cyn answered. "The satellite images I have are good, but not great, and we think we can see a few remnants of small buildings."

"Anything else we should know?" Gavin asked. As they neared the turnoff to the old road, Violetta slowed the car. Chances were, it wouldn't be easy to spot, even with the satellite images guiding them.

"Not right now," Cyn answered. "Devil is looking into the history of the area and if she finds anything, like areas to stay away from, we'll let you know. You guys have what you need?"

Gavin assumed she meant weapons-wise and assured her they were all set. In addition to the various items he'd grabbed from Violetta's car, he also had his own gun.

"We'll get back in touch once we're done," Violetta said. Cyn demanded they be careful, Violetta assured her they would, then they ended the call.

"It should be…"

"There," Gavin said, pointing to a break in the woods. The weeds were nearly taller than their car, and once they drove through it would be obvious someone had taken the road. The good news was that the lush foliage appeared to be growing up through gravel, so at least they wouldn't have to worry about a potentially muddy road. Of course, Violetta's new car *did* have all-wheel drive, but it would be nice if they didn't need it.

"I feel like we should start hearing a banjo pretty soon," she said, turning onto the road and crushing several feet of greenery underneath them as they inched forward. After a minute of their snail's pace, the thick grass and weeds gave way and the road cleared. Not completely, but they could at least see the old tire tracks.

"Banjo? From *Deliverance*? Didn't that take place in the South somewhere?" he asked.

"Yes and yes," Violetta said, navigating around a large rock. Judging by the map, they had under a mile to go. "But remember, you're now in a state whose motto is 'Live Free or Die.' New Hampshirites are not people you want to mess with."

He hadn't known that. The motto had a rather ominous tone to it that was a bit at odds with the beauty surrounding them, but what did he know? He'd only been in the US for five months; he'd have to take Violetta's word for it.

They maneuvered their way to what was indeed an old work camp. Once they'd exited the car, they'd seen the remains of two wood cabins along with the old stone foundations for four more buildings. Without a word, Gavin pulled the bag of goodies out and set it on the hood of the car. The hike through a bug-infested forest wouldn't be fun, but at least with the distance between them and DePalma, they had the freedom to prepare without worrying about being seen or heard.

He handed Violetta the gun she'd given him earlier, and she slipped it back into her ankle holster. Next came the small appliance bag, which she shoved into the left pocket of her lightweight sweatshirt. And then the switchblade, which she tucked into the back pocket of her jeans. "Need anything else?" he asked. Like her, he also carried a knife, only his was in a sheath at his waist.

She eyed the gun with the silencer on it, the debate clear in her eyes. It would be a nice weapon to have, but taking it spoke more of an intent to kill than an intent to capture. With a sigh, she reached in and grabbed the gun, but then unfastened the silencer and tossed the accessory back into the bag. Slipping the gun into the right pocket of her sweatshirt, she then zipped it up, securing the weapon for their trek.

"Ready," she said. He nodded and tossed the bag into the trunk. The distinctive *beep beep* echoed through the empty forest when she locked the car.

Taking a quick read from the GPS on his phone, he pointed southwest, and when Violetta gestured for him to lead the way, he began an easy jog through the forest. Keeping an eye on the ground to avoid rocks and roots, they made good time. Ten minutes later, he slowed to a walk a hundred meters from where the map showed DePalma would likely be parked. With Violetta at his back, they silently moved as close to the clearing as they could without leaving the woods.

DePalma's SUV came into view first, but the man himself was nowhere to be seen. What Gavin *could* see, though, was the rear bumper of a second car—a truck, more specifically. He held up a hand, and they both stopped. Turning to Violetta, he pointed to the second vehicle. She studied the scene for a beat, then pointed to her pocket that held the small bag with the GPS tracker and the bug.

He shook his head. Attempting to slip those on and into DePalma's vehicle now, when they didn't know where he was, wasn't a good idea. She narrowed her eyes at him, letting him know exactly what she thought of his caution. It made him wonder if maybe her parents had yet another reason for agreeing to send her to St. Josue. She would *not* have been an easy teenager to raise.

She made to step forward, but then paused before he stopped her. Cocking her head to the side, she tapped her ear. Understanding her message, he, too, turned his head to listen.

"Is it all taken care of?" a man asked. Neither of them had ever heard DePalma's voice so had no idea if it was him speaking or someone else.

"Yes, but like I told you, there's no way of knowing if I got there in time. It didn't look like anyone had accessed his files, but I didn't have the time for a full forensic workup," another man said.

Gavin's gaze lifted to meet Violetta's. The first man must have been DePalma, and from the sound of it, the second was a hacker he'd hired to wipe Jeremy's electronic files. Only he was too late. Not only had the files been accessed, but Violetta had downloaded everything onto her own computer.

Leaning close, her lips brushing his ear, she spoke. "I have a cloaking program that hid my accessing of the files. If he was a good enough hacker and he looked hard enough, he'd see through it, but it sounds like it held."

He let out a long breath. It wasn't that Violetta was out of DePalma's crosshairs altogether, but he would certainly feel less urgency to come after her if he thought his hacker had been successful and that she didn't have any important information.

"All files?" DePalma asked.

"As you know, his laptop and phone were destroyed in the hit-and-run, so I couldn't get to the hard drives. I wiped his cloud account and phone records, though. His phone records were easier than they should have been, but the security on the cloud account was tight—I barely got out before they caught me. The service provider has a protocol that will require them to tell Wheaton's sister there was a security incident involving the firm's account. The company will have to do their own forensics first, though. And between that and the funeral, my guess is it will be a week or so before she's aware there was a problem."

Suddenly the two men appeared in front of the Escalade. DePalma was walking toward the edge of the quarry and a short, skinny young man with straight black hair and glasses followed. Gavin wanted to yell to the younger man not to get any closer, but before he had too much time to think about it, Violetta darted from his side. He reached for her, but his fingers barely grazed the fabric of her sweatshirt. Silently maneuvering through the forest toward the back corner of the SUV, she slipped away.

Adrenaline spiked through his system as he divided his attention between Violetta and the two men. He wanted to throttle her. He wanted to bark at her the way he barked orders at the men and women he led. Thankfully, he was well-trained at tamping down his reactions, and he managed to stay quiet.

He was also self-aware enough to know that his over-the-top response was of a more personal nature than a professional one. The truth was, if this had been his op, he would have done the exact same thing she'd done. That didn't make it any easier to watch her go, though.

Pausing at the edge of the woods closest to the back bumper, she looked at him, relying on him to signal to her when to go. A small part of him wanted to pretend he didn't know what she was doing, but he couldn't bring himself to be that petty. Besides, Violetta would move ahead without his input anyway. She'd been operating on her own for twenty years and didn't need his help to do what needed to be done. The fact that she was offering him the opportunity to step up and play a role was huge.

He glared at Violetta to express his disapproval, but she rolled her hand at him, silently telling him to get on with it. He turned his attention back to the two men, who were standing about fifteen feet in front of the SUV, catty-corner to where Violetta stood. If she stayed low, there was no way they'd see her, although if she tried to open the door to place the bug inside, the sound would get their attention.

Wiggling his fingers, he gave her the green light as he kept his eyes fixed on the men. DePalma was walking closer to the edge, but the other man had stopped moving, perhaps starting to sense something wasn't quite right.

In no time flat, Violetta had the tracker affixed to the inside of the back bumper and was inching her way to the back door. She'd even used her sweatshirt to wipe any prints she might have left on the dime-sized device.

She glanced up at him, and he shook his head. There was no way she could open the door without alerting DePalma. She narrowed her eyes but didn't move. His attention was so fixed on her and trying to figure out how to get her to come back into the woods that DePalma's sudden movements caught him by surprise.

In the blink of an eye, DePalma had the younger man in his arms. The hacker screamed and fought, thrashing his legs and scratching at DePalma's shirtsleeves. Easily twice the size of the man he held, DePalma remained unaffected by the blows raining down on him as he walked toward the quarry's edge.

Gavin's eyes darted to Violetta, who motioned for him to stay put. He didn't believe she'd stand by while DePalma murdered the man, but for the life of him, he couldn't figure out what she planned on doing. When her eyes widened in a silent command, he hesitated, then nodded. He'd stay put until she told him otherwise.

"I did everything you asked, you can't do this!" the young man pleaded.

DePalma continued his steady trek to the side of the quarry. Gavin's heart rate increased with every step DePalma took, then it shot through the roof when Violetta stood and stepped away from the SUV.

"You really shouldn't do that, DePalma," she said.

CHAPTER TWENTY-TWO

AT THE SOUND of Violetta's voice, DePalma spun around but didn't release the man.

"Good help is so hard to find these days, you really should put him down and let him go on his merry way," she said, her hand in the right pocket of her sweatshirt.

DePalma grinned. "You're the federal prosecutor, aren't you? Wheaton's little insider."

In a gesture DePalma couldn't see, she held her left hand out, palm down, staying Gavin. His muscles twitched with the need to intervene, but he clenched his hands into fists and forced himself to remain still.

"Oh shit, you're a federal prosecutor?" It wasn't the smartest thing the hacker could have done. Not only was it a repeat of what DePalma had said, but it reminded DePalma that he had something to take care of.

Gavin bit his cheeks to keep any noise from coming from his mouth. He knew exactly what was going to happen next, and judging by the way Violetta darted to the front of the SUV, she knew, too.

Sure enough, as if disposing of a bag of garbage, DePalma

turned his back on Violetta and hurled the hacker over the edge of the quarry. The young man's screams echoed off the granite walls, and Gavin's heart climbed into his throat. Then training and habits kicked in and his body quieted. Yes, Violetta was involved, but this was a mission, like any other. They needed to neutralize the threat. With that reminder, he took a deep breath, forced his muscles to relax, and waited for Violetta to give him a sign or an order.

"You were next on my list," DePalma said, walking toward her.

Violetta didn't move, but Gavin's eyes were trained on her, and he could see the muscles in her legs tensing under the denim of her jeans. "I assume you already ticked Julian Newcross off that list?" DePalma didn't confirm verbally but he did incline his head slightly. "Pity," Violetta said. "I was hoping to turn him against you."

"Julian was easy prey. Not much fun to be had in cleaning up after him. All it took was a single morphine pill to knock him out, then a carefully placed injection of Botox to the heart."

"I adore how you're confessing to me like I won't live to tell the tale," Violetta said. Gavin all but rolled his eyes. Seriously, she had a gun, couldn't she get on with things?

"Because you won't. You may be tall, but at the risk of sounding cliché, you're no match for me," DePalma said, advancing even closer toward her. Violetta took a step back and then to the side. Suddenly, Gavin knew what she was doing. By circling around DePalma until he had to face the quarry to keep his eye on her, she might be able to lure him into charging her. And forcing DePalma over the cliff, rather than shooting him, would be cleaner. It would also buy them time to continue the investigation. She—they—wouldn't feel quite as compelled to report his death if they weren't the ones to, literally, pull the trigger.

Clever woman.

"I didn't think you knew words like 'cliché,' DePalma," she taunted, taking a step closer to the quarry.

"Where are the women?" he asked, suddenly drawing to a stop as he put two and two together.

Violetta cocked her head. "Oh, you mean Abyasa, Candra, and Shinta? So kind of you to ask. They're doing great. Teaching cooking classes and taking self-defense."

Gavin could only make out the side of DePalma's face, but he bit back a laugh at the way the man furrowed his brow.

"What the fuck are you talking about?" DePalma said.

"What didn't you understand, you barbarous, tongueless foot-licker?"

The last part of her comment was spoken in Italian, and Gavin dropped his head and shook it. Violetta definitely had a unique way of going about things.

"What did you say?" DePalma asked.

"Nothing you would understand, fool," she shot back.

"This is getting tedious."

"Ooo, another big word. You *are* impressing me today, DePalma. A couple of murders, some big words thrown in, I'm curious what's next. Although let's be clear, I'm only *mildly* curious about what's next because mostly I don't give a shit. Oh, and too bad you're such a dumb fuck that you can't see there's no way to clean up the mess you created. But you know, go ahead and try to keep killing people. It will only give the prosecution more ammunition."

"So Julian wasn't lying? Wheaton had videos?"

For the life of him, Gavin couldn't figure out why DePalma was continuing to talk unless he hoped to get something out of Violetta. But to her point, DePalma was a big-ass dumb fucker. If he hadn't figured out by now that she was running circles around him, he had no hope. Not that he had much anyway, not with the two of them standing against him.

"Jeremy had a lot of things. I have them now, though."

From his vantage point in the woods, Gavin saw what DePalma's next move was. Before he could think, he burst from the woods as the man pulled a gun from the waistband of his pants.

"Gun!" he shouted. He didn't look to see how Violetta reacted but kept his entire attention on DePalma, who turned in surprise at his sudden presence. The surprise didn't last long but it was enough for Gavin to dive-tackle him as the gun fired. Dirt kicked up near his left foot where the bullet struck the ground, but he was already in motion. A split second later, he had his arms wrapped around DePalma's legs and the man was coming down.

A miscalculation had DePalma bouncing off his SUV and falling to the side, rather than straight back. Gavin tried to turn but ended up in the awkward position of having his side pressed against the vehicle. With his movements restricted, it wasn't easy keeping his grip on DePalma. He did, however, hear a sound that was music to his ears—the distinct thud of DePalma's gun hitting the ground. At least the man was no longer armed. Or at least he was no longer armed with a gun.

DePalma might have been surprised, but it didn't last long. He strained against the hold Gavin had on him and pulled a knee up as far as he could then kicked out. His steel-toed boots could have broken Gavin's nose or taken out an eye, but Gavin managed to tuck his head so that the blow landed on his shoulder. Unfortunately, the impact was jarring enough that his arms loosened.

DePalma scrambled away and Gavin followed, the two men leaping to their feet simultaneously. Like fighting dogs, they circled each other until, like Violetta, Gavin had his back to the quarry. With a quick glance, he judged he had twenty feet to play with before the edge of the cliff became both a danger and an opportunity.

Concern for Violetta flashed through his mind, but he didn't have the luxury of checking on her. Not yet. Especially not when DePalma made a move, rushing Gavin like a WWE fighter and trying to hook his arm around Gavin's neck. Gavin ducked, but not fast enough, and DePalma's elbow glanced off his cheek.

Ignoring the pain, Gavin spun and stepped between DePalma's feet, then twisted his body to bring the bigger man down. Violetta's plan had included the possibility of DePalma dying, but if he could manage it, Gavin wanted him alive. Much as Violetta had wanted Julian alive to bring him to justice, Gavin would much prefer to see a man like DePalma—a man who abused women and sold children—in prison. Of course, his death wasn't entirely off the table, but he always felt it important to have a plan A and plan B.

DePalma landed on his stomach but didn't waste any time and flipped around, catching Gavin's neck in a hold between his legs. Familiar with the move, Gavin employed his least favorite —but most efficient—way to escape the awkward position. He reached up and gave a sharp jab in the man's balls.

Instantly, DePalma's legs released and pulled up. Gavin leaped to his feet and eyed the man lying on the ground. It was a painful hit—Gavin knew from experience—but it wouldn't keep a man like DePalma down for long.

Taking advantage of the brief lull, Gavin scanned the area for Violetta. Unwilling to turn his back to DePalma, he swung his gaze to the left, where he'd last seen her. But she wasn't there. Panic lanced through him, but he forced himself to stay calm and swiveled his attention to his right. Only to find her standing fifteen feet away, arms crossed over her chest, watching.

"I figured I'd stay out of it," she said, then she winked at him. He might have been halfway in love with her before, but he was pretty sure he tumbled the rest of the way just then. "You might want to keep an eye on him, though," she said, nodding to DePalma, who was starting to rouse.

"Aye aye, Captain," he said, then turned his attention back to DePalma. "So what's it going to be, you dog-hearted foul infection?"

"Oh, good one, Cooper," Violetta said.

He fought a grin. The fight wasn't over yet, but he was feeling good about the odds. "Will you stay down and let us bring you in, or are you going to make yet another bad decision?"

DePalma held a hand out in a gesture that looked to be surrender, but Gavin wasn't taking any chances. He backed up a step, once again, putting his back to the quarry. The man rolled to his stomach, then came to his knees. He paused there, with his hands on his hips, and regarded both Gavin and Violetta. Then he turned his full attention to Gavin, obviously having dismissed Violetta.

"Who are you?" he asked.

Gavin grinned. "No one special. Are you going to be a good little boy and let us restrain you until the cops get here or are you going to give us a hard time? Either way, it's not going to end well for you so if I were you, I'd think about your options."

DePalma may be a big guy, but he fought as though he'd learned his moves watching TV and wrestling with his friends. He had no idea who he was dealing with, and Gavin didn't mind that advantage one bit. He hoped DePalma would make the right decision, but he was 99 percent certain he wouldn't.

And sure enough, he didn't.

DePalma sprang at him and in his hand, Gavin saw a knife. He didn't have time to consider where it might have come from before it was being thrust toward his chest in an upward swing. His instincts took over, and Gavin grabbed DePalma's wrist and twisted his body around, using the leverage to bring the knife down and away from his torso. Only DePalma was stronger than Gavin gave him credit for—or perhaps it was the adrenaline—and the knife didn't quite clear his body.

A scorching pain sliced across his thigh. Gavin sucked in a breath and did his best to ignore it as he attempted to disarm DePalma. His leg had other ideas, though, and it wobbled under the strain of the fight for dominance.

As he struggled to keep his hold on DePalma and shake the knife from the man's hand, Gavin caught sight of the edge of the quarry, only a few feet away. Having zero interest in getting any closer while still locked in combat, he bent at the waist, then snapped himself up, catching DePalma in the face with his head. DePalma released him with a grunt, and Gavin spun in time to see him raise the knife again.

Only this time, it wasn't Gavin who stopped him.

Stunned into stillness, he watched as Violetta entered the fray, her body low to the ground. With one sweeping kick of her left leg, DePalma was knocked off his feet. But before the man could hit the ground, her right foot punched out, hitting him in the chest and sending him flying backward.

In the split seconds that followed, Violetta remained poised and ready while Gavin stared at the empty spot where DePalma had been. Less than ten seconds later, the sickening thud of his body hitting the bottom of the quarry echoed up the granite walls.

Violetta turned to him, and his eyes locked on hers. Neither rushed to the other as the reality set in that together, they'd killed a man. Not that he thought either had any regrets, but still, this was a moment that they'd both remember. He'd come forward to help her when DePalma had pulled the gun, and she'd stepped in to save him when the cut in his leg had put him at risk. It might sound dramatic, but they'd saved each other's lives, and that shit wasn't to be taken lightly.

"Vi," he said, holding out a hand.

Her gaze held his for one more moment and then, in the next, she was kneeling in front of him.

"Oh my god, Gavin, I think you need stitches," she said, her

SIX

hands on his thigh. She was probably right. He hadn't looked at the cut, but he could feel the blood dripping down his leg and pooling around the edges of his boots. "Give me the knife," she said.

When he didn't immediately reply, she touched his waist. Unsure what she planned, he removed the blade and handed it to her. She whipped her sweatshirt off and promptly used the knife to cut the sleeve off, which she then bound around his leg.

"You are definitely going to need stiches. But in the meantime, can you walk out? I don't mean to be callous, but it would be best if neither of us left any DNA around here." She was looking up at him as she tightened the makeshift tourniquet. The ends of her hair lifted in a breeze, her cheeks were flushed with the rush of the fight, and her cognac eyes searched his.

A faint smile touched his lips. "You know, this isn't quite what I had in mind when I fantasized about having you on your knees in front of me."

CHAPTER TWENTY-THREE

GAVIN GLANCED at Violetta as she navigated them back to the highway that would take them to Cos Cob. She'd been muttering unflattering things about him in Italian ever since he'd refused to go to the doctor. As far as he was concerned, there was no point. Any ER would have to report a knife wound and between Devil and Nora, he figured he'd get better care when they got home anyway.

"You know I can understand you," he commented, after she'd said something particularly colorful about his stubbornness.

She glared at him as she switched lanes and darted around a truck hauling a horse trailer. She didn't take her eyes off him the entire time, and he held his breath until they were well past the other vehicle.

"I'm fine," he said.

She muttered something more, this time quiet enough that he missed most of it, although the phrase "cocky motherfucker" was pretty clear.

"Keep the pressure on it," she barked. As soon as they'd reached the car, she'd folded her sweatshirt and insisted he use it to cover his wound. Deciding it was best to do as she said, he pressed it against his thigh. Pain shot up through his hip and down to his ankle, but he did his best to cover his wince. His best wasn't good enough, though, and her head whipped around. She studied him before her eyes dropped to his thigh. He fought another wince, but this one wasn't from pain. She'd seen that he'd bled through her sweatshirt, and he wasn't looking forward to the consequences.

A beat later, she handed him her phone and told him to find and open an app called "detector." He wasn't too shameless to admit that he liked that she was worried about him, but that didn't mean he wanted to poke the bear. Again, he dutifully followed orders and opened the app with his free hand.

"What is it?" he asked.

"Radar detector," she answered, gunning the engine and once again moving into the left lane to pass a row of slower cars.

"Aren't those illegal?"

She shot him a look. Okay, that *was* a dumb question considering they'd basically just killed a man. Arguably, it was self-defense, but still.

He fell silent as she continued to pick up speed and pass several more cars. He held his commentary for several minutes as she weaved between lanes. There weren't that many cars on the road, but as she was now traveling close to a hundred miles an hour, what cars there were came and went fast.

"This isn't exactly a Ferrari," he pointed out, knowing damn well he was taking his life in his hands by making the comment. Still, maybe he could distract her enough so that she didn't feel the need to drive like she was on a racetrack. Again, it was nice that she felt the need to do that for him, and her driving was impeccable, but still...

"I fucking know that," she gritted out as she flew by a Porsche.

He turned in his seat, then tried to hide the involuntary

breath he sucked in at the pain the small movement caused. He stood by his reasons for not going to the ER, but damn DePalma had delivered a solid wound.

"You've trained in a Ferrari?" he asked.

Her eyes flickered to him, then refocused on the road. "Not only am I an AISE agent, but I'm a fucking Italian billionaire. I've been driving Ferraris since I was thirteen."

He had no problem imagining Violetta behind the wheel of the powerful car at such a young age. In fact, he would have paid money to see her tackle the famous training track. He didn't doubt for a minute that after a few laps, she owned it.

He fell back into silence again, but it didn't last long. A few minutes later, Violetta's phone rang. Bringing the call up on Bluetooth, he answered for her.

"Hello, Cyn," he said.

"You might want to tell Six to slow down. There's a speed trap about three miles up," she said. At a hundred miles an hour, three miles flew by fast, and on cue, Violetta's radar detector started beeping. She slowed to a sedate sixty-five.

"What did you do to piss her off?" Cyn asked. "She's grumbling in Italian."

"I got injured," he answered. Cyn already knew that; they all did. They'd called the club the minute they were back on the road and updated everyone.

"I see," Cyn said with a chuckle.

"There's nothing funny about this, Hyacinth," Violetta snapped, making Cyn laugh even harder.

"There is, Six. There really is," Cyn responded. Gavin thought Cyn might not be making the best choices with her comments, but he didn't want to get in the middle of it, so he remained silent.

"We're thirty minutes out," Violetta said. "Are Nora and Devil ready?"

Cyn sighed. "Yes. As we told you when we first spoke and

then again by text, Devil and Nora have their kits and will be ready to take care of Gavin's wound the second you arrive."

Without another word, Violetta ended the call. They'd passed the speed trap and its five patrol cars a few minutes back. When another five minutes passed with no sounds from the radar detector, she picked up her speed again.

"Why Hyacinth?" he felt safe in asking.

"Because that's her name," Violetta snapped as she shifted down into fourth gear to give her the power to pass a couple of more cars. "Lady Hyacinth Steele," she added before shifting back into fifth at a comfortable cruising speed of a hair under a hundred miles per hour.

"Lady?"

Violetta nodded. "Her father is the twelfth Marquess of Alderbrook."

Gavin frowned. Franklin hadn't mentioned that. Not that it mattered, but still, it seemed like kind of a big thing to leave out. He'd known she came from money—they all did—but he hadn't known Cyn was a member of the aristocracy.

"What about the others?" he asked.

Violetta's lips tipped into a small grin. "Nora is distantly related to the Jordanian royal family, but Devil and I are plain, plebian billionaires."

He chuckled. "Why does it not surprise me that Cyn prefers to fraternize with the common rabble?"

Violetta's grin turned into a smile. "You should meet her parents. They are what Americans would call a trip. Real estate and financial tycoons by day and hippies fresh off the commune by night. I kid you not."

Gavin had no idea what that might look like so took Violetta's word for it. "What about Devil and Nora and their families? And why doesn't Nora have a nickname?"

"Have you ever met a 'Nora' that wasn't badass?"

He didn't know a lot of Noras, but now that Violetta

mentioned it...he shook his head.

"Exactly. She didn't need a nickname. But as to her family, she's the only daughter and has three brothers. I'm sure Franklin gave you the file on her?"

He nodded. It didn't contain the interesting details about who she was as a person—her personality, her character—but it did include a summary of her family, one of the wealthiest importer/exporter families in the Middle East.

"And as for Devil," Violetta continued, "she has one brother. Her family and mine are not dissimilar in that both her parents are involved in running the family empire, but that's about where the similarities end. Her family is, well, we would call them cold. They look out for one another, but mostly out of duty. And emotions are weakness and to be avoided at all times. I'm glad she has me, Cyn, and Nora to help breathe a little humanity into her life."

He didn't know Devil—or any of them—well, but it wasn't hard to see what Violetta referred to. In the few hours he'd spent with Devil, she'd been cool, assessing, and not one to put her opinions or thoughts out for public consumption without careful consideration.

"I know she mostly engages in research rather than practicing medicine. Is she going to be able to handle this?" As he asked the question, he lifted the sweatshirt up to see if the wound was still bleeding. The flow had slowed significantly, especially since he'd been sitting in the car and not moving or stressing it, but it was still oozing. Violetta glared at him, and he considered—too late— that he shouldn't have mentioned his wound again.

"Nora will be the one to clean and examine it. I know she's a vet, but her bedside manner is a lot better than Devil's. We only rely on Devil when it's a last resort. So long as the knife didn't go through any tendons or damage anything other than skin and muscle, Nora should be able to handle it."

SIX

He glanced at his leg one more time before pressing the sweatshirt back down. He was 99 percent sure there wasn't any significant damage. It hurt like hell, especially after their mile-long trek through the woods, but if tendons or cartilage had been involved, they wouldn't even have made that mile.

"What's your favorite color?" he asked. According to the map, they were fifteen minutes from her house. Why not pass the time with idle chitchat? They might need to strategize about what they were going to do next in terms of helping Heather file the lawsuit, but his mind wasn't quite up to that at the moment.

She flashed him a look, then returned her attention to the road. "I like red, but it doesn't look great on me, not unless it's a deep red. If not that, then anything in the yellow palette."

"Yellow?" That wasn't a color people usually mentioned when talking about favorites.

"I like bright yellows for home accents, deep yellows for clothing, and sunny yellows for plants. It's a cheery color."

Now that he thought about it, most of the flowers in her front yard were yellow. Not all, but most.

"What about you?" she asked as she took the exit for Cos Cob.

"Blue. I know it's kind of a generic color, but like your opinion of yellow, I feel that way about blue. There's blue for every mood."

She nodded. "What about favorite food?"

"Anything I don't cook. You?"

She chuckled. "Anything Sylvia makes for me."

"Sylvia?"

"Javier's mom, the woman who cooks for me."

They played twenty questions for the remaining ten minutes of the ride. In that time, he learned she preferred Italian red wines to French (not a surprise), fiction over nonfiction,

211

summer over winter, and sunrise over sunset. Although that last one had pretty much been a tie.

When they pulled into her drive, Nora, Devil, Cyn, and Joe were all waiting for them. Violetta didn't bother pulling into her garage and instead came to a stop less than five feet from the steps leading up to her front porch. By the time he got his door open and one leg out, she was standing beside him, holding out a hand to help.

He looked at her, then to the four people watching them. Joe had his arms crossed and a grin tugging at his lips. Cyn's eyebrows were raised while Devil stood with her hands on her hips. Nora was the only one who appeared to be focusing on him and his injury rather than watching Violetta fuss over him.

"Come," Nora said, directing them inside. "We've set everything up in the downstairs bathroom."

Gavin followed Nora with Violetta at his side. He didn't really need the help, but having her arm wrapped around his waist wasn't an experience he was going to deny himself.

"We need to get you out of your jeans," Nora said, then held up a hand to stop the commentary forming on his lips. "No jokes, not right now. Six is on edge enough, and we all need to do as she says if we don't want to have to sleep with one eye open tonight."

"I'm not on edge," Violetta snapped. Wisely, he and Nora remained silent as he unbuttoned and unzipped his jeans. He didn't bother to smother the hiss of breath that escaped his lungs when the denim slid over the cut. And despite his belief that the injury wasn't too serious, he was grateful for the chair Nora had set up as he sank onto it. Kneeling before him, Violetta removed his boots, then tugged his jeans the rest of the way off, leaving him in his boxer briefs and shirt.

Violetta stood back as Nora inspected the wound. Blood had dried in streaks down his leg and was smeared all over his thigh. Gently, Nora examined the cut, no doubt to gauge its depth, then spoke. "I need to clean it up before I can tell how deep it is or if it needs stitches."

Not that he hadn't expected that, but he wasn't looking forward to it. "I'm all yours, Doctor," he said, leaning back in the chair and letting the fatigue that came with an adrenaline crash wash over him.

Together, Nora and Violetta went to work. Violetta concentrated on cleaning the blood off his leg while Nora focused on the wound itself. He kept his eyes closed throughout the process. It helped him keep his thoughts away from the pain. But it also helped keep his attention away from the fact that Violetta was, once again, kneeling before him.

Despite her gentle touch, pain lanced through his body as Nora poked and prodded the cut. "Internal stitches and then skin glue," she finally pronounced.

"Not that I'm not a tough son of a bitch, but I'd love you forever if you have some numbing shots you can give me?" he asked with a grin.

Nora chuckled. "You've been stitched without it, I take it?"

He felt Violetta's eyes on him as he nodded. "More times than I care to admit."

Violetta once again muttered something in Italian. He couldn't make it out, but whatever it was, it made Nora smile.

"Lucky for you," Nora said, "I have everything we need."

Twenty minutes later, Nora placed the last dab of skin glue on his thigh, sealing the wound off and bringing the two sides of his skin together. "You doing okay?" she asked, sitting back and snapping off the gloves she'd put on.

"Yep, never better," he replied, his head resting on the back of the chair and his eyes closed again.

"Here, take these," Violetta said. He popped his eyelids open to find her standing over him with two pills in one hand and a glass of water in the other.

"What are they?" he asked. He had zero interest in taking

anything that would put him to sleep.

"Just ibuprofen," she said. "Prescription strength, but nothing stronger than that."

Gratefully, he took the pills from her and washed them down. "Any chance someone can grab my sweatpants from my bag?" he asked.

"They're already here," Violetta said, handing them over.

Gingerly, he rose and managed to get his sweatpants on without too much pain—the glue on his skin pulled and felt awkward, but it held.

"Devil has prescribed you some antibiotics since we have no idea where the knife has been," Nora said as she washed her hands. "Joe and Cyn ran out to get them before you arrived. They also swung by your apartment and packed some additional clothes, since we all presumed you'd be staying here this weekend." He raised his eyebrows at that. Nora smiled. "There isn't a lock in the world that Cyn can't pick," she said, answering his unasked question.

Gavin made a note to himself about Cyn's skill, then looked to Violetta to see how she'd react to her friends' presumption. He honestly hadn't planned to stay, but he certainly wasn't going to look a gift horse in the mouth. They had a lot of work to do before they filed the suit on Monday, and not having to drive back and forth to his apartment would save some time. But it was Violetta's house, and he didn't know how she'd feel about having him in her space for the next several days.

To his surprise, she said nothing, just turned and walked out of the bathroom. Nora shrugged at her friend's uncharacteristic silence and followed her out. Alone in the room, Gavin gave himself a good once-over in the mirror. He was a little pale, probably from the loss of blood and the pain, but all in all, he didn't think he looked any the worse for wear. Leaving the bathroom, he walked to the living room, where he found Joe holding out a glass of whiskey.

"I thought you might need this," he said.

Gratefully, Gavin took the drink, then glanced around the empty room. Joe nodded to the office, and Gavin turned around to see Devil, Nora, and Violetta all looking over Cyn's shoulder as she typed something.

"What's that about?" he asked, taking a sip of the excellent whiskey.

"Cyn is emailing Franklin about what's going on. She thinks we're going to need the FBI's help when it comes time to bring these men down."

Gavin frowned. "We could have gotten DePalma on several murder charges and likely conspiracy ones as well. But now that he's dead, I think the only avenue we still have open is the alien tort claim, and that's a civil suit against the company. Why would the FBI want to be involved?"

"Money laundering," Joe answered. "It's one of the many things we discovered while you were out. It appears that Shanti Joy regularly takes funds from a few shady characters and launders it through the company."

"There are also criminal fraud and misrepresentation charges that can be brought," Violetta said as she and the others joined them. "Devil's family does a lot of business in the region, and she has an uncle in the security sector. He's digging into it and thinks he can get enough evidence to argue that Shanti Joy, as a company, has perpetrated fraud and engaged in misrepresentation that meets the federal standard. You should be sitting down," she added with a pointed look at his leg.

He fought a smile and did as she asked. "It sounds like you found out quite a bit while Violetta and I were gallivanting around. Is it time to trade notes?"

"It's time for dinner," Cyn said as a Violetta's phone beeped, letting them know someone was coming up the drive. "We ordered pizza from Tucci's. Alexander said he'd have Tommy bring it over."

Tucci's was the one Italian restaurant in Cos Cob. Gavin had never been there, but given that he hadn't eaten anything since breakfast, he was pretty sure he could eat an entire pizza—an American-sized one at that—on his own. "Who's Tommy?" he asked as Violetta and Nora went to answer the door.

"Alexander is the owner. Tommy is his son. They don't usually deliver, but they'll come to Six's house anytime," Cyn answered. "Alexander's family in Italy were having some problems with the local organized crime organization, and Six helped them out. If Alexander weren't a happily married man, I'm pretty sure he would have asked Six to marry him years ago."

"He's nearly seventy years old," Devil said, coming into the room from the kitchen where she'd grabbed plates and napkins for everyone. "If anyone would marry Six, it would be Tommy. He's a little younger than we are, but not by much," she added, flashing Gavin a sly grin.

"Nobody is marrying anybody," Violetta said, entering the room with three pizza boxes. Nora followed carrying another two along with a paper bag. Violetta set her pizzas down on the dining table, then opened each box and flipped the lids underneath. Nora handed the two boxes she'd been carrying to her, then pulled a large container of salad from the bag she carried.

The scent of tomato sauce, cheese, and warm bread filled the room, and Gavin's stomach rumbled. The whiskey had been appreciated, but the pizza would be devoured. A few minutes later, they were all seated around Violetta's large table, with food piled high on all their plates.

They ate the first slices in silence, but by the time Gavin was on his second, he wanted to hear everything Joe and the club had discovered while they'd been gone. Starting with Newcross. "Did you send someone up to check on Julian?" he asked before taking a bite of pizza.

Joe nodded and finished chewing before answering. "He's

definitely dead, although that's not a surprise given DePalma told you he'd killed him. Jennifer Farrington, the Keene chief of police, called me after they discovered the body to ask me a few follow up questions. By then, I knew about the morphine and Botox, but I didn't want to get into it, so held my tongue. They will be doing an autopsy, though."

Gavin nodded. "Did she want to know how you knew to send her team up there?"

Joe bobbed his head. "A bit. I told her that his name came up in a case I was investigating. Once we figure out the story we want to spin about DePalma, I'll fill her in, but I didn't want say anything until we had a plan."

"What should we do about DePalma?" Nora asked, then she took a sip of her wine. Gavin hadn't seen anyone bringing wine to the table but noticed there were now two bottles sitting between Cyn and Devil.

"Ideally, I'd like to postpone the discovery of his body if we can," Violetta said. Gavin might not know what she had planned, but her comment didn't surprise him.

"If some random hiker finds him between now and Monday, we obviously can't stop that, but barring that, if we can keep it quiet, I'd like to," she continued.

"Why?" Devil asked at the same time Cyn asked, "What are you thinking?"

Violetta took a sip of her wine before she answered. "The charges that *could* be brought against the company, in particular those related to the Alien Tort Claims Act, are hard to prove." She paused and looked around the table. Her gaze lingered on him before taking in everyone else. "I want to try to get a confession."

"From whom?" Nora asked.

"How?" Devil jumped in.

"Fabulous idea, what do you need me to do?" Cyn offered. Joe shot his woman a repressive look, then turned to Violetta.

"What does that have to do with keeping DePalma's death, and the murder of that young man he tossed into the quarry, a secret?" Joe asked.

"Confusion," Gavin said. Violetta's gaze found his, and she nodded.

"Explain," Devil said.

"Julia Newcross will soon learn, if she hasn't already, that her husband is dead," Gavin said. "The first thing she'll probably do is try to reach DePalma. But when she can't reach him—the man behind much of the nefarious activity of the company—she will likely start to panic."

"And when she continues to not be able to reach him, she'll probably go to Austin and Kaden Fogarty—more likely Kaden since he's her COO—and they'll talk," Devil finished. Both he and Violetta nodded.

"You want to record that conversation," Cyn said.

Violetta nodded.

"Recording from a bug or other listening device won't be allowed in court," Gavin pointed out. "And if you're thinking of trying to be a part of those conversations, Massachusetts is a two-party consent state," Gavin said. "There's no way anyone from Shanti Joy will give their consent to record a conversation." He paused, then looked at Cyn. She smiled at him, and it all clicked. "And that's why you want to bring the FBI in, isn't it?" he asked.

Again, Violetta nodded. "If we have a warrant, we can intercept calls and record conversations without consent."

"So now we just have to get them to talk," he said, sitting back in his chair and swiping Violetta's glass of wine. "I assume you have some ideas about that, too?" He took a sip and savored both the smooth flavor and his anticipation of her answer.

She smiled at him, a calculating and somewhat diabolical smile. Taking her wineglass back, she took her own sip, then answered. "As a matter of fact, I do."

CHAPTER TWENTY-FOUR

SIX WAS PUTTING the last of the dishes in the dishwasher when Gavin walked back into the kitchen after seeing Cyn and Joe off. She didn't have to look at him to know he was in pain; she could hear it in the gait of his step as he trod across her hardwood floors.

"Need a hand with anything?" he asked, leaning against the doorframe.

She shook her head. "Why don't you head up to bed? You can have the same room you took last night, or I should say early this morning." She kept her focus on drying the dish in her hand. It was well past eleven, and they'd only had a few hours of sleep in the last thirty-six hours. If she was lucky, he'd take her suggestion and make his way upstairs to the bed.

"Violetta," he said.

Luck was apparently not going to be on her side. She held in a sigh. "Heather is coming at eight tomorrow morning Not only do we have to start drafting the complaint, but we also need to work with the FBI contact Franklin set us up with to coordinate the intel we have on both the DePalma family and Shanti Joy. It's been a long few days, Gavin, and you need to rest your leg.

219

Go, I'll finish up here." They'd done so much research in the past few hours that she felt confident that the civil complaint Heather would file would be complete. But there was still much more that they needed to do for the federal criminal charges.

Gavin let out a long breath. "I know you've only known about me, about my real role, for a few days, but you've known me for several months. You might not have had the advantage of having my files in the same way that I had yours, but you *know* me, Violetta. I want to know why you're pushing me away."

Six glanced over her shoulder as she slid a cutting board back into its place. "I'm hardly pushing you away, Gavin. You're staying the night," she replied, being intentionally obtuse.

"Why are you evading this conversation?" He straightened and walked toward her, stopping less than a foot away. The countertop pressed against her lower back as she leaned away from Gavin.

"We've talked through everything we can talk through tonight," she said, knowing full well that she was a coward, and that Gavin wouldn't let her get away with it.

"You trust me, you respect me, and you're attracted to me—"

"That last one isn't all that special, Gavin. I suspect a great many men and women are attracted to you," she said with a smile, trying to lighten the mood. Gavin didn't bite, and his brown eyes seemed to darken as he studied her. His hands came to rest on her hips, but other than that, he didn't move.

"What do you want from me, Gavin?" she asked.

He tipped his head. "I haven't heard you ask a dumb question yet, Violetta. Don't start now."

She opened her mouth to snap back, then shut it. He was right, it was a dumb question. She knew exactly what Gavin wanted from her. Not just tonight, but in the long term. He hadn't ever said a word, and god knows she hadn't—wouldn't— either. And yet, she knew.

"It's not a good idea, Gavin," she said, her voice barely more than a whisper.

"Because we work together?"

"That's part of it." That was the whole of it, but she couldn't bring herself to say it because then she'd have to explain.

Leaning forward, he brushed his nose below her ear, and his lips grazed her skin as he asked, "And what's the other part?"

It would be easy, so very easy, to give in to him, to what he—what they—wanted. Unwittingly, she tipped her head to the side to give him better access, and his fingers tightened on her hips. His lips trailed a line of butterfly kisses from below her ear to the edge of her collarbone.

"Talk to me, Violetta."

"I don't want to," she managed to say, drawing a huff of a laugh from him that caressed her skin. He kissed his way back up her neck, then along her jawline until finally, his lips brushed hers in a touch that was more innocent than even her first kiss.

"I can feel your pulse under my lips, Violetta. I can feel your quickened breaths against my chest. Even without seeing how you responded to me getting hurt today, I know you want me as much as I want you. Give me a reason—a real reason—this shouldn't happen."

She had one. A good one. Or at least she *thought* it was a good one. It was getting harder and harder to remember that as the moments dragged on and Gavin didn't release her.

"Violetta," he said one more time. The first time he'd said her name, it had sounded like an entreaty. This time, his tone held a hint of a warning.

She leaned back to look at him and met his gaze. They were inches apart, and his pupils had dilated so much his eyes were almost black. Without warning, he slid one hand up, fisted it in her hair, and brought his mouth to hers in a kiss that was anything but innocent. She didn't need Gavin to call her a liar;

her own body betrayed her, and in an instant, she was kissing him back.

A grunt, or groan, or some noise of satisfaction escaped from him when her hands gripped his waist. She didn't have the wherewithal to identify it, she just knew that she liked it. She liked it more than she'd ever admit.

Using his grip on her hair, he tilted her head to the side and began dragging his lips down her neck. He nipped her earlobe as he pressed against her, trapping her between his hard—very hard—body and the counter. For a moment, she didn't care. She didn't care that they worked together. She didn't care that she'd made a promise to herself not to get involved with someone until she was well out of her career with AISE. She didn't care that she'd been hurt before.

"Talk to me, Violetta," he whispered.

Those four words were like a bucket of cold water, and she pushed him away. To his credit, he said nothing, just stepped back. She didn't want to talk. But she also didn't want to continue down the path they'd been traveling seconds ago. No, scratch that, continuing down that path was something her body very much wanted. But she knew Gavin well enough by now to know that if she wasn't all in—body and mind—he wouldn't accept that. And he shouldn't. He wasn't looking for a one-night stand or to let off some steam. He *cared* about her, of that, she had no doubt. And because of that, he deserved someone who cared for him.

She shook her head and tried to move around him, but he stayed her with a hand to her arm. They both knew that if she wanted to walk away, she would and he wouldn't stop her, but the mixture of concern and heat in his gaze held her in place.

A beat passed and then another. Neither moved as he gave her space to consider her response. He might not be pushing her, but he wasn't going to make it easy either.

"I've been here before," she finally managed to say.

His eyebrows dropped in confusion. "What do you mean?"

"I... Can we go outside?" she asked, suddenly wanting to feel the cool ocean air on her skin. He studied her, then nodded and stepped back again, gesturing her to go ahead of him. She grabbed a blanket from the back of a chair as she passed and as soon as they stepped out, she wrapped it around her shoulders. Gavin remained in just his shirt.

She took a seat on the swinging bench, and he sat in a chair beside her. Gently, she pushed herself into a slow, rhythmic sway.

"About eight years ago, I was on an op," she started. "He was another AISE agent. We were both undercover at the time, and I was playing his weekend girlfriend. I flew back and forth between Italy and the US regularly for over a year so that I could keep my job here and play the role AISE needed me to play.

"After several months, the relationship stopped being fake and started to feel more real. Well, as real as those things can get when you're both undercover. I think we both relied on each other to be the other's anchor—we were the only two people who knew that we weren't really the horrible people we were portraying, and we, well, it brought us pretty close."

She rocked in silence for a few more minutes, remembering that year—the good, the bad, and the very, very ugly.

"He didn't make it, did he?" Gavin asked, his voice quiet in the night.

She shook her head. "No, he didn't. At the end, his cover was blown by a double agent from another country who knew him. We were on a yacht in the Mediterranean, and we managed to escape, but he'd been shot. And stabbed. I was in the bathroom during the first attack and staying in that room, in the dark, hearing what they were doing to him, was one of the worst moments of my life.

"But he'd begged me to stay in there." Her voice cracked, and she cleared her throat before continuing. "He knew they were coming, and they believed me to be up in the lounge with the owner's girlfriend. If they found me, they'd kill me, too, he said. If I lived, at least I could try to get his body back to Italy. Back to his family. He was right, of course, but that didn't mean it was what I wanted."

Her mind drifted back to that night as she continued to talk. "There were four of them and we had no weapons—we'd been searched before we'd boarded so had nothing. Both of us were good at hand-to-hand combat, but there was no way we could go two against four. Not when the four were armed and had no intention of doing anything other than fire their weapons. If they'd been untrained thugs, maybe. But these weren't thugs."

They hadn't been thugs at all. In fact, they'd been trained by the military of her—their—own country. They'd been as brutal and as efficient as any Special Forces soldier she'd ever encountered. Only they'd had none of the honor or loyalty that was so common among that elite branch of the military.

"They shot him in the stomach. They wanted him to bleed out slowly. Painfully. When they left, we managed to make our way out of the stateroom. I was about to drop the Zodiac boat into the water from the back of the yacht when one of the guards discovered us.

"He came after me first since it was my hand on the lever that was lowering the boat, but Giorgio stepped in front of him. To this day, I don't know where he found the strength, but somehow he did. In the process of deflecting the blow from the guard's knife, Giorgio was stabbed in the shoulder. He managed to break the man's neck, though, and the two of us scrambled into the boat. I had to let minutes, so many precious minutes, tick by before we were far enough away from the yacht that I dared start the engine and make our way to shore."

Again, she paused, reflecting on that night. From the moment they'd realized his cover had been blown, she'd known

—they'd both known—that Giorgio wasn't going to make it. He'd lasted an hour in the small boat, clutching her hand the entire time, before he breathed his last breath.

"By the time we made it to Sicily, the closest island, he'd been dead for four hours," she said.

"Do you blame yourself?" Gavin asked.

And that was the crux of it. Some days she did. Some days she hated that she'd stayed in that bathroom. She hated that she hadn't come out to fight even though it wasn't a fight they ever could have won. But in the quiet moments, she knew that she'd done the right thing. That Giorgio had made his choices, and she'd made hers. He hadn't wanted her to die with him, and she wouldn't have been able to save him if she'd come bursting out of that bathroom. But at least she'd been able to get his body home to his family and provide a detailed report to AISE.

She shook her head.

"I'm glad," he said softly.

"But that doesn't mean it didn't hurt, Gavin," she said. "That night, more than any other, messed me up. I took a few months off and went to Greece to lick my wounds. I know Giorgio and I did the best we could in the circumstances we were in, but that doesn't mean it didn't hurt to lose him. That it didn't hurt like hell to hold his hand as he died. To promise him I'd tell his family that he loved them. He might not have been the love of my life, but he was a good man and a damn good agent."

"Do you see him when you look at me?"

She turned her head and looked at him. No, she didn't see Giorgio. She saw a man she could care about in ways she hadn't cared for Giorgio. She saw a man she could honestly share her life—all of it—with. But she didn't ever want to be in the same position as she'd been in with Giorgio again.

She shook her head, but held his gaze. "I don't," she said. "But after that night, I made a promise to myself that I wouldn't ever get into a serious relationship while I was still with AISE. I know life holds no promises for anyone, but I'm not prepared to go through that again. I don't want to experience that kind of pain, that kind of hurt, again."

"And you think you will if we let this thing between us develop into something?"

The moon was dark that night, and she could barely make out his features in the ambient light coming from inside the house. From what she could see, though, his face held no judgment, just concern, and maybe curiosity.

"I don't know, Gavin. But why would I invite that chance, that pain, into my life again?"

He studied her for another long moment, then rose from his seat. Her eyes tracked him as he took the few steps that brought him to her. Slowly he leaned down and kissed her forehead.

"You don't invite pain into your life, sweetheart. You find something that's worth pushing through your fear for." He drew back and searched her face as her eyes stayed locked on his. He leaned back in again and brushed one more kiss across her forehead, then he straightened. "Good night, Violetta."

And she watched as he walked away.

Several hours later, and despite her fatigue, Six tossed and turned as Gavin's words echoed in her head. She and Giorgio might not have been soul mates, but there was something about sharing that mission together—having the same goals and being in lockstep on how to achieve them—that had brought them together in a unique way. And they'd grown close. Very close.

But while the pain she'd felt after Giorgio's death wasn't something to be dismissed, there was another reason she'd never considered having a serious relationship. If she couldn't share *all* of her life with someone, was that a relationship she—or he—would want? And since she'd set herself against being with another agent, someone who she might be able to share all aspects of her life with, she'd just tossed the entire idea of a relationship out the window.

Her mind started to drift down the rabbit hole of what-ifs when she thought of Gavin. What if they did have a relationship? What would it be like to live and work with someone with whom she could share everything? What would it be like to be with someone who would *expect* her to share everything? What if something happened to him while they were working together? Giorgio's death had been hard; Gavin's would be devastating.

As soon as that thought—that reality—settled in her mind, the bitter taste of cowardice washed through her body. The truth was, anything could happen to either of them at any time. The truth was, they both had dangerous jobs, and they both knew better than to take anything in life—like love and time— for granted. The truth was, she'd be devastated if anything happened to him. That last little nugget, more than anything, told her all she needed to know about how she felt. And the only viable reason she was shying away from him—from them —was fear.

In his room down the hall, Gavin got up to use the bathroom, and she tracked the subtle squeaking of the old floorboards as he crossed his room. She wasn't sure how she felt about knowing he was awake, too, but she did know that he wouldn't be knocking on her door. No, he'd wait for her to come to him. He deserved to know that she had chosen him over fear, and he had enough respect for himself to not settle for anything less.

With a sigh, she turned onto her side and gazed out the window. A spring storm was brewing off the coast, and the stars were barely visible behind the drifting, thickening clouds. She'd left the window cracked open, and the rhythmic sound of waves crashing gently on the rocky beach at the edge of her property provided a quiet soundtrack.

Staring out at the ocean, her mind started to drift away from the question of Gavin, and how she felt about him, to the vastness of the water that stretched as far as the eye could see. Mentally, she traced the waters from those that lapped her shore, across the Atlantic to Europe, through the Mediterranean and Suez Canal and into the Red Sea. From there her mind traveled through the Indian Ocean and into the Pacific Ocean, then through the Panama Canal and finally through the Caribbean and back up into the Atlantic. A single journey that could take her everywhere in the world. A thing so vast that it made her life feel insignificant. Not in the things she'd done or accomplished, but in her place in the world. She was a tiny speck on the planet and an even smaller one in the span of time.

Rather than depress her, the reminder the ocean had given her grounded her. Her time on this planet *wasn't* very long, nor was any time promised to her. A sense of strength surged through her, warming her body and settling the anxious energy she'd carried since her conversation with Gavin. She didn't have an epiphany about what to do with, or about, Gavin, but she no longer had blinders on that kept her from seeing her own motivations or feelings. Thinking of her own inconsequence had opened a door for her to see the truth. She had no answers, but at least now, she felt she could ask—and maybe answer—the right questions.

CHAPTER TWENTY-FIVE

ON SUNDAY MORNING, Gavin and Joe stood on Violetta's back porch sipping coffee. As promised, Heather Wheaton had come over on Saturday, and they'd all—Violetta, the club, Heather, Gavin, and even Joe—worked furiously on the complaint Heather would file on Monday. Now all but Heather, who'd left early in the morning to prepare for her brother's funeral, had finished brunch and he and Joe had moved outside while the club updated Franklin on their plan for Monday.

"I heard from the ME this morning. The autopsy on Julian Newcross is scheduled for this afternoon," Joe said.

"I assume Julia is being kept updated?" Gavin asked. Given the mood of the group yesterday, it had been appropriate that a storm raged on most of the day. But now the sky was a bright blue, the ocean waters calm, and the smell of damp earth rose from the ground as it warmed in the sun.

Joe nodded. "She arrived back in Boston yesterday and is staying at their home in the city."

Gavin took a sip of his coffee and stared out at the ocean, letting his mind wander. Was Julia upset over her husband's death? Had she ever loved him? Or had she known what DePalma had planned?

"When we were working yesterday, did anyone come across any background as to why she married Julian in the first place?" Gavin asked. According to Julian, Julia had been having an affair with DePalma pretty much her entire life.

"They met at a farmers' market. She was getting Shanti Joy up and running, and he owned the land that hosted the market," Joe responded. The details of how and why the Newcrosses had met and married weren't relevant to the complaint, so Gavin hadn't bothered to ask before.

"She's a user and a liar. He must have had something more going for him than just being a landowner," Gavin said.

"He did. His parents owned a chain of high-end organic grocery stores. The perfect place to launch an organic, ethical cosmetics line. And much easier to marry into it than try to pitch to it," Joe answered.

"They still around?"

Joe shook his head. "Both died while hiking in the Andes a few years back. He inherited the chain and sold it about a year later." He paused and looked out at the ocean as well. "You know, I never thought about marriage or a lifelong commitment until very recently. It wasn't something I felt ready to take on while I was in the Navy." Joe had put in his twenty years before retiring and moving into work as a police officer, then as a detective, and now chief of police. "I can't imagine marrying someone for such mercenary reasons."

Gavin glanced over at the man and realized that his reasons for not choosing to get into a committed relationship while in the Navy were not dissimilar from Violetta's. Yes, Violetta had experienced a loss that brought her to that conclusion, but it was the same conclusion.

"Violetta feels that way, too," Gavin said. Joe's gaze came around, and he raised a brow. "She's reluctant to start anything that might involve a commitment while still working for AISE."

Joe gave a small smile. "Yeah, Cyn was like that, too. Despite their jobs, I think those women," he said with a small jerk of his head in their direction, "don't like to lie. Not to people they care about—I think that's one of the reasons they all live so far from their families, too. I don't know Six's specific reasons, but Cyn had never been in a committed relationship because there were —are—huge parts of her life that she can't share, and that didn't seem fair to her. I don't know if that's what's holding Six back, or if it's something else, but at least that's something you and I have going for us."

That might be part of what was holding Violetta back, but given what she'd told him last night, it wasn't the only reason. "What do we have going for us?" Gavin asked.

Joe smiled. "They may not be able to tell us what they are doing on specific operations, but they don't have to lie to us about being on them. They don't have to make up reasons for suddenly having to jet out of the country or for all the extra security they have on their technology. Generally speaking, they don't have to lie to us about anything. Like I said, we may not ever know the details of what they do, but we know they do it. And given that we're both military, we know the cost some of those ops can take. We're good people for them to talk to— again, not about the specifics, but about how their jobs affect them."

Joe's observation shed new light on the situation with Violetta. After seeing the very real pain reflected in her eyes when she'd told him about Giorgio, Gavin had considered the possibility that nothing they felt for each other would ever be stronger than her desire to avoid a similar situation. He'd been viewing his active agent status as something getting *between* himself and Violetta.

But Joe's comment made him realize that there was a benefit, a very real one, to it, too. He could be there for her in a way very few other people could. And though she was his only active op at the moment, that didn't mean he didn't have his own demons from the past. Demons she'd understand. Demons she'd not shy away from.

"What do you think about the plan for tomorrow?" Gavin asked, changing the subject. He'd been thinking about Violetta more than he ought to given the situation, and he'd come to accept that there was nothing he could do but wait. He'd made a promise to himself that the next move would have to be hers. He understood her reticence and he understood her fear, but Violetta wasn't a woman who could or would be cajoled out of her chosen course. She had to decide her own path, make her own decisions. And if she did choose him, then that act in and of itself would tell him everything he needed to know about where he stood with her.

In the meantime, they had work to do.

Joe shot him a half grin. "It's a little crazy, but not nearly as crazy as what we did in January, so I count that as a win."

Gavin chuckled. He'd heard what had happened five months earlier when the five of them had traced and taken out a small but violent group of young white supremacists. Bringing Julia Newcross and the Fogarty brothers to heel *did* seem rather tame in comparison.

"You think it will go as planned?" Gavin asked, pretty sure he knew the answer Joe would give. His training—both their train-ings—didn't allow them to assume anything would go as planned. Ever.

"Probably not," he answered. "Something will go wrong. But the good news is everyone here is more than capable of handling whatever Julia Newcross and the Fogartys throw at them."

"And then some," Gavin added.

Joe nodded. "The leaders of Shanti Joy might be grade-A

assholes who deserve to rot in prison, but there's no way they can outsmart or catch that lot off guard," he said, once again nodding to the women inside who were all now walking toward them.

Gavin turned as Violetta led the group out onto the porch. All four wore purple dresses, which had, apparently, been Jeremy's favorite color. Violetta and Devil had paired theirs with four-inch heels, Nora with flats, and Cyn with matching purple boots that just covered her ankles.

Tomorrow, everything would be put into play. By the end of the day, everyone involved in, or who had turned a blind eye to, the activities of Shanti Joy would know their mistake. Several of them would likely be behind bars if all went according to plan.

But now, today, this afternoon, it was time to honor the man who had started it all.

Three hours after the end of the funeral, Six was sitting in Nora's living room waiting for her friend to bring coffee for everyone. As she waited, she stared out the big picture window that looked out onto Nora's property. The iconic red barn was catching the evening light, and a deer was drinking from the far side of her pond. Out on the lawn, between the house and the barn, Abyasa, Candra, and Shinta were sitting on a blanket with a litter of two-month-old foster puppies. Michaela, Cyn's personal trainer, was watching over them, just as she and Dan had done when they'd brought the women to Jeremy's funeral.

Six hadn't wanted them to come. With DePalma dead, she was pretty sure no one was looking for them, but because she couldn't be certain, she'd wanted to be cautious. She'd been overruled by Gavin, though, who felt it was important for the women to have an opportunity to say goodbye to the man who had tried to help them and had died for his efforts. In the end, they'd reached a compromise. The three had attended the memorial, but they'd done so from the balcony at the back of the church and out of sight of the other mourners.

The women were smiling and laughing at the antics of the five black-and-tan puppies who seemed to want to climb them like jungle gyms. Every few minutes one or the other would pick a puppy up and cuddle it, rubbing her face along its soft fur. Six was well acquainted with the healing power of puppies, but even so, she was grateful that Nora had also found a counselor for the women who spoke their languages. Abyasa, Candra, and Shinta were strong. And they were drawing even more strength from being part of the efforts to bring Shanti Joy down. But no one who'd experienced what they'd experienced should have to process it all on their own. And Nora had at least made it possible for the women to talk to a professional should they choose to. Of course, playing with the puppies seemed to be having a healing effect, too.

"We're all set," Cyn said, drawing Six's attention as she rejoined everyone in the living room after taking a call out on the screened-in back porch.

"Franklin came through?" Gavin asked.

Sitting beside Six on the sofa, flipping through a magazine, Devil let out a sardonic laugh. "Franklin doesn't ever *not* come through when it comes to us."

Gavin flickered a glance at Joe, and the two men shared a look that Six didn't understand, but then returned his attention to Cyn. "Shall we go over the plan one more time?"

Devil groaned, but everyone ignored her. Six could almost sympathize with her friend. When working alone in the field, none of them had anyone to answer to and certainly didn't need to coordinate plans. Well, that wasn't entirely true. They often needed to coordinate intel with other agents or with headquarters. And occasionally, they needed to coordinate the timing of specific actions. But generally, they worked alone. What was planned for Monday morning was entirely different, though, and Gavin had a point. In fact, as former military, he and Joe had far more experience than Six and her friends in orchestrating the kind of operation they intended to implement.

"Heather just called," Nora said, walking into the room carrying a tray of desserts and a pot of coffee. Gavin got up to take it from her, then set it down on the large square coffee table. Nora turned back around to get the mugs from the kitchen.

"What did she say?" Six called out. The distinctive clacking of dishes filtered into the room as Nora took mugs down from the open shelving.

"She put the finishing touches on the complaint and will have it uploaded and ready for filing as soon as we give her the green light," Nora answered. She returned to the room with a second tray that held six ceramic mugs made by a local potter.

Cyn leaned forward from where she'd taken a seat on the floor with Joe behind her in a chair and poured a cup of coffee. Handing the first cup to Joe, she then poured another before leaning back against his legs. His free hand came up and rested on her neck.

Six's attention lingered on her friend, and the partner she'd chosen to share her life with, until a steaming mug came into her line of sight. She switched her gaze to Gavin and his dark brown eyes, slightly creased at the edges from years of smiles and experiences she knew nothing about. As she took the mug, she realized that Cyn had been—was—much braver than she. Yes, Cyn and Joe struggled every now and then with their relationship. But those struggles, those little tiffs and fights, had more to do with figuring out how to be with someone when they'd both never had a long-term relationship before. Unlike her, Cyn had never once balked at the general idea of letting Joe into her life.

"It's not a latte or a flat white, but it smells good, and I think we'll need it," Gavin said, pulling her out of her thoughts.

"Thank you," she said, wrapping her hands around the mug. He waited until Nora and Devil had their drinks, then poured himself one before taking his seat beside her. Devil sat on her other side while Nora had curled up in another chair.

"So, the plan again?" Gavin prompted. At least this time, Devil didn't groan. Although that was probably only because she had just taken a sip of her drink.

Six was about to run through it when her phone rang. Glancing at the number, she frowned, then held it up for her friends to see, eliciting the same reaction from them.

"What?" Gavin asked.

"It's fine. Probably good," Six said in response to the wary tone in his question. Then, hitting the Answer button, she put the device on speaker. "Aren't you on maternity leave yet?" she asked.

"Don't fucking talk to me about these kids," Beni Ricci, now Beni Matthews, snapped back. "And I'm not going on maternity leave until they make me," she added. Six held back a laugh, but Cyn snorted.

"Fuck you, Cyn," Beni said. "You wait. And even if you decide not to have kids, I'm going to thrust mine on you for the fun of it."

"Babe," Calvin Matthews's voice came through. Beni and her now-husband, Vice President Calvin Matthews, had met Cyn and Nora on an op the year before when Beni was on a special FBI task force. The op had brought the couple back together and they'd married a few months ago—when she'd already been pregnant with the twins she carried. Now the two bundles of joy were expected within six weeks. Six didn't want the twins to come too early, but for Beni's—and Cal's sake—maybe they'd make an early appearance.

Beni sighed, and the creak of what sounded like a bed followed. "Sorry," she said. "You cannot believe how uncomfortable it is to carry two babies in this awful Washington, DC, humidity. It makes me cranky. And you better keep your mouth shut, Calvin Matthews. You knocked me up so think very carefully about what you say next."

He chuckled. "Want me to rub your feet?"

Beni let out a contented sigh. "Would you?"

Gavin shot Six a look as the sounds of rustling came across the line, then when Beni next spoke, she sounded almost relaxed.

"I hear we got authorization for a wiretap," Beni said, though it was more like a question.

"We did," Nora answered.

"Oh, hey, Nora," Cal called, making Nora smile.

"Hey, Cal," she replied. "Glad you both are doing well. I heard the wedding was gorgeous."

The two had announced a June wedding in Chicago, where they'd both grown up. That event had been changed to a reception, though, after the couple had eloped in March on Tildas Island, where Beni had been working when the two reunited.

"The honeymoon was better, but yeah, it was a good time," he answered, and even through the phone there was no missing his happiness.

"Can we get back to the matter at hand, please?" Beni asked. She hadn't wanted any sort of wedding and had tried to convince Cal that just the two of them should elope. Cal had been adamant that they weren't getting married without family and close friends in attendance. In the end, they'd compromised with the small event on Tildas. Although it sounded as if Beni wasn't quite over losing that battle.

"How did you hear about it?" Nora asked. "Seriously, I thought you were on leave from the FBI?"

Traditionally, husbands and wives of the president and vice president weren't employed. Not only was working a potential conflict of interest, but it also created a security risk. And in

Beni's case doubly, or triply, so, since she worked for the FBI, which had its own risks, and was now pregnant with the vice president's children.

"I am," Beni grumbled. "Officially. Unofficially, I'm still advising. Once these crotch goblins are out, I'll quit and go work unofficially for Cal's sister."

"Nita," Cal said, calling her by the nickname only he used. Her full name was Benita, and everyone but Cal called her Beni.

"Not now, Cal," Beni retorted, heading off what sounded like a long-standing argument. "How did you manage that? The authorization?"

"You're unofficially advising, but they didn't tell you?" Devil asked.

"I only found out because Franklin called me. Said he didn't want me to hear it through the grapevine. Of course, with Franklin, I'm sure there was another motive. But since I'm unable to move any faster than a beached whale, need to pee every ten minutes, and all my work is done by phone or computer, I'm not sure how he thinks I can help."

"Franklin called you?" Six asked, then not bothering to wait for an answer, she continued. "Do you know who is involved from the FBI?"

"I do. It will be a small team from the Boston office, headed by Chad Warwick. What on earth did you find that enabled you to get the authorization?"

Federal wiretap authorizations were notoriously difficult to obtain. The question was a legit one. Six took a few minutes to fill her in on what Jeremy had discovered and what his original plan had been. "Like Jeremy, we originally thought we'd only have a shot at the company through a civil suit," Six continued. "But while DePalma was out murdering Julian Newcross and the hacker he hired to wipe Jeremy's electronic records, Cyn, Joe, Devil, and Nora found that that was just the tip of the iceberg."

"I'm all ears, Six." All the rancor was gone from Beni's voice, and her tone was now deadly serious.

"In addition to the obvious fraud and misrepresentation claims against the company, there's also significant evidence of money laundering. None of that would have likely gotten us the authorization, so here's the good stuff. It turns out that DePalma, and likely others in the company, were bribing and extorting public officials as well as engaging in espionage and weapons sales," Six finished. Yes, her friends had found a wealth of information about DePalma and the activities of Shanti Joy and its board of directors. They didn't think the entire board was knowledgeable about or engaged in the activities. It would have been too risky given there were sixteen of them. But in addition to Julia Newcross and the Fogartys, there was evidence that at least four others had participated in the criminal activities.

Everyone involved needed to be brought to justice for every wrong they'd committed. But if she were honest with herself, Six was more focused on bringing them down so that they couldn't continue to do to others what they'd done to Abyasa, Candra, and Shinta. In her cynical mind, there would always be someone willing to sell out their country—if not DePalma and the others, then someone else. But governments had the resources to go after those people. Workers like the three women currently playing with puppies on Nora's lawn had no one. The federal crimes had allowed them to get the wiretap authorization, and she'd not shirk her duty in attempting to lure Julia and the Fogartys into talking about those activities. But she wasn't about to let the crimes they'd committed in Indonesia— crimes that couldn't be punished criminally in the US—go unaddressed.

"Hhmm, sounds like a good time," Beni said. "I won't ask which public officials were involved since I'm sure that's sealed, at least until charges are filed, but what's your plan?" It didn't escape Six's notice that Beni hadn't asked about the murders of Julian Newcross and the hacker. Franklin must have suggested she not pursue that line of inquiry. They hadn't yet reported the death of the hacker or DePalma. That call would happen later that night because they wanted Julia Newcross caught off guard when she learned her lover was dead. The timing of the call had been yet another "discussion" between her and Gavin. He'd wanted to call it in Saturday night, arguing that holding off would bring suspicion on them. She'd wanted to wait, knowing that they needed the element of surprise when dealing with Newcross and the Fogartys.

She won the argument and when pressed by him on how she'd explain the delay, her friends had stepped up with the solution. Devil had already identified the young hacker as Michael Yang, a local university student with a large ego backed by mediocre talent. She'd easily, and surreptitiously, inserted a backdated missing persons report into the law enforcement database.

From there, Six, Nora, and Cyn had created a simple cover. Later that evening, Heather would call the local sheriff and let him know that during her investigation for the civil case, she'd come across information about a meeting at the quarry between DePalma and the hacker. She'd pass on the location and time and suggest that the hacker might be in danger. If the sheriff followed procedure, which they had no reason to believe he wouldn't, he would run both names through the database. Once he found Yang's missing persons report, he'd be obligated to check out the quarry. Their story also had the added benefit of being able to explain why Gavin and Six had visited Julian. They were friends of Heather's just doing her a favor by looking in on someone implicated in the civil suit.

"The plan?" Six repeated Beni's question, then smiled. "It's not one you are going like, but I hope Chad Warwick has a sense of humor."

CHAPTER TWENTY-SIX

"IT DOES NOT NEED to be so complicated, Violetta," Gavin insisted. For the fourth time. The bloody woman just wouldn't listen.

She rolled her eyes at him, though how he knew that, he didn't know since her back was to him as they entered her house. They'd stayed at Nora's for several hours going over Violetta's ridiculous plan, and each time he'd pointed out the potential flaws. There were so many variables, and variables meant opportunity for error. As far as he was concerned, the chances of tomorrow going all fubar were higher than a kite. Higher than the International Space Station.

The only good piece of news was that at least she hadn't balked when he'd made the solo decision to come back to her house rather than return to his apartment.

"Only an English man would say that," she shot back as she reengaged the alarm after he'd shut the door.

"What the hell does that mean?" he snapped.

She slid him a look, then turned and started up the stairs.

"Violetta."

She looked at him over her shoulder but kept walking. "Are we having our first fight?"

"Don't be flippant." He might be irritated—okay, *worried*—about what would happen tomorrow, but that didn't stop a little tendril of awareness from uncurling inside him at her words. If she referred to this as their first fight, that meant she thought they'd be having more of them. Which meant she anticipated his sticking around.

She entered her bedroom and he followed. His gaze swept over the muted walls, wide-plank floors, and colorful area rug. A huge abstract painting hung over her king-size bed, and she had a large picture window that, had it not been dark, he could have seen the ocean through.

"It will be *fine*, Gavin," she said, walking into what he presumed was a closet. He sat down on the end of her bed and waited for her to come out. When she did, she was wearing the same tank top, sans bra, and boxers she'd had on when he'd stopped by the house for the first time earlier that week. All that skin distracted him and even though he was very aware of what his mind—and body—were doing, he let it happen.

"You wear that to sleep," he said.

She nodded and walked by him, entering a different room which, since it wasn't her closet, he assumed was her bathroom. A few seconds later, he heard water running. Unable to stop himself, he started picturing all sort of things, most of which revolved around the two of them in the shower.

The muscles in his stomach contracted, and his shoulders tensed. He'd been watching her, learning her, *falling for her*, for months. He wanted nothing more than to walk into that bathroom and take her—the wall or shower would do fine. She'd have to make the decision about what would happen between them, though. He'd made a promise to himself, and he wasn't one to go back on that. Even if he was currently hating himself for it.

Holding a hand out, he curled it into a fist, then uncurled it, his fingers itching to touch her. Then, placing his palms on his thighs, he took several deep breaths, willing his body to stand down. He was almost there when she walked back into the room. She paused in the doorway, and their eyes met. Any relaxation he might have achieved flew out the window.

The fact that she was as aware of him as he was of her—as evidenced through the thin material of her tank top—didn't help. And yet he didn't move. This was *a moment*. This was a moment when she might make a decision; this was a moment when she might decide being with him was more important than clinging to her instinct to protect herself. Again, he—they —should be talking about what would happen tomorrow, but he found himself holding his breath, waiting for her to make a move. To walk to him or turn away from him.

Agonizing seconds ticked by, but when she finally made her decision, there was nothing tentative about it. In less than four strides, she was standing between his legs, his knees on either side of her thighs. She brought her hands to his face, then ran her fingers through his hair and tipped his head up to look at her. His hands curled around her legs above her knees as his gaze met hers.

"Do you really think the plan is bad, or are you just worried about me?" she asked.

"There are a lot of moving parts," he answered, holding her gaze.

"That doesn't answer my question."

He let out a deep breath. In truth, there were a lot of moving pieces and yes, that meant the margin for error was high, but that wasn't what she was asking. Even if the margin for error was high, what was the level of risk if there was a slip? That's what she wanted him to think about. There were errors that cost people their lives and there were errors that, though not planned, had no bearing on the outcome of an op. Given that they were planning to waltz into the Shanti Joy headquarters in the middle of the day, it wasn't likely that they'd encounter the kind of error that could cost someone their life—cost Violetta her life. Contrary to what the movies would have a person believe, the chances were low that someone, even Shanti Joy security, would be carrying a weapon at work. They were even lower when it came to possibility of it being used to kill.

"It's the best way, Gavin," she said, massaging his scalp with her fingers. "I know it's complicated, but we need to catch them off guard and we need to let them think they have the upper hand. I know these people—not these ones specifically, but ones like them. Ones that think that money is the god of all things and that it gives them power. They think they are untouchable, and we need to let them *keep* thinking that until we have what we need."

He closed his eyes and savored the feel of her hands in his hair and her skin under his fingers. "It's not that I'm not used to covert ops, but usually, mine involve weapons and sneaking up on people. By the time they send me in, body count really isn't an issue so long as I get the target. This is different though, and I know it." He opened his eyes and looked at her. "What we're doing tomorrow is exactly the kind of the thing MI5 would do, it's just not…well, it's not *my* go-to. So to answer your question, I trust you when you say this is the best plan, but that doesn't mean I'm not worried."

She held his gaze for the space of several heartbeats, then she leaned down and kissed him. His hands tightened their hold on her thighs as she angled her head to deepen their connection. When she pulled back, there was no mistaking the look—part desire, part need, part curiosity—in her expression. It was clear she'd made her choice.

"Are you sure, Violetta? I'm not asking you to make any declarations about our future, but if we do this, it is a commitment to let this thing between us happen. It is *not* a one-night event. It is *not* two people burning off steam before an op. It *means* something."

Slowly, she nodded, then leaned in for another kiss. He adjusted his legs, moving them between her thighs, then pulled her down to straddle him. She yanked back and tried to pop up, but he held her steady.

"Your leg, Gavin!"

He slipped his hands under the hem of her shirt to her waist and tugged her closer to him, her chest pressed against his. "It's fine, you're not sitting on it."

"Gavin, maybe we should wait."

He lifted one hand and tangled it in her hair, tilting her head to give him access to her neck. He'd been waiting *months* to run his lips, his teeth, over the sensitive skin there. If she thought even for a second that he was going to be willing to wait, she had another think coming.

When he didn't respond to her suggestion, she spoke again. "Gavin." But this time, it was spoken on a sigh. And despite the hint of admonition in her voice, her fingers tightened on his scalp, and she tipped her head even further to the side.

Flattening the palm of his hand across her lower back, he pulled her tight against him. Smiling to himself, he took her lips again in a searing kiss as she started rocking her body against his. She mumbled something in Italian, something about it being too long. But after all these months of waiting and wanting, his mind was too focused on the feel of her to translate it clearly. Although when she pressed into him, her core riding against the ridge of his jeans and her breath coming in shorter and shorter bursts, he had a pretty good idea of what she'd meant to convey.

Because it had been a long time for him, too. And like her, the feel of her body pressed against his had him a hair's breadth away from cascading over the edge. Knowing what she needed and wanting to give it to her before he embarrassed himself, he slid his hand down her lower back, under the waistband of her boxers.

"Gavin," she managed to say, tearing her mouth from his and letting her head fall back as she continued to rock against him. When he slid two fingers inside her, the moan she released just about finished him.

"Ah, *cazzo*," she said through her heavy breaths as she ground into him. *Ah, fuck* was right; he felt the same. But so caught up in watching her, in seeing her head thrown back, her long hair falling over her shoulders, her eyes closed as she focused solely on the feelings building inside her, he was no longer worried about an early ending to their encounter. He was physically aching to be inside her, but more than wanting that, he needed to watch. He needed to feel her body flutter, then hear the sound of her voice when her orgasm washed over her. After that, it was fair game for how long he'd last, but for now, there was nothing, truly *nothing*, he wanted more than to see her in ecstasy.

With one hand still wrapped in her hair, he tugged back hard enough to let her know that while she may be straddling him, he was in control—in control of her body, in control of her pleasure. He hadn't been sure how she'd respond. A woman like Violetta might object to being controlled—as minor as his actions were—in bed, but the little hitch in her breath and the first flutter against his fingers told him all he needed to know.

Taking even more control, he gripped her hair, pulling her body down as he pushed deeper inside her. Then, holding her tight, he only allowed her to rock against him in short, staccato bursts.

Her nails dug into his scalp as he increased his pace. Sweat dampened her skin, and he was tempted to lean forward and taste her, but he didn't want to take his eyes off her face. Her lids fluttered, then her body did, too, and she was riding that thin edge, enjoying the anticipation as much as she would enjoy what was to follow.

The need to control, to dominate, if only in this one realm and if only for now, took over, and he refused to let her decide when she'd let herself fall over that edge. Curling his fingers into her and using his other hand to keep her pressed against him so tightly that she couldn't move, he rocked his hips against her.

She froze, but he kept rocking, as he teased and seduced her to completion. And then she was there. There was no gentle buildup, no more small spasms, no breathy moans. Her body clamped down on his fingers, and her back bowed in his arms. Her mouth opened, and she gasped his name along with a series of enthusiastic moans and a few words of encouragement that he didn't need, but appreciated. Stilling his hand, he continued bucking against her as her orgasm peaked, then slowly subsided.

When there was nothing more than the sound of her breathing evening out, he withdrew his hand and rested it on her hip. With his other hand still tangled in her hair, he studied her. Her face was flushed, her full lips were slightly parted, and her eyes remained closed. She was the most stunning woman he'd ever known. She was beautiful, there was no doubt of that, but as cliché as it sounded, even in his own mind, it was far more than her physical looks that drew him to her.

At the thought of sinking into her, of seeing her face when their bodies joined, he swelled even more in the confines of his jeans. With a small flutter of her lids, her eyes opened, and she met his gaze. Slowly, a small smile played on her lips. He didn't think she meant it to be seductive, but there was very little she could do at that moment that *wouldn't* be.

"I think it's your turn now," she said.

He smiled back, then shook his head. "Now I think it's *our* turn."

CHAPTER TWENTY-SEVEN

SIX AND HEATHER came to a stop at the reception desk of Shanti Joy headquarters. "Heather Wheaton and Violetta Salvitto to see Julia Newcross, please," she said to the receptionist—a young man whose name tag identified him as Scott. She glanced out the window behind her as Scott looked them up in the system. It was a beautiful day, and the midmorning sun streamed through the two-story windows of the lobby. Beside her, Heather stood with her briefcase, looking more determined than a person should less than twenty-four hours after burying the last of her family.

Scott was taking his time, but Six had faith Julia was expecting them. Earlier that morning, Heather had called Julia's private phone and told the CEO that she had information about Shanti Joy's activities in Indonesia. Not surprising, Julia had played dumb. Heather had ignored her denials, though, and simply said that if she was interested in hearing more prior to the filing of the civil suit, then Heather would be at the headquarters at eleven to talk. Intentionally, she'd ended the call prior to receiving an answer. Theoretically, it was possible Julia would refuse to see them, but Six doubted the woman would pass up the opportunity. There was too much at stake for her company, for her life, for Julia to take the risk of not learning about the pending suit ahead of time.

"There you are," the young man said, eagerly clicking the mouse to his computer. "Your appointment is in five minutes and Holly, Ms. Newcross's assistant, will be down in a few minutes to show you up."

Six nodded to Scott, then she and Heather moved to the side. On cue, and on schedule, Cyn, Nora, and Devil all pushed through a side door and made their way to a second door that would lead them to the freight elevator. Dressed as cleaning staff, they caught no one's eye, except Scott's, who frowned.

From where she stood, Six watched as he rose from his seat, his eyes trained on the three "janitors."

"Excuse me," Scott called. When none of the crew answered, he excused himself and rounded his desk, approaching her three friends. Six glanced up and noted all the cameras in the area that were surely catching everything.

"Excuse me," Scott said again. Nora was the only one who looked in his direction although neither she, nor the others, stopped their progress.

"What?" she snapped in a very un-Nora-like way.

"It's the middle of the morning. You're not supposed to be in the lobby during work hours," Scott said, tapping his watch. "What are you doing here?"

Six had to give him credit, he was doing his job. But the fact that he had to continue to walk alongside them as the group more or less ignored him definitely didn't lend any authority to his comments.

Nora shrugged. "We're just going where we're told."

"Well, who told you to come this way? You should be using the back hallways," Scott replied.

Again, Nora lifted a shoulder. They were nearing the door, and Cyn moved ahead to open it. "Don't know. Some woman, big, tall, too. We don't usually service this building, but the company sent us today since I guess you had some people out."

Scott sighed, but then appeared to relax a little when Cyn opened the door using a key card. No doubt he assumed they'd been cleared by the cleaning company, because why else would they have a pass card? It also helped that they were clearly leaving the precious lobby area. Apparently, it was not to be soiled with the presence of the cleaning staff during work hours.

Scott stood, his back to Six and Heather, and watched as the three disappeared through the door and into the labyrinth of back hallways—the schematics of which they'd gotten their hands on the day before.

When it was clear they were gone for good, Scott returned to his seat and flashed Six and Heather a look. "Sorry about that. The cleaning staff is supposed to stay in the back halls."

Heather cast Six a look, then offered the young man a sympathetic smile. "Good help is hard to find these days," she said.

Scott all but beamed at her. "Don't I know it. I've been here five years and wouldn't want to be anywhere else, but some people don't feel the same." As he spoke, his eyes drifted to the door that the group had gone through. Six considered pointing out that the cleaning service for the building didn't work for Shanti Joy but held her tongue when Holly Kline stepped out of the elevator.

Six had always thought the name "Holly" was a pleasant one, conjuring up cheery images of smiles and Christmas. Neither "cherry" nor "smiles" applied to the woman who walked toward them, though. They'd all seen her photo in their research, but the photo, a professional headshot, did not prepare Six for the person before them.

She wore a business suit straight out of the eighties, with a knee-length skirt and blazer, complete with shoulder pads. A string of pearls hung from her neck and her nylon-clad legs ended in a pair of eminently sensible pumps. Her hair was pulled back into a tight bun that stretched her face into an awkward tableau. And the expression she wore—thin, pinched lips, and narrowed eyes—gave her the look of an irate school-teacher trying to hold her shit together.

Heather shot Six another look, this time one that included a raised brow and the hint of a smile she refused to let show. Six had always liked Heather Wheaton, but in this moment, she was also in awe of her. That she could find humor in the situation—the situation that had led to her brother's murder—said more about the woman's fortitude than anything else Six could think of.

"Ms. Kline," Heather said, not bothering to hold her hand out when the woman stopped in front of them.

Not deigning to acknowledge the greeting, her eyes took them in, then, looking somewhere between the two of them, she spoke. "Follow me. Ms. Newcross is waiting for you." Without another word, she spun on one of those sensible heels and started back toward the elevator.

Six and Heather followed her into the waiting car, then rode in silence to the top floor. Holly maturely showed her disapproval by keeping her back to them the entire ride. When they stepped out and onto the executive floor of the building, Six took a moment to study the space. It looked exactly like the schematics they'd pulled from the permitting office's public records. This top floor of the eight-story building was the exclusive domain of the company executives. Including Julia Newcross, Austin Fogarty, and Kaden Fogarty.

Holly knocked on a closed door, then without waiting, opened it, revealing the three people in question. Six wondered if Julia knew how the presence of the brothers—and not the presence of any other executives—revealed that she knew exactly what Six and Heather were here to talk about.

"Your eleven o'clock appointment, Ms. Newcross. Please let me know if you'd like anything else," Holly said. She shot Heather and Six a nasty look as she shut the door behind her, not bothering to offer anyone coffee.

Six shifted her bag on her shoulder and looked at the three people in front of her. Julia sat in a high-back leather chair at her desk. As one would expect from someone who ran a cosmetics company, her hair and face were immaculately made up, although her eyes appeared puffy. Six was quite sure she hadn't been crying over her husband which meant that the bodies of Michael Yang and Victor DePalma had been found.

Kaden Fogarty was leaning against a large picture window that looked out onto a treed hillside. His hands were tucked into the pockets of his khakis, and he wore a navy polo shirt and brown leather loafers. His dark hair was slicked back with so much product that Six was pretty sure that the Rubik's Cube Cyn liked to toss around would have bounced right off.

Austin Fogarty was a little older than his brother and his dark hair, though no less at the mercy of hair gel, was shot through with strands of gray. Lounging on the leather sofa, he had an arm draped across the back while in the other hand, he held a phone. His khakis and shoes matched his brother's, though he wore a salmon-colored button-down.

"I don't know who you are, nor do I much care, but I'm sure you've heard of the death of Julia's husband," Kaden said, firing off the first salvo. "I hardly think this is the time to discuss a lawsuit. Especially a frivolous one."

Six looked to Heather to take the lead, and the younger woman nodded. "The fact that you are all here tells me you know this lawsuit isn't frivolous, and I doubt it's Mr. Newcross that Ms. Newcross is mourning. I understand Victor DePalma was found dead this morning."

At DePalma's name, Julia, who'd been staring out the

window, whipped her head around. "How do you know about Victor? It hasn't been in the news yet."

Heather lifted a shoulder, then placed her briefcase on the edge of Julia's desk. "It's of no consequence. I'd say I'm sorry for your loss, but I'm not. He was a loathsome human being who kept like company." Her gaze took in the two men as she spoke. Then, popping her briefcase open, she pulled out a copy of the complaint she planned to file as soon as the meeting was done.

Julia's eyes narrowed. "Who are you?"

Heather flashed her a toothy smile. "I'm Heather Wheaton, attorney-at-law. I'm also the sister of Jeremy Wheaton, a man Victor DePalma had killed last week to stop him from filing this." She held up the complaint. "Lucky for my brother, he has some very good, though very suspicious, friends, who thought there was more to the hit-and-run. I'm sure you can imagine what they found when they started looking."

"Actually, we can't," Kaden said. "As I'm sure *you* can imagine, we get threatened with lawsuits nearly every day. Most of which are spurious, as I'm sure this one is, too."

"I hardly think the systematic rape and torture of young women, or sale of young women and boys, is spurious, Mr. Fogarty," Heather shot back. "I'm sure you are well aware that had those events taken place in the United States, criminal charges would be brought with the evidence we have. But since they took place in Indonesia, at the plantation where you source your palm oil, the best we can do is the civil suit." She held the complaint out to Kaden, but he didn't take it. After a beat, she set it down on Julia's desk.

"Who are you?" Austin asked, focusing his attention on Six.

Six smiled. "I'm one of those very good yet very suspicious friends," she answered. "I also happen to have a lot of contacts in a lot of interesting places."

Austin's beady gaze traveled from her face down her body, then back again, but he said no more.

"I have no idea what you're talking about," Julia said.

"That's interesting," Heather said. "Especially since, in the last twelve months, there have been no less than seven complaints filed with your compliance hotline about the activities of several of your executives, your husband, and Mr. DePalma."

"How would you know about that? Those complaints are anonymous. And any access you might have to them, if they even exist, would have been obtained illegally as we've never received a subpoena. *That* I would remember," Kaden said.

"We spoke to the complainants themselves," Heather said. It was only a little lie. On Saturday, Abyasa had told them of two people at the plantation who'd filed official complaints. Candra had also gone to their overseer and begged the woman to protect the workers, telling her everything that was happening. The woman may or may not have already known, but regardless, she'd done nothing to help.

"That's all hearsay," Kaden said, revealing his lack of knowledge of the laws. Complaints made by the people to whom the wrong had been done was *not* hearsay. But smart woman that she was, Heather let that slide and kept the conversation moving in the direction they needed it to.

"We're continuing to work on obtaining additional evidence, of course," Heather said, closing her briefcase. "As we progress, I have little doubt that we'll find further support for our position that Julian Newcross, Victor DePalma, and you two gentlemen —and I use that word in the loosest sense possible—engaged in violations of the human rights of your employees. I also know we'll be able to prove that you knew about it, Ms. Newcross," Heather said, nodding to the woman, "and likely your board did as well. So, Ms. Newcross, not only does your company *not* source its supplies ethically or sustainably, it systematically engages in torture, violence, and fear. I can't wait for the public to find out what a sham you are. More importantly, though, I'm looking forward to bringing you all to justice. Nothing will ever make up for what you've done to the women and men you've abused, but the least I can do is try."

Silence fell in the room for a beat—a short one—before Austin laughed. It was a forced laugh, and though he'd likely meant it to come across as arrogant, he sounded nervous. "This is all very interesting, but you can't possibly believe you'll win this suit. You have no evidence that we've ever been anything other than what we claim to be and certainly no evidence of any wrongdoing."

Heather looked at her watch, then glanced at Six, who nodded. "We have some," Heather said. "Enough to file the complaint, and you can be sure we're working to obtain more."

Austin, who appeared to be the smarter of the two brothers, noted Heather's movement and sat up straight. "You can't possibly think you'll obtain evidence from anyone working here."

Heather averted her eyes and gathered her briefcase but didn't answer.

"Julia, call security," Austin barked, rising from his seat.

"That's not necessary," Heather said. "We'll be leaving." She started toward the door, but Austin stepped in front of her.

"What are you planning to do?" he hissed.

Heather glanced at Six again, then dragged her gaze to Austin. Visibly taking a deep breath, she straightened her spine. Behind Six, Julia started speaking into the phone, no doubt following Austin's directive.

"Nothing you can stop," Heather retorted.

"You're playing with fire. You know that, don't you?"

"I don't *play* at anything," Heather said. "You'll learn that soon enough."

Austin remained in front of her, blocking their path to the exit.

In her mind, Six noted the fact that this was one of those

moments that Gavin had been worried about. It could go wrong, right here, right now. And if it did, they wouldn't walk away with nothing, but they wouldn't have what they truly wanted.

Kaden moved away from the window and came to stand beside Julia's desk. She and Heather weren't fully flanked by the brothers, but it would be easy enough for Kaden to move behind Six were he inclined to do so.

Without taking his eyes from Heather, Austin spoke. "Julia, have security check all the cameras in the building. I'm getting a feeling that this little meeting wasn't the main event."

"What?" she asked.

"Just do it," he snapped. A split second passed, then Six once again heard Julia speaking into her phone. Six didn't bother to listen as she kept her focus on Austin.

"What do you think they've done?" Kaden asked, taking a step closer to Six. He wasn't in arm's—or leg's—reach, but he was close enough that she could smell his cloying aftershave.

"I think they're here to fish. I wouldn't put it past them to be sniffing around our employees and records as we speak," Austin said, his words deliberate and clear.

"If they have someone who broke in, they couldn't use anything they stole anyway," Kaden said. Six wasn't going to get into an argument with the man; besides, it helped them to let him think what he was thinking.

"There was a new cleaning crew," Julia said. "Scott called in and complained about them not following protocols. I have security searching for them now."

Heather's head whipped around, and she looked at Six. Six gave a small shake of her head and Austin laughed. "Nice try, Ms. Wheaton," he said. "Not only will we be filing to have your complaint dismissed, I'll be making my own complaint to the bar association. I hope you have a good retirement plan because I can assure you, you'll never work as a lawyer again."

Six reached out and touched Heather's arm in what she hoped was a gesture of comfort and confidence. But Heather was spared from answering when Holly walked into the room after a single knock.

The assistant paused in the doorway, her eyes glittering with triumph. "Ms. Newcross, I understand you called security?" She stepped to the side and a guard moved forward and into view.

"I did, Holly. Thank you," Julia said, rising from her seat for the first time. Looking at the guard, she gestured to Six and Heather. "Please take them to your office and detain them there. We'll be calling the police and pressing charges."

CHAPTER TWENTY-EIGHT

HEATHER LOOKED at Six over her shoulder as they followed the guard out. With her back to Julia and the Fogartys, she winked at the younger woman and mouthed, "We got this."

Heather didn't look convinced, but she said nothing as she turned around. In silence, they walked around the corner toward the back hallways and the freight elevator that would take them to the guards' room in the basement. Well, it would take Heather. And Gavin.

"Nicely done, ladies. Right on schedule," Gavin murmured as he held the door for them. Six couldn't help herself, and she reached down and gave his ass a little swat. He looked adorable in the guard's uniform. He arched a brow at her, then tossed her his own wink. "No 'I told you so?'" he asked as she passed.

"That's beneath me, babe," she said. "Or at the moment, it is. We'll see how I feel later tonight."

The hallway was empty except for the three of them, and he snagged her around the waist. "Heather?" he asked.

"Hhmm?"

"Turn around, please."

Heather chuckled but did as requested, and Gavin leaned in

for a deep, though brief, kiss. "You have everything you need?" he asked when he pulled back.

She nodded.

"Good. Cyn and the crew should be doing their thing"—he looked at his watch—"right...about...now." Less than two seconds later, the fire alarm began pealing. "Go," he directed Six. "In five seconds, this hallway is going to be flooded with people."

She dropped another kiss on his scrumptious lips, nodded to Heather, then slipped into a utility closet across from the elevator as Gavin guided Heather down the stairs. A few seconds later, the formerly empty hall filled with everyone from the executive floor as they made their way to the stairwell.

Taking her phone out, she opened her trusty listening app and slipped one earbud into her ear. Adjusting the sound so as to filter out the screeching of the alarm, she started listening to the conversations happening on the other side of the door. Several people chatted good-naturedly, wondering if this was a fire drill. A few ignored the potential for danger altogether and were talking about what they'd done over the weekend. All in all, it was an orderly evacuation and, as expected, Julia, Austin, and Kaden were the last to leave.

Thankful for her handy device and the application on it, she listened to their hushed conversation as they made their way to the stairs.

"I don't think we should leave," Julia said, for the first time showing both a backbone and some sense.

"People will notice if we're not outside," Kaden replied. "You know how it goes. Once we're outside, the fire marshal won't allow anyone back in until each person is accounted for. If we're not there, it will draw attention to us."

He was right, although Six thought they were already dallying enough to bring attention to themselves. In fact, from the sounds of it, they'd stopped walking and were standing in the hall talking.

"You can't possibly think this is a coincidence," Julia snapped.

"Of course it's not," Austin snapped right back. "But security assured me that both Heather Wheaton and the woman she came with, as well as the three members of the cleaning staff that Scott reported, were under control. There's little we can do without drawing unwanted attention to ourselves."

"So we just leave?" Julia asked.

The trio started walking again, answering Julia's question. "It's standard protocol for internal security to lock our IT systems down in situations like this. If somehow they managed to evade the guards, they'll be locked out of any system they might have tried to access."

The sound of the stairwell door opening echoed in the hallway. "Ms. Newcross?" came Holly's voice.

Both Austin and Kaden mumbled something under their breath, but it wasn't distinct enough for Six to pick up.

"We're on our way, Holly," Julia responded. "We were doing a final sweep of the floor. We wouldn't want to leave anyone behind now."

Six smiled to herself. No, they most definitely wouldn't want to leave anyone behind. Especially not the one person that *had* been left behind.

"Of course not. That's very thoughtful of you," Holly said. A few seconds later, the door banged shut, and with the exception of the screaming alarm, the hallway fell silent. Six turned off the app and returned her earbud to her bag, but remained in the utility closet, waiting for the message that would give her the all clear. Several minutes passed with no message, but she wasn't worried. It took more than a few minutes to clear an eight-floor building—nine if she included the basement. To pass the time, she posed with a mop, then with a bucket that had the dried-up wrapper of a candy bar stuck to the bottom. She was about to pretend to be flirting with Mr. Clean when her phone dinged with the anticipated message. Quickly snapping the picture, she sent it to Gavin with a text telling him she'd met another man.

Without waiting for his response, she stepped out of the closet and made her way back to Julia Newcross's office. Knowing that the guards—the real ones—were all outside waiting for the fire marshal, she didn't bother trying to hide from the cameras. Entering the room she'd left less than twenty minutes ago, she paused in the doorway and assessed the scene.

The complaint was still lying on the desk, but other than that, there were no visible files or paperwork. Julia's computer sat on her desk, but like a good corporate citizen, she'd powered down the device when she'd left. Six grinned. It was a good thing she'd brought her own.

Getting quickly to work, she withdrew a laptop from her bag, as well as a small rectangular device. Taking a seat in Julia's massive leather chair, Six turned her computer on, plugged in her password, then pulled up the file she wanted. Once it was on her screen—frozen in a sick sort of tableau—she hooked up the extra device, then put it to sleep. Eyeing the office for a place to hide, she decided that sometimes, hiding in plain sight was the best option.

Six spun Julia's chair until the back of it was facing the door, effectively giving her the cover she needed. She hoped. Because other than crawling under the desk, which she wasn't about to do, there was nowhere else she could be both out of sight and yet close enough to hear what she hoped would be an enlightening conversation.

Ten long, boring minutes later, her phone dinged with a message from Gavin.

"If you want to leave me for a bald man with an earring and questionable grooming habits—those eyebrows say it all—and who is old enough to be your grandfather, I won't stand in your way. Although

given how you like things raw and just the right kind of dirty, I'm not sure a man obsessed with cleanliness will serve you in the long run. At least not like I do."

Six laughed out loud. *"I've reconsidered my position,"* she typed. *"As you well know, I don't like to play second fiddle to anyone or anything and well, he's made it clear that I can't compete with a muddy floor. I fear I'd always be trying to get his attention and would end up rolling in the mud to do so. While I'm not opposed to a getting a bit—or a lot—dirty, I think that if I'm going to go to the effort, it better be because you're on top of me. Or under me. I'm not that picky."*

A long paused came before he answered. *"You are picky, I just happen to be the lucky one you picked. Maybe tonight we can have a picnic outside for dinner. After dark. It did rain recently."*

She smiled and was about to answer when a message from Cyn came in. *"While the grin Gavin is wearing is somewhat entertaining, whatever you two are texting about will have to wait. The marshal is letting everyone back in."*

"Roger that," she answered. *"Going dark."* She then texted the same thing to Gavin, who managed to get her a quick *"be careful"* message before she switched her phone to silent. Then pulling on all her years of experience, she stilled her mind and her body and waited.

In her meditative state, time both passed and didn't, and she had no idea how many minutes had ticked by when footsteps finally sounded outside the office. A few seconds later, the door clicked open. Six slowed her breathing and crossed her fingers that Julia wouldn't come straight to her desk. Six both needed and wanted more time to let things unfold in the way she knew —from years of experience—they could and should.

"Christ, I need a drink," Austin said.

"I'll second that," Kaden said. The door shut behind them and someone—judging by the footsteps, Julia—walked to the small bar area set up on the other side of the office.

"None of this would be happening if you hadn't sold that information Michelle Reiner let slip," Julia snapped. Six's ears perked up. Michelle Reiner was a third-term senator from one of the Midwestern states. "We were doing fine until you decided to sell that. Now everything is falling apart."

The sound of the small refrigerator opening then closing filled the room, followed by the sound of ice cubes landing in glasses.

"You're so fucking dramatic," Austin said. "That was months ago. Your husband and DePalma didn't die until this week."

"The first time may have been months ago, but that wasn't the only time," Julia said. Despite her rancor, Six could hear the woman pouring drinks for the two men in her office.

Austin laughed. "I hardly think Michelle has anything to do with Julian's or Victor's deaths or those two bitches who came here. She might have let slip troop movements in Afghanistan all those months ago, and we might have made some money off the information, but if she calls attention to it now, she'll be tried as a traitor. The first time, it might have been a mistake. But the third or fourth time she gave me information? No way. She has nothing to do with what's going on now. She has too much to lose."

Six was pretty sure that the most important thing Michelle had to lose—her integrity—had already been lost.

"Then what the fuck is happening? First Julian, then Victor? And what were those two women doing here?" Kaden demanded, then, judging by the sound of ice hitting glass, took a sip of his drink. Six cringed when he finished his swallow with a big "ahhh," as if he'd gulped down sixteen ounces of fluids rather than taken a sip of something.

"What about Percy and Shelton?" Julia asked. She was on the move, and Six tensed as her footsteps came closer to the desk. Eight strides closer, Julia stopped. In her mind's eye, Six saw Julia leaning against her desk, her back to where Six now sat.

She didn't know if this was a true imagining of where Julia was, but Six was going to go with it.

Judging again by location, it was Austin who swirled his drink in his glass before taking a sip, then answering. "We pay those fools enough to turn a blind eye when we use their ports for our shipments. I talked to Percy yesterday and I can promise you, he's not involved. He's a nervous creature, and I would have known if he was lying to me when he assured me the next shipment would go as smoothly as the last ones. And like Reiner, he has too much to lose to be a whistleblower."

"I agree with Austin on Percy and Shelton," Kaden said. "Both of those men like the money too much and besides, it's not like the weapons stay here. Every shipment has gone to some fucked-up country that then requires businesses to hire Department of Defense contractors any time they want to do business there. It's a win-win for those two since they both have ties to the companies that get called in to do that work."

Six's stomach flipped at the thought. She'd studied too much history not to be aware of how easy it was to destabilize a country and make money off that destabilization. Colonization wasn't the first or last example of that—though it might have been the most destructive. What Kaden was alluding to meant it was likely that thousands of lives had been affected because of Representatives Percy and Shelton's hunger to get rich. Or richer, as the case may be.

"Then what the fuck is going on? Why, of all times, did those women show up now?" Julia demanded, slamming her drink on the desk. Six barely managed to not jump at the sudden sound ricocheting through the office.

"I don't know why now," Austin answered. The sound of the leather sofa creaking and squeaking told Six he'd sat down. "But I guarantee they were here for no other reason than to fish for dirt."

"They seemed pretty confident to me," Julia muttered.

"Confidence is easy to fake, you know that," Austin shot back. Six cringed at the low blow to Julia's public persona.

"Look," Austin said on an exhale. "It's nothing. It's just a civil suit that will allege something happened in Indonesia. Not only does that rule out Reiner, Shelton, and Percy being involved, but it's a *civil* case. How many times has a lawsuit been brought against us since we started this company?" He didn't wait for an answer and continued. "I don't know the exact number, but I know it's dozens. And none of them have amounted to anything. You know what they do have in common with what happened today though?" Austin asked.

Kaden murmured a "What," but Julia remained silent.

"Like the two women today, the lawyers in each of those cases came to talk to us before filing suit. And they come to talk to us because they hope we'll give them something to use, or in some cases, that we'll settle."

"This is different," Julia said. "Not about the suit being filed, but with Julian dying and Victor and that other person being found dead at the quarry..." Her voice had cracked on Victor's name, and a sudden wave of sadness washed over Six for the marriage Julian and Julia must have had. They were both despicable human beings and likely deserved each other, but to be stuck in a shitty marriage, well, it was shitty.

"Look, even if they have something, they can't have much," Kaden said.

"I agree," Austin said. "They would have just filed the suit if they had the evidence."

"But even if they have something, what would it be?" Kaden posited, then continued. "Maybe it's statements from the women, but if it is, those are easily argued against. After all, who do you think a jury is going to believe? Us or some ass-backward native who can't even speak English? I can promise you, a jury will understand that that lawyer, and whoever else she's dragged into this, is only in it for the money."

Six's blood pressure shot up so fast she could feel the capillaries in her body expanding even as she forced herself to remain still. This conversation—all of it—was why she was here.

"Kaden has a point. What kind of evidence could they have? If it's only the word of the women, then it's a 'he said-she said' situation and I think we all know who will come out the victor of that fight."

"What if there's more?" Julia asked.

"There's not," Kaden said. "Aside from interviewing the women, whom we've agreed we can undermine, what more could they have? Come on, Julia, it's not like there's a video or anything."

Always loving a dramatic entrance, Six took the opportunity to spin around in the chair. "It's funny you should say that, Kaden, because as a matter of fact, there *is* video," she said. And with that, she pressed a button and projected onto the wall the first video they'd found in Jeremy's files—one involving all three of the men, Austin, Kaden, and Julian, assaulting and abusing two women who worked at the plantation.

Six didn't watch the scene playing out in grand scale on the other side of the room. She'd seen it more often than she cared to. Instead, she watched the three people. Julia's attention stayed fixed on the images, and Six had a moment's thought that perhaps she was a sexual sadist. Her interest in the video did *not* seem normal. Kaden, though one of the participants, seemed unable to watch it and had dropped his gaze to the floor and turned his head away. Austin, on the other hand, kept his attention on her.

"Who the fuck are you?" he demanded.

She lifted a shoulder. "Like I said earlier, other than the fact that I have lots of interesting contacts, it's not that important."

"This is entrapment," he barked.

She smiled. "Hardly. I didn't induce or persuade you to say or do anything. In fact, until this moment, I've said nothing at all." It was not lost on Austin that she'd just overhead them confess not only to the abuses of the workers in Indonesia, but also to the federal charges involving bribery, espionage, and treason. The Feds were going to *love* her.

"It will all be hearsay," Kaden said, joining the conversation.

"You keep saying that word, Kad. I don't think it means what you think it means," Six said.

Kaden blinked at her bastardization of the line from *The Princess Bride*. "It will be," he insisted. "We'll deny this entire conversation, and then it will be your word against ours."

Six inclined her head. "Had the Feds not been listening through this legally authorized device," she said, unbuttoning her shirt two buttons to reveal the wire she wore, "then you'd be right. But as this whole morning was run strictly to protocol, although perhaps a bit unusually, there's no hearsay involved."

"You bitch," Austin said, striding across the room toward her. Like the bully he was, he hesitated at the edge of the desk when she didn't flinch.

"You may be right about that...no, scratch that, you *are* right about that, Austin," she said, leaning back in the chair. "I *am* a bitch. But let's be clear, I'm the bitch who's going to bring you all down."

He lunged for her then. Not the smartest move on his part. Partly because the Feds were still listening, but mostly because, well, she was trained, and taking him down would be like fighting a toddler. Although she'd *never* fight a toddler, not physically, and as Austin came flying at her, she decided she'd *very much* like to fight him.

His hands were up and coming toward her throat when she shot up from her seat, sending the chair flying backward. His fingers closed around her neck as the chair bounced off the wall behind her. She let Austin feel a moment of victory, a moment of triumph, before bringing her own arms up in between his and chopping his elbows out. He fell forward with the force he'd been using to keep his arms locked and she head-butted him in the nose with a single solid jerk.

"Fuck," he shouted as blood began to pour down his face, and he staggered back two steps.

His gaze found hers and in it, she saw the bloodlust of a cornered animal. It was a look she'd seen before in those she'd hunted, although, admittedly, she'd never expected to see it here in the United States.

"I'm going to kill you," he hissed. She almost smiled. She wasn't quite sure how he thought he'd accomplish that. Even if he had a weapon, which he didn't, he was no match for her training and experience. Of course, if he did try to kill her—which arguably, he just had—they could get him on an attempted murder rap, which wouldn't be such a bad thing either.

Six shrugged, "Go ahead and try. I have to admit, I'm kind of curious how you think you'll do that." She kept her attention on Austin but sensed his brother moving in behind her. "And Kaden," she continued, "you should stay out of this. I know you feel like you should step in, and that maybe two on one gives your brother better odds, but I can assure you it doesn't. All it will do is piss me off and make me want to end this as efficiently as possible. And when I'm efficient, it's possible people might die." She wanted to add "Like Victor DePalma did," but she restrained herself. There was no reason she needed to muddy the waters of the story they'd already committed to regarding DePalma's death.

To her left, Julia gasped. Her dramatic delivery almost had Six laughing, but then Austin lunged forward again, drawing her attention back to the task at hand. And speaking of hands, suddenly there was a knife in Austin's. She forced her gaze from the switchblade that he must have pulled from his pocket and focused on his eyes. Because it would be his eyes that would tell her his intent.

His gaze dropped to her chest, to the area that held the wire he now knew she was wearing. Attacking her there and slicing the wire wouldn't damage the transmissions they'd already recorded, but it sure as shit would send a message. Six adjusted her body, preparing for an attack in that region, but then his gaze shifted up and locked on her neck.

She read everything in his eyes, in his face, in the split second before he attacked. He'd accepted that he wasn't going to escape justice this time around, but just because he'd accepted it didn't mean he wasn't going to go down without a fight.

He lunged toward her again, one hand raised to grab her hair and force her head back. The other, held the knife at an angle so that the blade would slice cleanly across her neck. He got his hands into her hair and a bright look of triumph flashed in his eyes. Again, Six let him feel that moment—savor it if he could—then brought her hand up. Gripping his wrist, she used his own momentum to spin them around so that her back was to his front.

Stepping back into him, she threw him off-balance, although her hold on his hand that held the knife stayed firm. He staggered back to keep from stumbling, and she used the space between them to spin once more. Twisting his knife-wielding hand, she felt the distinctive crack of bone.

"Fuck!" Austin shouted, trying to yank his now-broken wrist back against his body to protect it.

The switchblade clattered to the floor as Gavin and several FBI agents burst through the door.

"You okay?" Gavin called as the agents fanned out, weapons drawn. She appreciated how he refrained from using her name. It wasn't as if Julia and the Fogartys wouldn't learn it later when they went to trial, but for now, she was glad to remain some nameless woman Austin hadn't been able to bully or abuse.

"I'm good," Six said. "He dropped his switchblade. It slid

under the desk." Kaden and Julia already had their hands up and agents were approaching them.

"Mr. Austin Fogarty," Special Agent Chad Warwick said as he approached the man. "You have the right to remain silent."

Six tuned out as the agent finished Mirandizing Austin and stepped out of the way as another agent approached to collect the knife. Within minutes, Julia, Austin, and Kaden had been led away in handcuffs and the knife lay on the desk in an evidence bag.

"Well, that was exciting," Six said, her hands on her hips as she stared at the now-empty doorway, although she could see Holly arguing with an agent on the other side.

"Not the word I'd use," Gavin said, approaching her.

"Me neither," Agent Warwick concurred. His attention lingered on the door, then turned back to her. "You okay?"

She nodded, realizing she hadn't answered Gavin when he'd asked. "I'm fine. Hardly got my heart rate up." Agent Warwick's lips kicked up into a ghost of a smile. With his dark hair, sharp features, and nearly black eyes, he was a good-looking man. And she'd be blind to miss the flicker of interest that flared in his eyes.

"Want me to remove the wire?" he asked. His left eyebrow raised a fraction of an inch when he asked. She'd bet that if the room hadn't been filled with FBI agents, and now crime scene techs, it would have full-on waggled.

"I'll get it," Gavin said, striding toward her. She flashed Warwick a smile before turning her attention to Gavin. He looked none too pleased, although she wasn't sure if that was because she'd been in a knife fight or because Agent Warwick had flirted with her. Either way, her way of dealing with it was the same, and when he was within reach, she tugged him to her and pulled him down into a kiss. The kind of kiss that left no doubt in anyone's mind, let alone Gavin's, where her loyalties lay.

SIX

He was smiling when she finally released him. "Are you really okay?" he asked, his hands gripping her waist.

"I'm fine. I wouldn't mind losing this wire and then heading home for a nice long shower. Being in the same room as those three made me feel dirty. And not the good kind of dirty either."

His smile broadened, and he dipped his head and dropped another kiss on her lips. "I don't need to worry about Mr. Clean, do I?"

EPILOGUE

"To Jeremy," Six said, raising her glass of champagne.

"To Jeremy," everyone echoed. As she took a sip, her gaze traveled around the room of revelers, and she smiled. Although the criminal case had been resolved two months earlier—with guilty charges being levied all around—barely three hours ago, a jury had found Austin Fogarty and a number of executives of Shanti Joy, including Kaden Fogarty and Julia Newcross, liable for the torture and violations of human rights of their workers at the Indonesian plantation. It was the finding that Jeremy would have wanted. The one he had no doubt hoped for when he'd first learned what was happening at the plantation.

Thinking of her friend, Six's smile widened. She truly believed that on this gorgeous fall day, Jeremy was smiling down on all of them—her, Gavin, Cyn, Joe, Nora, Devil, Heather, Abyasa, Candra, and Shinta—as they celebrated this victory. In some ways, it was a bit hollow—the atrocities shouldn't have occurred in the first place—but if wishes were horses and all that. And today was not about lamenting everything wrong with the world and the people in it. Today was a day to celebrate justice.

And the new beginnings of the plantation.

During the investigation, the plantation had shut down. Without Shanti Joy there were no buyers, and with no buyers there were no paychecks. And given that the entire C-suite of the company (more or less) had been involved in the indictments in one way or another, there'd been no one to manage finding a contract for new buyers.

But no longer. Tomorrow, the plantation, operating under the new owners—who happened to be cousins of Devil—would reopen. And Candra and Shinta would return home to manage employee relations for the new company. Abyasa, on the other hand, had decided to stay in the Boston area and was currently taking cooking classes with a dream to open her own restaurant. The woman would do it, too. Not only was her food outstanding, Abyasa had more drive than anyone Six knew, and that included herself and her friends.

"Are you happy?" Gavin asked, slipping an arm around her waist and dropping a kiss on her temple. In the past five months, they'd been both living and working together. The lease on his apartment wasn't up for another few months, but neither of them were kidding themselves that he was living anywhere other than with her in Cos Cob. Much to the dismay of their single colleagues.

It was still a little awkward to be in a relationship with someone who was, from an HR perspective, not as highly placed as she. But because they didn't technically work together, they'd managed to get their relationship officially signed off on. She had no say over his assignments or his performance reviews, nor did she wish to. They might have learned to work together as agents for their respective governments, but if one of them were put in charge of the other, either as agents or as legal professionals, well, all bets would be off.

"Very happy," she answered, tipping her head for him to kiss her, which he obligingly did.

"Good," he replied. "Like happy enough to sneak upstairs and enjoy a little—"

"Fuck!" Devil exclaimed, cutting Gavin off.

Everyone swiveled their heads in her direction, but Devil kept her head down, focused on something on her phone.

"Devil?" Nora prompted.

Devil started muttering something in French as she furiously typed a message into her phone.

"What's wrong?" Six asked.

Devil stabbed her phone with her index finger, presumably sending the message she'd finished typing, then looked up.

Her blue eyes landed on Nora first, then traveled to Cyn before settling on Six. "That was our new chief operations officer at the lab. He said there's been a data breach."

"How bad?" Six asked. Devil's research wasn't top secret, but there were top secret projects happening in other labs in her building. It was part of the reason she'd been assigned to that particular block.

Anxiety flashed across her friend's beautiful features. "Five labs were hit, including mine. Two months' worth of research is gone."

"Gone?" Cyn asked, and Six understood why Cyn's tone sounded confused. Unless someone was planning to ransom the data for money, very rarely was data *taken in its entirety*. More often than not, it was copied so that the hackers could expose it.

Devil gave a sharp nod. "Gone. Completely."

"Can we do anything?" Nora asked. But Six already knew the answer to that. Maybe they could, but they wouldn't know until Devil had a better picture of what was going on.

"Go," Six said. "We'll celebrate another time. You need to be at the lab right now."

Devil's decisive nod was a testament to how serious the situation might be. She was dedicated to her work, but she was equally dedicated to her friends. Leaving the party meant she was worried.

Nora stepped forward and took her champagne glass as Six and Cyn headed to the front door. Reaching into the hall closet, Six had Devil's coat waiting for her when she joined them.

"I'm sorry to run," she said, directing her comment to Six as she slipped into her coat.

"Jeremy would understand," Six said. "The operations officer, he's new, isn't he?"

Devil nodded although her attention was focused on buttoning her coat. The daytime temperatures this October had been perfect, but the evenings were chilly. Great for the changing colors of the leaves, but definitely a harbinger of the winter to come.

"Retired Navy. Started a few months ago," Devil answered.

Six looked at Cyn, who frowned at the information. Could this new director be someone else Franklin had sent? Six arched a brow, and the look Cyn shot back let her know that maybe it was time for her to ask her uncle a few hard questions. In the meantime, though, there was only one thing they could do.

"Let us know if we can help," Six said, leaning in and giving her friend a hug.

"Call and keep us updated," Nora insisted, dropping a kiss on Devil's cheek.

"I'll give you two hours, but if you don't respond to my texts, I'm coming down there. You don't want me to come down there, do you?" Cyn admonished, though she did raise an eyebrow, making Devil smile.

"I'll call. I promise. Congrats again, Heather," she called out to the woman who'd remained in the kitchen.

Pausing at the door, her long, straight black hair falling like water from under her blue knit cap, Devil's gaze swept over all of them, saying without words what they all knew. Depending on what had been taken, she could be walking into a bad—a very bad—situation.

"We'll figure it out," Six said. Cyn and Nora nodded in unison.

Another small smile played on Devil's lips. "I love you ladies."

Six smiled back. "We love you, too. Now go find out if we're going to have to start worrying about biological warfare. If I had my druthers, I'd rather not."

Devil barked out a laugh. "You and me, both, Six. You and me both."

And with that, she turned and walked to her car. As she slid inside, then turned it on, Cyn grabbed Six's hand.

"It will be okay," Six said, knowing Cyn's other hand was holding Nora's, connecting them. The taillights of Devil's car faded into the darkness.

"And if it's not," Nora said, "like you said, we'll figure it out. Because that's what we do."

THE END

Thanks for reading *Six*!

A top-secret lab is broken into, a scientist goes missing, and a prominent doctor falls ill from a virus eradicated decades ago. Pick up book 3 in the Doctors Club series and follow Devil and Commander Darius Washington as they uncover a plot that could spark a war.

Read on for a sneak-peek!

EXTRACT OF
DEVIL

#3 Doctors Club Series

EXCERPT

Virginia Beach, Virginia
Naval Amphibious Base

"This wasn't how I anticipated spending the last year of my service, sir," Darius Washington said to his commanding officer.

"I understand, Commander, but they are your orders," Captain Peters replied. Darius didn't miss the look that passed between Peters and Admiral Bennington. Both men sat across the conference room table from him, though Bennington had yet to say anything.

"Any reason she might need protection?" Darius asked. The "she" in question was Dr. Lily Devillier, a research doctor based in Boston. For the past twenty years, she'd also been an agent for China's Ministry of State Security. How, or why, she'd been allowed to live and work in the United States was intel he wasn't privy to, but he suspected it had something to do with the older British man sitting in the far corner of the room watching the proceedings. Like Bennington, he hadn't said a word. But if Darius was a betting man, which he wasn't, he'd wager the man was a highly placed spook of some sort. That was the only reason he could think of to explain the begrudging respect both Peters and Bennington showed him—and why he hadn't been introduced.

"Nothing specific," Peters responded.

Darius raised an eyebrow. "Anything nonspecific?"

A ghost of a smile touched the lips of the man in the corner, but Peters frowned. "No."

Darius wasn't born yesterday, nor was he a navy or intelligence newbie. There was something going on with Dr. Devillier and either Peters and Bennington didn't know, or they couldn't say. Neither option boded well for him and his quest for answers.

He turned his attention to the corner. After a beat, the older man surprised Darius and spoke. "She's not a double agent," he said. "But she is an asset to many countries. She's been in the game a long time. Statistically, it's only a matter of time before one of her enemies comes out of the woodwork."

At least it was an answer, although not a great one. Every intelligence agent who'd been in the field for any length of time faced that same situation. So while it might be legitimate, it did not explain why he was being deployed to Boston to watch over her for the last year of his navy career.

Darius let his gaze linger on the man as he thought about the work he'd be leaving behind. He and the team he led were responsible for the operations of the base and ensuring the teams that deployed from there were properly supplied. He wasn't concerned about his departure disrupting the system— the navy had enough redundancies that someone would be able to step into his shoes. But the fact that he was leaving behind essential work—work that *mattered* to the men and women who served—to babysit an intelligence agent from China did not sit well with him. Sure, he'd be stepping into the role of chief operations officer of the research center where she was employed, and the work coming out of the center was important. But Peters had made it clear that his orders were, first and foremost, to protect Dr. Lily Devillier.

"We've leased an apartment for you near Irving and Phillips Streets, not far from the hospital district where the labs are located," Peters said, bringing Darius's attention back to his commanding officer. "She lives north of the city, so we've arranged a car and a parking spot as well. In addition to your salary, you'll have all expenses covered."

This time, both of Darius's eyebrows went up.

The man in the corner rose, and Darius watched as he straightened his cuffs and prepared to leave. "I do hope this turns out to be the easiest deployment you've had, Commander. But make no mistake, it is a deployment, so should you need anything, contact Captain Peters."

Darius glanced at his commanding officer. None of the navy men said anything as the man who had to be either CIA or MI6 walked toward the door. When his hand was on the knob, he turned and met Darius's gaze one more time.

"She won't be who you think she'll be, Commander. And while I'm not naturally inclined to dramatic declarations, there are people counting on you. Please don't prove them wrong."

And with that enigmatic statement, he exited.

Darius stared at the closed door, then turned his attention to Peters and Bennington. "When do I leave?"

"The lease starts August first. It's unclear when, or if, there will be an opportunity for leave over the next year, so we're giving you two additional weeks before you begin. Your last day on base will be July fifteenth."

He had one week to transition his job, say goodbye to his friends and colleagues, and close up his house. He'd spend his leave with his family on the Outer Banks of North Carolina before saying goodbye to them for an indeterminate amount of time. The spook hadn't been exaggerating; it was exactly like a deployment. At least this time, he'd be stateside, and presumably, he wouldn't have restricted phone privileges.

He gave a sharp nod and rose. "Then I guess I better get started."

CHAPTER ONE

Lily Devillier—known as Devil to her close friends—followed her parents out of the restaurant to the waiting limousine. The dinner—an annual obligation—was the only time she ever saw them in person anymore. They'd spend two weeks in New York reviewing their property holdings, then fly up to meet her, their only daughter, for a three-hour dinner.

Like all the others, the dinner had been excellent—the food exquisite and the wine even better. Also like all the others, the company had been so dull that even Devil had felt the urge to fidget. Not that she would. Especially not in front of An and Li Devillier. But to say she would be glad to see them on their way back to China tonight—via one of the family's private planes— was an understatement. Especially because their departure meant she'd have a full year before she had to sit through yet another dinner with them.

"Will the plane be ready?" she asked when they paused at the side of the vehicle. Their meal had finished twenty minutes earlier than usual. Not that she'd been keeping track.

Her father inclined his head. Both he and her mother had staff that managed such things. "Your grandmother wishes for you to visit," he said.

Her grandmother had said no such thing. When translated from "Devillier" into English, they'd just reminded her that she had a duty to the family to marry a man of their choosing.

Devil inclined her head, mirroring her father, but didn't

otherwise respond. The last time she'd visited her family in China had been eight years earlier. They'd spent three weeks trying to coerce her into marrying a suitable man. She hadn't returned since.

"Please," she said, gesturing to where the valet stood holding the open door. "It's quite warm, Mother. You should be inside." Her parents, who were something like fourth cousins twice removed, regarded her with identical blue eyes. Devil's were brighter than either of her parents', but complements of a French ancestor from many generations prior, everyone in the Devillier family had inherited the shade.

Finally, her mother gave the smallest of nods.

Devil was careful not to let her relief show as she touched her cheek to her mother's, then offered her father a small bow. A minute later, they were being whisked away to the airport where their plane awaited them.

"Ma'am," a voice behind her called. Devil turned. "You left this on your chair," a young waiter said, handing over her silk wrap.

"Thank you," she said, taking it from him and draping it over her purse. It was close to ten at night, but it was also August, and she had no need to cover her shoulders.

"Can I get your car, ma'am?" the valet asked.

Devil pondered the question, then shook her head. "Thank you, no. I'll pick it up tomorrow afternoon." The man nodded, and she walked away into the humid Boston night. After dinner with her parents, there was only one place she wanted to be. Well, scratch that, she wouldn't mind being back home in Cos Cob, the small seaside town an hour north of Boston where she and her friends lived. But the Smith House Inn was a close second, and it was only a ten-minute walk away.

Pulling out her phone, she texted Angelica, her friend and assistant manager of the hotel, to let her know she was stopping by. A few seconds later, Angelica responded, confirming the residential suite Devil owned in the hotel was ready. She also suggested they meet at the bar and catch up if Devil had the time.

Devil readily agreed and told her she'd have her favorite drink—a virgin rum and Coke, which yes, was just Coke—waiting for her.

Devil was smiling and about to put her phone away when it dinged again, this time a group text from her friends in Cos Cob.

"How was dinner?" Cyn asked.

"Are you glad you had your wrap?" Six asked.

"Are you coming home tonight?" came from Nora.

Devil didn't fight the small chuckle that bubbled up. Cyn wanted to know the facts. Six wanted to know if the wrap she'd insisted Devil bring had protected her from the arctic chill that was An and Li Devillier. And Nora wanted to know if she should worry about Devil driving home.

"Dinner was dinner. The wrap was responsible for the ten seconds of interesting conversation all night. And no, I'm staying at Smith House tonight. I'll be home tomorrow after work."

"We'll want more details than that," Cyn said.

"There aren't any more details than that, Cyn, that's the point," Six said.

"Children." Again, from Nora.

"I'm certain there are more details," Cyn insisted.

"If there are, she won't remember them because they were mind-numbingly boring," Six countered. Her friends had all met her family, and it wasn't that the Devillier family was *exactly* boring. In fact, in the elite world of billionaire business empires, her family was quite influential. But since none of them were capable of talking about anything other than business, conversations tended to feel a little like Groundhog Day. Maybe a company name would be different or a valuation higher or

lower, but for the most part it was, to Six's point, mind-numbingly boring.

"Can you two take this to another thread?" Nora asked. "Are you okay, Devil?"

Devil smiled. "I'm fine. Meeting Angelica for a drink, then headed to bed. Kearney's tomorrow for dinner? Maybe Abe's for drinks after?"

Kearney's was the local pub in Cos Cob, and Abe's was a dive bar on the outskirts of town. Joe, Cyn's partner and the chief of police, hated it when they went drinking there. Its well-deserved reputation was less than stellar. But they'd been going there long before he'd shown up in town eight months earlier, and none of them saw that changing any time soon.

"You're on," Six wrote. "Gavin can chauffeur us. It amuses him to no end to pick us up after we've been drinking." Gavin was Six's partner. They'd only been together a few months, but he was definitely in it for the long haul.

"I'll have Joe drop me at your place," Cyn said to Six—the two lived a mile apart whereas Devil lived in town and Nora a few miles west of town. "He'll fuss, but I'll have fun convincing him it's not a big deal."

Joe didn't like them going to Abe's, but Devil was also pretty sure that half the fuss he put up was to see what Cyn would do to convince him it was fine.

"I'll meet you at your place, Devil," Nora wrote. "That way Gavin doesn't have to drive out here." Gavin would drive anywhere Six asked him to, and Six hadn't been kidding when she'd said the group of friends amused him. Pretty much everything amused Gavin—he was the perfect fit for her tempestuous friend, taking Six's moods easily in stride.

"Perfect, see you all tomorrow. Love you." Devil received a chorus of "love yous" back, then she slipped her phone into her clutch.

She turned onto Park Street and headed toward Beacon

Street. To her left, people strolled through the Common, and the notes of street musicians filled the air. She passed tourists and locals alike as well as several college students who'd stayed in town for the summer. Devil didn't stop the small smile that played on her lips. Compared to where she'd grown up, Boston wasn't a very big city. It had a life to it that was uniquely Boston, though. During the day, it heaved and flowed to the drumbeat of a major city. But at night, *people* came out. Not businessmen and women, not dealmakers and movers and shakers. Those types were there, too, but the nights were owned by tourists seeing the sights, college kids clubbing, young adults sharing cheap beer and food, and families enjoying walks. At night, it became a *town*.

By the time she entered Smith House, she was almost regretting her decision to walk. She'd needed the distraction and the time to clear her head, but beads of sweat now dripped between her breasts, and her hair was sticking to her neck. Thankfully, the boutique hotel was well air-conditioned, and coming in from the humid night, the AC felt almost arctic.

Pausing at the entrance, she savored the frosty air wrapping around her. When she'd cooled down enough that her dress wouldn't stick to her skin, she made her way through the charming and comfy lounge and into the cozy bar, waving to the two employees at reception as she passed. There were three other people occupying stools, a man on his own and a couple who were paying their check. She passed by all three and took a seat at the farthest end.

The bartender spun around, and Devil smiled. "Esteban, how are you?"

A huge grin split the young man's face. "Dr. Devillier, it's great to see you. I'm well, how are you? Your regular?" he asked, walking to stand in front of her.

She nodded. "And Angelica is meeting me, so hers, too, please. How is your sister?" she asked as he flipped a tumbler over and added two small ice cubes.

Esteban beamed. "She made the dean's list in her first year."

"That's wonderful!" Devil exclaimed, truly pleased. Esteban had come to work at Smith House after a run-in—or four—with the law. He'd been going down a path he hadn't wanted to be going down but, like so many in his position, hadn't known how to step off. And since he was the primary provider for his family, which included his younger sister and chronically ill mother, they had suffered, too.

That had changed three years ago, though, when Smith House had given him an opportunity to make different decisions. He'd grabbed on to that opportunity and started working at the inn, first as a cleaner, then as waitstaff, and now as the head bartender. The choices he made allowed him to keep a roof over his family's head and food on the table. They also allowed his sister to attend community college where she was studying accounting. Devil had a feeling Esteban would eventually go to college, too, but for now, his priority was getting his sister through.

He beamed again and set the tumbler in front of her, and the two fingers of Ardbeg beckoned. "And you? How's the research?" he asked.

Devil inclined her head. Her research wasn't top secret by any means, but having been bored to near death listening to her family go on and on about their businesses more than once, she didn't tend to talk about her work much. "It's going. I'm finishing up a study on the effects of a new cancer drug. Unfortunately, it's not looking great. There are some redeeming qualities to it, though, so if we can salvage those, I'll be happy."

Esteban nodded and set a Coke down beside her. "Always good to be happy."

She smiled back as the thought occurred that she probably should have checked her phone before asking Esteban to pour Angelica's drink. As the assistant manager, her schedule wasn't always her own. "And how is your mother?" Devil asked, reaching for her purse that she'd hung on the back of the chair.

All the happiness in his face bled away before her eyes. He blinked and looked away, keeping one hand on the back bar as if to steady himself. Her fingers closed around her phone, but she hesitated to pull it out. "Esteban?"

He cleared his throat, then met her gaze. "She's not well," was all he said. Esteban's mother had been diagnosed with MS nine years earlier. It had progressed rapidly in the first few years but then had seemed to slow down. The disease wouldn't lead to her death anytime soon, but Devil had a pretty good idea of the kind of pain she might be living in.

"Have they given her new medication?"

Esteban didn't exactly nod.

"Talk to me. You know I can help," she said.

The young man looked away, then, after a beat, turned back with a shrug of his shoulders. "I can't get her to go to the doctor," he said. The pain in his voice hit Devil in the chest. She didn't wish her family ill, by any means, but they weren't close. And they certainly didn't love each other the way Esteban clearly loved his mother.

"I'll send someone," Devil said, immediately. Esteban started shaking his head. He even took a step away from her.

"You can't, Doc. You don't need…"

"I don't need to, but I *can*, Esteban. You know I can."

"We'll figure something out."

Devil shook her head at his reluctance. "Look at me, Esteban." She waited until he complied. Fear, ego, and uncertainty swirled in his eyes. "We all need help every now and then," she said. "I know it's a cliché, but it's true. I *know* you. I trust that when you say she isn't well, you are already doing everything you can to make it better. But sometimes you need to let friends help. Since starting at Smith House, you've taken every opportunity available to you and you've made something of it. Take this opportunity, too. If not for you, then for your mom."

He blinked, moisture gathering in his eyes, but he didn't look away. She held his gaze until finally, he nodded and whispered, "Thank you."

She nodded back, then smiled, lightening the weight that had fallen between them. "I'll have someone call you tomorrow to get it set up. Now, do you want to take bets on whether Angelica got pulled into something and that Coke is going to waste?"

Esteban hesitated, then smiled back. "It won't go to waste, but it might not be Angelica who finishes it." As he spoke, he picked the drink up and took a sip, setting it down on the back bar.

Devil laughed as she pulled out her phone. Sure enough, there was a message from her friend saying there was an issue with a room on the third floor she needed to deal with, but that she'd stop by the suite later to say hi. Devil showed Esteban the message, and he laughed.

"She can have a drink up there. You going to take yours up?" he asked.

Devil slid from the stool. "I will, thank you. And we'll talk tomorrow after you speak with the doctor."

Esteban nodded and she turned to leave, not bothering to pay. She had a running tab at the hotel, and the staff knew to add a twenty-five percent tip to every meal and drink. With a little wave, she walked toward the lounge and the elevators that would take her to the top-floor suite.

"Ma'am," a voice called out. Devil glanced back to see a porter holding her silk wrap. Once again, she'd been about to leave it behind. Only this time, it must have fallen from her purse when she'd replaced her phone.

"Thank you," she said, taking it. The young man smiled and carried on toward the restaurant. She looped the wrap around the strap of her bag, checked to make sure it wouldn't fall again, then started to leave. Only she hesitated.

The man sitting alone at the bar was watching her. The porter had drawn attention to her, but something in his steady gaze was, well, not exactly unnerving, but not casual, either. Quickly she cataloged him. He looked to be six foot two or three, and his well-muscled arms were visible in his soft cotton T-shirt. His jeans were well-worn and molded to his legs, and on his feet, he wore a pair of black Adidas. Switching her attention to his face, she realized he was an attractive man, not like a movie star, but in a very *real* way. Light brown eyes were set against deep brown skin. His jaw was square and maybe a little stubborn. And he had the smallest amount of facial hair—more than a five o'clock shadow, but not quite a beard. His short black hair held a hint of gray at the temples and curled tightly against his head.

Focusing her gaze on his eyes—eyes that were still watching her—Devil considered if maybe her night was about to take an interesting turn. She didn't usually meet men in bars, but there was a first time for everything. Besides, she could more than take care of herself if something went wrong.

She was about to make the first move—a small smile and a step toward him—when he surprised her. He didn't give her a look of invitation. He didn't smile or rise or make any move toward her.

No, as if dismissing her like a gnat, he shifted his gaze back to the baseball game playing on the television and took a sip of his beer.

Devil waited a beat to see if he'd turn back around. When it was obvious that he wasn't going to, she swiveled on her heel and started toward the elevator. She didn't bother to hide the rueful smile that touched her lips as she passed through the lounge. It wasn't often a man dismissed her. Her ego wasn't too bruised, though. In her thirty-eight years, she'd learned that attraction was a subjective thing. Just because she'd found him attractive didn't mean the attraction would be reciprocated. That was the way of the world.

Still, as the elevator door closed and she caught one last glimpse of him, his beer still in hand and his attention still focused on the game, she wondered what it would have been like if her night had ended differently.

Made in the USA
Columbia, SC
11 September 2024

41603457R00165